D0049256

PRAISE FOR *MEADOWLARK*

"I picked up this riveting novel one morning, and by the time I looked up—gasping at the explosive, inevitable ending—it was late afternoon. Call in sick, get a babysitter, clear the day, because once you pick up *Meadowlark*, you won't be able to put it down until the very last astonishing page."

—Ayelet Waldman, author of *Love and Treasure*

"*Meadowlark* is a riveting, vividly rendered journey into the haunted past and uncertain future that await a mother and daughter in the Nevada desert. Melanie Abrams is a writer of remarkable power and insight, and in these pages, she is at the top of her game."

—Anthony Marra, author of *A Constellation of Vital Phenomena*

"This intense, powerful novel heats like a crucible over misunderstandings inside and outside a contemporary West Coast cult. The hotter the book gets, the richer the questions it raises about American utopianism, parenting, and power and how far people will go for their ideals. *Meadowlark* is a superbly gripping and insightful read."

—Maria Hummel, author of *Still Lives*

"Melanie Abrams's *Meadowlark* seduces you into the dark, secretive world of cults and how those who have been touched by them are never truly free. Her textured prose and detailed descriptions of the rituals and rivalries behind the compound gates are not only vividly imagined but also completely transporting. Simrin and Arjun, with their complexities and weaknesses, are frighteningly believable and reeled me in from the moment they appeared on the page. A gorgeous and gripping read."

—Hallie Rubenhold, author of *The Five: The Untold Lives of the Women Killed by Jack the Ripper*

"A fascinating novel that illuminates the afterlife of America's 1970s counterculture and challenges the power and danger of alternative communities."

—Jess Row, author of *Your Face in Mine*

MEADOWLARK

WORKS BY MELANIE ABRAMS

Playing

MEADOWLARK

A NOVEL

MELANIE ABRAMS

Little
a

Text copyright © 2020 by Melanie Abrams
All rights reserved.

Published by Little A, New York

www.apub.com

Amazon, the Amazon logo, and Little A are trademarks of Amazon.com, Inc., or its affiliates.

ISBN-13: 9781542007351 (hardcover)
ISBN-10: 1542007356 (hardcover)

ISBN-13: 9781542007344 (paperback)
ISBN-10: 1542007348 (paperback)

Cover design and illustration by Kimberly Glyder

Printed in the United States of America

First edition

For the Boo and the Bean

SIMRIN

The emails come in through the blog, encrypted with her own public key. The first: Simrin. I think of you often and with deep affection. Arjun. She reads it three times, each time the name making her breath catch, her heart beat irritatingly faster, but she shakes it off. There have been so many trolls lately, strangers that have dug up parts of her past. Her fan-created Wikipedia page is a trove of info on Ananda Nagar, most of it pretty accurate descriptions of the "Eastern-leaning ashram in Central California," a community focused on "enlightenment through liberation from the self." There is a short statement on equality, how Ananda members are treated as equals no matter their sex, race, or age. But there is no mention of what this means. No mention of the grueling schedule—the hours of meditation, the mandatory karmic yoga duties, the memorization of long strings of unintelligible mantras and the subsequent assessments in front of the whole community, all required by the time you turned five. This she keeps to herself, and she imagines the others do the same. As children, they weren't allowed to talk about Ananda with outsiders, and that vigilance is hard to shake. Besides, she can't imagine any of them want to talk about it. Ananda kids didn't want to be known then, and she's sure they don't want to be known now. Herself included. She's never tried to find any of the "brothers and sisters" she grew up with. The one exception to this is Arjun. For years she has googled him with no results, but she doubts he is still using his real name. Even she transformed from Simrin to Simone soon after they left.

Still, the email catches her, and she saves it under "Fan Mail," his name scratching at her persistently until a second email arrives the next day: Simrin. Do write back? Missing you lately. Arjun. This one she keeps in her inbox, opening and closing it throughout the day, annoyed at herself for getting pulled in by some basement-dwelling hater. Someone has dug his name out of some old Ananda propaganda, she tells herself, found an incense-scented pamphlet at a garage sale or unearthed some old microfiche and seen the ads in *Whole Life Times* and *New Dawn* magazine.

But the third email—the third sends her head reeling.

She is checking her diagnostics when it comes in. Cakravat parivartante duḥkhāni ca sukhāni ca, it says. Please, Sim? Arjun.

The world seems to slow. It is the mantra they both lived by and loathed. Even now, twenty years after she ran away, it is the one she still weaves through her head when she's had to photograph cancer patients in hospice and community-obliterating wildfires, the last scrap of Ananda embedded inside her: "Pain and pleasure revolve like a wheel." If you didn't like something, the grown-ups would say, wait patiently for the wheel to spin. They hadn't liked a lot of things, but they had endured. Pain, then pleasure; pleasure, then pain.

Her phone rings, and she is jarred back from the ache of those memories. Tom. She steadies herself, takes a breath, and answers.

"Hi, Tom."

"Papa?" Quinn asks. Quinn is splayed on the floor, playing with the iPad, those damn Disney princesses flouncing across the screen.

"Yes," she mouths.

"Darling," Tom says.

She walks into the kitchen. "Tom, what a pleasant surprise."

"Oh, don't be mean," he says. "It's not good for your complexion."

"Where are you?"

"In your driveway."

"Jesus, Tom. Quinn has a birthday party in an hour."

"Oh, let her skip it."

She sighs and closes her eyes. She's seen enough talk shows about children trapped between divorced parents to know that a hostile environment works great if you want your kid to become a drugged-out pole dancer.

"I'll bring her out in ten minutes. Please take her to the party," she says.

"Fine, fine, and have her pack a bag? Stay the night?"

"Sure." She sighs and hangs up.

She walks into the living room. "Papa's outside. He's going to take you to Bea's party, and you can sleep over."

"Yay!" Quinn says.

"Go change and pack some stuff. Don't forget your toothbrush."

Quinn runs to her room, and Simrin sits back down on the couch. She stares at Arjun's name on her computer screen and thinks of the last time she saw him—that crazy night in San Francisco. She and Jaishri were fifteen, Arjun sixteen. The three of them just babies. It was two weeks after they had run away, and Simrin had returned to the day-rate motel room after stocking up on frozen burritos and strawberry yogurt and found both Jaishri and Arjun gone, which wasn't that unusual. The motel was cheap and scared Jaishri—the cockroaches in the shower drain, the screaming and slamming of doors from the other rooms, even the weird buzz the light bulbs made—so Arjun would take her on walks to the park to pet the dogs and look for dropped change. But this time, they didn't come back for hours, and when they did, it was just Arjun. "Jaishri decided to go back," he said. "I tried to stop her." Then late that night, he had vanished too.

"I'm ready," Quinn says. She is wearing a pink dress with yellow pajama bottoms underneath and carrying two stuffed animals, a backpack, and the birthday present.

"Okay," Simrin says but doesn't move.

"Mama!"

"Okay." She gets slowly to her feet.

Quinn races ahead of her and opens the front door. Sunlight spills in, too bright, too yellow.

"Bye, Mama," Quinn yells and races into the back seat of Tom's car.

"I'll bring her back tomorrow morning," Tom calls out the open window.

And then they are gone, leaving her with the mantra looping through her head: *Cakravat parivartante duḥkhāni ca sukhāni ca.*

She shuts the door, bolts the top lock, and lies down on the floor. It is, without doubt, him. No trolls. No fans with too much time on their hands. Just Arjun, somewhere, staring into her site, his unnaturally green eyes the same ones that peppered the brochures, the pamphlets, the flyers, the bumper stickers, the notebooks, the letterhead, the gift shop incense packs. Every single printed page of her Ananda childhood.

Simrin and her mother had moved to Ananda when Simrin was four. Her mother had always been interested in "spirituality," and Simrin had spent many hours in dimly lit shops browsing the chakra-cleaning crystals and purifying candles while her mother paged through books, looking for enlightenment. But then came the rough divorce. And the lost job. And then a friend from her mother's meditation class asked her to go with her to visit Ananda, to experience the "path to inner joy." Ananda was having an open house. The two of them might leave with new insights. And her mother had. And then come back and immediately packed up their San Francisco apartment and moved them three hundred miles away, explaining the move as if they had won the lottery: "Everything you've ever wanted, you can find at Ananda!" "Candy houses?" Simrin asked. "Better than candy houses!" her mother said. But it wasn't better. Instead it was a lot of white people trying to *find* themselves by taking Indian names and forcing little kids to chant a bunch of stuff they didn't understand, a community of grown-ups earnestly in pursuit of enlightenment and inner peace.

At first, it had seemed an adventure. The California high desert was nothing like the tightly packed blocks of the Haight. Ananda sat on a wide expanse of open land, nothing but barrel cacti and jackrabbits disrupting the flat brush. Their first night there, her mother had taken her beyond the outbuildings—the pink communal houses and massive dining room and sacred learning spaces—and shown her the stars. So, so many. And then one had shot across the sky, just for her, her mother said. And then they had seen a kit fox, his eyes shining yellow in the strobe of their flashlight.

And the community welcomed them warmly. "It's so refreshing," her mother said. "No one cares where we were before." But Simrin cared. "I go to Step Up Preschool," she told everyone. "I have a canopy bed," she said. The grown-ups were nice enough. They gave her raisins and patted her head, but it was Jyoti, one of the oldest members of Ananda, who actually listened. The first few weeks, the two of them wandered Ananda together while Simrin's own mother spent most of her time learning the long, involved mantras that would lead her, and eventually Simrin, to enlightenment.

Jyoti listened to Simrin name all the Strawberry Shortcake dolls and explain the rules of rollover tag and rank her first-, second-, and third-best friends, and then she gradually encouraged Simrin to walk barefoot, to feel the earth under her toes and the hot desert wind in her hair. "You are the dirt, the wind. Everything you see and feel, you are too," she said. Her mother was also full of such platitudes. "*Choose* to be happy," she'd say when Simrin cried for ice cream. "*Embrace* the unknown," she had said when they packed up their lives and moved to Ananda. It was confusing and scary, and Simrin couldn't imagine how you could embrace the unknown. She heard the words literally and felt stupid. But when Jyoti spoke, something inside her shifted, and although she was still confused, she didn't feel stupid. She held Jyoti's hand and learned the Gayatri *japa* on her fingers.

And then she found Arjun.

Arjun. Perhaps slightly more blessed than the blessed, just a touch closer to enlightenment, just a bit more equal than the rest. The first child born at Ananda, their prince, their hero.

The first time she had seen him, he was bare chested, draped in beads, doling out new *malas* for meditation. Simrin watched him weave in and out of the rows of seated grown-ups, his shoulders arched back, barely looking as he poured the long strings of beads into their waiting hands like water. "Is he a grown-up?" she asked Jyoti, who had laughed but not answered. Only later, when Simrin watched him and Jaishri throwing broken beads at each other, did she realize that Arjun was, like her, little.

He was only five, but he seemed so much older. He didn't care about the scratch-and-sniff stickers she gave the other kids, but he looked her in the eye and thanked her anyway. And he made sure all the littlest kids got their stickers, particularly Jaishri. He held her hand and helped her decide and complimented her choice of the strawberry sticker, and Simrin understood there was something different about him but different about Jaishri too. She was four and barely spoke, but she touched the tiny blue stones in Simrin's ears as if they were magic and was awed by the chipped nail polish still on Simrin's toes. And soon, she was pulling My Little Ponies from Simrin's Little Mermaid backpack, asking "Name? Name? Name?" while Arjun stood by, growing more and more wary of Simrin and more and more sullen over Jaishri's developing admiration.

It took a whole month before he stopped brooding. She had watched Arjun carefully. There was something shimmery about him, a gravitational pull he seemed to effortlessly exude. She felt it too. So when they were finally paired together for dinner cleanup, she gave him the last Tic Tac in her secret stash. And the next day, she let him catch her playing tag. And the next, she asked if he was sure he wasn't six. And soon he was showing her how to play chopsticks during meditation without the grown-ups knowing, how to make it look like you washed the plates just by dunking them, how to not worry about learning the weekly mantra and get away with mouthing nonsense, how to lean against him during *satsang* and just rest.

And then it was the three of them, Arjun leading the way and both Jaishri and Simrin following behind. They followed him from sunrise meditation to breakfast to *pathshala*, where they learned to read from two dog-eared copies of *A Duck Is a Duck*. Then to lunch, then karmic yoga duties (mostly dishwashing and picking up trash and sometimes, when there was someone handing out assignments who didn't like kids, floor scrubbing). Then to *abhyasa* for meditation and breathing and hatha yoga instruction and sometimes (if they were lucky) Amar Chitra Katha comics. Then (blessedly) free time. Then evening meditation. Then dinner. Then *satsang*. Sure, they played at Ananda, but it was *vishrama*, ten-minute spurts meant to give the mind a rest. Unless it was Sunday. Sunday was all-day *vishrama* for everyone, including the adults, which meant no one cared what the kids were doing or where they were doing it because they were resting their grown-up minds.

So on Sundays, the kids wandered deep into the desert. There was always a bunch of them, sometimes five, sometimes twelve. They hunted lizards and tried to steal their tails, collected cigarette butts and empty beer cans and pretended they were hobos, put piles of tumbleweeds in the center of the highway and placed bets on whether the cars would swerve around or stop and move them. Sometimes they trekked to town, the adults not caring if they brought a baby and no water, or if they stayed off the road, or even if they wore shoes. Sometimes they just trudged around Ananda, half-heartedly playing hide-and-seek in the kitchen and dining hall or, when they were older, just walking and talking, dragging sticks around Rudraksh, the pavilion where all meetings and meditations took place. They ate crackers with filthy hands and let the babies go naked instead of changing their diapers. It was Sunday. *Vishrama*. Grown-up minds were resting. And no one was bothered by the fierce dichotomy between six days of vigilance and one day of neglect.

She can't imagine ever ignoring Quinn for an entire day. How stupid the grown-ups must have been. She turns over and opens her laptop to the first of the three emails: Simrin. I think of you often and with deep affection. Arjun. She feels the lump rise in her throat, and she swallows it down. It has been a long, long time, and she suddenly aches—for him, for her mother, for fucking Ananda. It is rare that she is overcome by nostalgia, but all at once she longs for the desert silt caked stubbornly between her toes, the women's sour sweat layered beneath homemade incense, the *dal chawaal* slopping over her steel bowl as she ran to find a place next to Jaishri. And Arjun, always Arjun, fawned over and petted and exalted while slyly stealing packs of gum for the three of them.

You've found me, she writes. Or he has chosen to be found. Underneath her need, still bitterness. And now what, Arjun? she writes. Now, what.

She clicks send and shuts the laptop.

◆ ◆ ◆

The next morning, Simrin wakes up and checks her email. Nothing. She is surprised at her profound disappointment. Such a different life, such a long time ago. Still, with Quinn about to start the madness of kindergarten, the last thing she needs is something else to worry about. She has just received the welcome packet from Griffin Day School, and she pages through the handbook—pictures of scrubbed and braided girls eating lunch under a sycamore tree, pairs of children engaged at computers, bigger boys shirtless and goofily smiling at the camera on a track field. Tom can go through it. He is thrilled about the school. She should be thrilled, too, he says. The foofy co-op was fine for preschool, but Quinn needs structure, discipline.

Structure and discipline. The words make her nervous. *Structure* and *discipline* are just nicer ways of saying *rules* and *regulations*. And Simrin spent her childhood trudging through rules and regulations. Although no one would have called them that at Ananda. Two hours a day of required meditation liberated. An hour of karmic yoga unshackled. Rules were for those chained to the physical world. Practices were for those seeking liberation.

But she is afraid Tom is partially right about structure. Quinn is five and can't write her name, routinely skips numbers when counting, and still often looks at books upside down. Still, even the idea of Quinn being asked to sit quietly at a desk makes Simrin recoil. And there are Quinn's "issues." The whole "business," as Tom calls it, of tasting words, seeing sounds, feeling colors. "She has an active imagination," Tom said when Quinn started running into furniture because the "orange with red thingies" of her father's voice got in her way. But when she refused to call him Daddy because it tasted of "too much toothpaste," and she cried inconsolably if she looked too long at the Kandinsky print in their neighbor's bathroom, he worried that there might be something more going on.

It has never seemed too unusual to Simrin. She has seen the pastels of certain voices and the deep hues of unexpected booms for as long as she can remember. Her alphabet is colored too. She only realized this wasn't normal in seventh grade, the age Ananda determined was appropriate to leave their homeschooled isolation and trudge off to the local public school. In English class, they read Rimbaud's poem "Vowels." Why, she asked the teacher, didn't Rimbaud use the right colors for the vowels? The teacher looked at her, confused. "He writes that *A* is black," she said, "when it's really red. *E* is white instead of purple, like that." The teacher stumbled, not knowing how to answer, until some kid in the back came out with, "Letters aren't certain colors, dumbass." "In your head they are," she said, defensively. There was a too-long silence, and at the end of class, the teacher pulled her aside and explained that she might have something called synesthesia. She was embarrassed. And terrified. And she went straight to the library after school and spent the next four hours researching. There wasn't much to find then, a bunch of references to nineteenth-century philosophers and their colored music performances, some articles about the "study of consciousness" that she couldn't really understand. But for the first time she realized that what she had had a name.

"Lots of artists have it," she told Tom when he insisted they ask the pediatrician. "It's not a *disease*." But Simrin conceded to the tests, each one pointing out some slight motor delay, some minor cognitive lag, nothing that indicated any straight-up diagnosis—just . . . "issues." They agreed to more testing next year. "Kindergarten will be good for her," the specialist said, and Tom had latched on to this like an antidote. Kindergarten!

She has thought about homeschooling. Her neighbor does it. But twenty-four hours with a five-year-old sounds life draining. Not to mention the fact that Simrin's own schooling includes huge gaps. School at Ananda was a joke. They learned to read and write and do simple math, but American geography? Writing cursive? Simrin had, in fact, just recently taught herself how to use commas. Instead they memorized sutras and mantras and asanas. They learned to hold *sirsasana* for five minutes, and to recite the thirty-five steps of soul reincarnation, and to alter their breathing depending on whether they were overexcited or nervous or couldn't sleep.

And public school wasn't much better. What they learned when they were finally released into the wild of middle school was mostly about the enormity of their seclusion. They didn't know who the president was or how to jump rope or that you needed to ask for permission to go to the bathroom. Once a boy mockingly asked Simrin to "go" with him, and she answered with an apologetic "I'm actually going to my fourth-period class."

No. Simrin wants better for Quinn. The truth is Simrin likes Griffin well enough. They have an innovation lab and a playground with a zip line and free-choice time every day. Quinn will probably flourish there, which produces its own kind of discomfort. Quinn is so miraculously Quinn, and the idea that she could change, mutate based on where they deposit her is something Simrin doesn't like to think about. It is too much power, too much influence. She has seen firsthand the consequences of adult stupidity. But—she takes a breath—this is not stupidity. It is school. And Simrin is not her mother. And Quinn is not her.

She's glad at least one of Quinn's parents is certain Griffin is a good fit, the one who's paying for it. There's no way Simrin could afford private school, but Tom, thankfully, is generous with money when it comes to Quinn. He gifts her with pretty much anything she asks for, and often she will come home with four new stuffed tigers—"She couldn't decide, Simone"—or a stomachache from the ice cream *and* doughnut *and* cupcake he has allowed. And his child support is always on time and often more than the prescribed amount.

And there is alimony.

Quinn was just over a year when they divorced. Tom hadn't wanted the separation. "I don't want a divorce, darling," he said three months after Quinn was born. "Just a girlfriend." Fine, she thought, fine; just get me a cleaning lady, but after six more months, when Quinn began to come into her cherubic perfection and Tom began to look older and more ridiculous (how many more years could he possibly have of seducing graduate students?), she pushed for the divorce. Once his impulsivity and recklessness had been charming. He was the daring photography professor who forgot to attend class because he was so absorbed in getting a light trigger to work in direct relation to a delay circuit, the eccentric Brit who took her on their first date to a garbage dump to photograph other people's festering leftovers, the older man who proposed marriage in the driveway of his ex-wife's house. Simrin hadn't even wanted to get married. She was fine with being the mistress, fine with being the live-in girlfriend, even fine with being the baby mama, but when she got pregnant, he insisted on having the baby be legitimate. "It's not nineteenth-century London, for God's sake," she joked, but she agreed, and now she thanks her lucky stars that he was so insistent.

If her mother knew about the alimony, she might have an actual stroke. "I raised you at Ananda so you would be liberated," Simrin can hear her say. "Spiritually *and* economically." Money from a man for nothing but having been his wife was in the same category of sin as drowning kittens. But so was eating meat. Or ditching meditation. Or any of the other million things that Ananda claimed anchored you to your unenlightened self. Liberation was the goal, "release from the material form and delivery unto enlightenment." Even for six-year-olds.

It's been a long time since Simrin tried to convince her mother that liberation is not children learning Sanskrit. Or taking silent eight-mile walks. Or performing endless breathing exercises. She rarely talks to her mother these days. Her mother never calls, and even now, when things have loosened at Ananda, getting her mother on the main phone is a test of patience and endurance—having to talk to whoever answers, then whoever happens to be in the main office, and then finally waiting an excruciatingly long time (once she clocked it at twenty-three minutes) for her mother to get to the phone and then chatter on about what everyone in the community has been up to, rarely remembering to ask about Simrin or Quinn but also certainly not discussing what constitutes liberation.

But the irony is that Simrin *is* liberated, and Tom's money is partially the reason. At least it was for the first three years of their separation, before her blog *Hole and Corner* went viral, before that one picture of Stephanie Bradford moments before she died won Simrin the internet and got her over a million hits (not to mention the 9,417 comments and 11,423 shares on Facebook). When she went to shoot the Wellness Institute, it had mostly been out of curiosity. A college girlfriend had succumbed so heavily to the "take back your life" rhetoric that Simrin secretly wondered if she too could "root by becoming unrooted." She hadn't (too much screaming, too much talk of energy), but she had been there when Stephanie Bradford had the first seizure, had caught the Wellness facilitators on camera as they held back the students who wanted to help, insisting the woman "process her pain" until finally some participant punched the facilitator blocking the one exit (Simrin caught that blow too; 800,000 hits, 6,234 comments, 8,732 shares) and ran to call 911.

And then, miraculously, the viewers stayed. Three months later she had 687,452 followers on Facebook, 283,043 on Instagram, and around 55,000 viewers a month. So despite Tom's insistence that there would never be a market for serious photography online, there was, particularly when those serious photographs exposed and illuminated worlds people never got to peek at, secret societies that *Hole and Corner* unsecreted. "You have to be barely visible," an investigative reporter once advised her, and she had thrilled at the concept. Being invisible was something she had spent her childhood simultaneously trying to perfect and shed, so "barely visible" was completely doable. Barely visible was being just pleasant enough, just pretty enough, just unassuming enough to gain access to places she had no business. And in doing so, she has captured Hasidim—the mohel sucking the blood from the baby's penis, the bride's pile of just-shorn auburn hair in the bathroom sink; the Society for the Preservation of Animals—their complete vandalization of the seven Portland butcher shops, the close-range murder of the guard dog at the Aris storage facility because it was better he not live at all than live a life so tormented; and the unassisted birth movement; the Orgasmic Meditation Center; the Wiccan Covenant of the Goddess. All odd sequestered communities where despite being markedly out of place, she's never felt more than mild discomfort. Except with the children. The kids always get to her.

Once, at the Church of All Nations, she secretly followed a little girl into the bathroom and watched as she locked herself in the stall and stood on the toilet seat to avoid a ritualized head shaving. Simrin had wanted to grab the girl and run, or slip her her phone number, or promise she too would eventually get out, but instead she had just stood there until the girl's mother found her and bribed her out with a chocolate bar. And then, what was there left to do but take the pictures? So Simrin had gone back to the sanctuary and shot and shot and shot, over two hundred pictures of just that little girl and her perfectly smooth brown head. And then she had chosen one heartbreaking shot and sheltered it away in a folder of images she calls "The Children's Ward."

There are fifty-seven images in that folder, each pulled from different shoots, each a different child, all looking badly in need of help. They aren't all neglected and traumatized, although there are those. Some are just kids caught in distressing moments. She has one of Quinn crying, looking like she should be recruited for foster care. She admires their lack of artifice, how blatant and unconcealed the children's pain is. But the truth is it feels more like penance, a collection plate for her childhood self. Once she went through and titled each picture "I see you" one to fifty-seven. Fifty-seven moments of evidence, fifty-seven pieces of proof that someone was not only watching but seeing.

But she doesn't share these pictures. The pictures she shares are the ones she knows will be retweeted, reblogged, and reshared on sites like jScoop and Dtown and PhotoShoppe. These are the pictures that hit the sweet spot that rides both pop culture and respected photography, the pictures that a year ago began to generate income. Not in huge amounts, but enough to make the wedding photography gigs fewer and farther between. Then came the viewer submissions. Each week she featured one photograph chosen from hundreds of submitted shots, and one of them had produced another viral moment. The photograph came through the Whisper app, an anonymous couple having sex on the assembly line of a Dollhouse Donuts. The whole internet viewed the photo, everyone trying to figure out which Dollhouse it was and how to get it shut down. Her hits doubled, her ad sales tripled, and the offers came, the most attractive from Mutineer.

They offered her a serious chunk of money to photograph the "secret society of those daring enough to wear the Mutineer brand." It will be a photo shoot in her trademark style! But with models! And microslub tees! It was depressing. And exhilarating. Money coming in. A name for herself. A sellout by any photojournalist's standards. But maybe photography is photography. Ultimately, you look through the viewfinder and shoot. Dewy-eyed newlyweds, fighting pit bulls, newborns' wrinkled fists, environmental disasters, high-waisted jeans on adolescent models. There is something subversive about infiltrating any proscribed unit, whether it's capturing a father's hard smack at his son's head in a Pentecostal church or the quick grimace of a bride's meticulously turned-out father. Still, she hasn't quite talked herself into it yet. The contract is still sitting in her inbox, waiting for the electronic signature that will keep both her and Quinn in Mutineer clothing (and their apartment) for the next year.

For now, she still has money coming in. She has a gig in a few days, photographing some rising star conceptual artist's work. The woman, JJ Campbell, is an ex-programmer who bought some property in the woods near Fort Bragg and uses vintage computer parts to make mixed-media sculptures. Simrin might find something she hasn't expected to find. It happens regularly enough that she knows that what she should expect is not to expect anything. She doesn't even care that Tom connected her with this woman, but with gas and a possible overnight, she will barely come out financially ahead.

JJ is supposed to have emailed her the JPEGs of her current work. She clicks on JJ's flash-heavy current site and hears her email ping. She clicks over to her inbox, and there he is.

Simrin (is it Simrin still? I'm using Aaron for reasons you can imagine), I've been following your blog. Which felt odd. Voyeuristic.

So, here I am, coming clean. Voyeur no more. Love. It is definitely Arjun, engineered speech and puckish attitude. Her hands shake, and she types quickly, having to correct typos every few words. But he is online. Now. Just a click away.

Here you are, just appearing in my inbox, she writes. Her insides are a tangled snarl. If he were here, she would hit him, then hold him. For a long time. Good God, Arjun. I guess you've read my bio: San Francisco, kid, photographer, the blog. Fucking hell, where are you? She hits send and waits. And waits.

It isn't until the next morning that he emails back, and this time it is a long, detailed email. He is living on the outskirts of Ravenna, Nevada, with his wife, Bethany; their two daughters and a baby son—Juniper, eleven; River, seven; and seventeen-month-old Blaze—and eighteen other families each committed to not only communal living but doing what is best for the children. He tells her how the kids are unschooled—many of the seven-year-olds still can't read, but who cares? Two four-year-olds can, and the children have collectively grown an entire field of watermelons! There is a central homestead with five communal households, each with a separate indoor/outdoor kitchen and family space; there are rope swings and tree houses and a man-made lake with a play pirate ship and digging spaces and lumber/tools/nails everywhere for impromptu creations. Even the three-year-olds have access to hammers. And sometimes, they eat pancakes for breakfast, lunch, and dinner. They call it Meadowlark.

My God, Simrin thinks, he's created an anti-Ananda. The idea both thrills and terrifies her. Arjun once found a half-bound copy of a book called *Lara's Island* about a postapocalyptic band of children who had all their needs met by anonymous keepers who watched them through a giant glass bubble. They took turns reading it to each other, and even now Simrin can recite the section about Christmas: "The children awoke to find their stockings laden with treats: chocolate creams, peppermint sticks, and caramel apples covered with toffee bits; the tree sheltering piles of prettily wrapped presents: yellow-maned rocking horses, child-size cars that really went, and a menagerie of colorful stuffed zoo animals." She dreamed of the animals. Wondered if a monkey was considered a zoo animal and whether you could make one out of a used rice sack. "But what do they *do* all day," Arjun repeatedly wondered. And Simrin said nothing, still just barely able to remember a time that wasn't structured by mind, body, and spirit edification.

Meadowlark is *Lara's Island*. She can imagine Quinn there, painting pink and purple flowers on the kitchen walls, playing bakery with sand cakes and mud pies, tasting and feeling without confused stares and pitying smiles. And then, behind that feeling, another. "Meadowlark," he writes, "is a community of like-minded folks committed to helping children know and grow into their truth." She reads it and feels the icy wave of disengagement, her mind taking a step back from her body and curling up to take a nap. She can recognize that there is nothing truly remarkable in this one statement. So it's communal living. People all over the world live in communal households. And so what if they value children and truth. That's pretty much her life summed up right there. And yet *like-minded* feels awfully close to *indoctrinated* and *truth* dangerously close to *enlightenment*. But this is silly. He has spelled it all out for her in his email. Yes, these children are liberated, but it is the kind of liberation they could only dream of at Ananda. The kind she wishes for Quinn.

But it is his last line that dissolves any lingering worry. "Oh God, Simrin, I miss you," and just like that, she can see his voice, the familiar warm copper streamers. Her head lolls against the couch, and she watches him spill around her. The color weaves through her, back and forth, back and forth. And when it has disappeared, evaporated back into reality, she reads the line again, wanting another hit, but it is gone.

Let's talk, she writes.

She waits for him to write back, finds herself dreaming about him and Meadowlark more than she is comfortable with. She is distracted and absentminded, and she forgets that she has to drive north the next day until Tom, in usual Tom fashion, calls to say he can't take Quinn, that he is going to the Carowyn Music Festival, the haven of nubile drug users ("To *photograph* it, Simone. Lord," he tells her). She almost cancels JJ's shoot, but every day puts her closer and closer to the judge's alimony-cutoff day, so she loads her iPad up with videos and kindergarten-readiness apps and sets out.

It is a long windy drive, and Quinn chatters about the merits of different ponies until she falls asleep, her head knocking rhythmically against her high-backed booster. There is no one on the road, and Simrin realizes how little of her grown-up life has included silence and space. At Ananda she had too much of this. There were no physical boundaries, and she would often run until the compound was a small pink heap on the horizon behind her, her feet beating against the dirt, kicking up dried sage and scattering the occasional lizard. There were scorpions and rattlers out there, but she ran barefoot anyway. On some days, she felt invincible, and on some days, she just didn't care. A slow painful poisoning in the middle of the vast expanse of stars seemed preferable at times to the slow painful smothering she felt at Ananda. The desert was a giant living biosphere, full of hot and dusty spiders and beetles and yucca and juniper. It took her in, made her feel a part of itself. And made her happy. Free of the eyes and ears of everyone who loved her "wholly—spirit, mind, and body" while simultaneously forcing her to detach from herself.

But *forcing* is the wrong word. Nobody at Ananda forced anyone. No one was beaten or deprived of food. There is not one single instance in her childhood that she can point to that would legally be defined as either abuse or outright neglect. But there was disappointment, and shame, and silence. Every reprimand seemed to somehow involve silence. Once she was sentenced to 110 minutes of silent reflection for sneaking banana chips into meditation, 10 minutes for every slice; another time she silently walked the perimeter of Ananda for 140 minutes, contemplating why running wasn't appropriate during *abhyasa*. All for her own good. All to help ease her closer to enlightenment.

Years after she left, in one of the many phone conversations with her mother about the oppressiveness of Ananda, Simrin had said, "You realize silence is a method of control." Her mother had gasped—literally gasped—then said, "Ananda is the embodiment of liberation," and hung up. And she was right. Ananda, at least in theory, was the embodiment of liberation. And liberation was achieved in many ways—liberation from the self and liberation from society's arbitrary dictates. It was why the children were expected to do everything the grown-ups did. It was why the council was made up of men, women, and children in equal number. Every January there was an election, and every January each subsection of the community voted their council members in. There were five representatives—one for children, women, men, those with jobs outside Ananda, and those with jobs inside—and four specialists: treasury, community, spirituality, and grounds. Together they formed the people's council, a rotating governance, all authority spread evenly over Ananda's blessed. Or so they said.

She drives for two hours and then pulls to the side of the road to dig out a granola bar. She checks her phone and warms when she sees another email from Arjun. Meadowlark is going through some growing pains, so might not be able to email for a few days. We're getting hassled by some city government types. Love.

She closes her eyes, lets the warm expand inside her until Quinn stirs in the back seat, and she starts the car quickly and eases back onto the highway.

Quinn sleeps until they turn onto the dirt road that leads to JJ's studio. They follow the rocky lane, then park the car, and Simrin collects her bags and tripod.

"I'm hungry," Quinn says.

"There's Goldfish in your bag," Simrin says.

"Ick! *Bag* tastes like peanut butter!"

"Sorry, there's Goldfish in your *sack*." She looks around—a wooden yurt, converted barn, and small cabin with a large porch. The front door opens, and a very tall woman with an inch of platinum-blonde hair comes out.

"Nothing's ready," she says. "We were supposed to get the cherry picker yesterday, but the hitch broke on the truck, and anyway . . . it'll have to be tomorrow."

You could have called, Simrin wants to say. "Well . . . we're almost four hours from home. I'm Simone, by the way."

"Who's 'we'?" the woman demands.

Quinn pops out of the car and drops the Goldfish in the dirt. "Mama!" she shrieks.

"This is Quinn," Simrin says.

JJ runs a hand over the top of her head and sighs. "This isn't really a place for children."

Simrin feels her temper flare. "Well, she's here now," she snaps. Then softens. "Sorry." Even after five years of being someone's mother, she often forgets that children are not welcome everywhere. "Last-minute emergency," she says.

This seems to shake JJ. "No, no. It's fine, it's fine," she says and invites them in. The house is nearly empty of furniture, but there is a kitchen table and chairs, and they sit down and eat oyster crackers and grapes.

"You can stay the night in the yurt, if you like," JJ says. "There's a wood-burning stove and a pallet."

"Yay!" Quinn squeals.

JJ raises an eyebrow.

"We just read the first Boxcar Children," Simrin says. "They sleep on a pallet."

"I loved the Boxcar Children when I was young," JJ says. "I have my own Watch, you know."

Quinn's eyes grow large.

"Want to meet him?"

"Yes, yes!" Quinn continues. "Please, Mama, please!"

Simrin nods, and they follow JJ out the back door into a sprawling landscape of redwood trees, boulders, and a large chicken coop.

"Watch!" JJ calls. She whistles with her fingers. Quinn shakes her head. Bright yellow, Simrin knows, in waves. She squeezes Quinn's shoulder.

Soon a big shaggy mutt comes barreling through the trees, followed by two smaller dogs.

Quinn shrieks with happiness and bends down to pet them.

"This is Watch." JJ points to the big dog. "And Turtle and Duck."

"That's silly." Quinn giggles and lets the big dog tumble her to the ground. Soon she is up and running around, trying to get the dogs to chase sticks.

"She loves animals," Simrin says.

"Well, you're welcome to stay."

"You'll be ready to go tomorrow?" she asks JJ.

"Definitely," she says. "Probably."

Simrin checks her phone. No service. "Okay, sure. Thanks."

They unload and look around the yurt. There is a broken ukulele in the corner, and Quinn picks at the strings.

"It's a rainbow. Listen, Mama, listen."

Occasionally, Simrin can still hear colors, but much of it has faded as she's grown. A revving motorcycle is still clearly a spiky white, static on the radio bulbous bubble gum pink. But voices are rarely tinted now, and she has never heard instruments. Synesthesia is inherited, but what Quinn can see and hear and taste seems like a 3-D blockbuster next to Simrin's 8 mm home movie.

"Remember, Q, not everyone can see what they hear."

"But you can."

She wonders how much of her synesthesia was lost to childhood and how much was forced out of her. As a child, she learned not to talk about it, at least with the grown-ups. "You sound like smoke," she would say to a teacher, and in return she would get an extra hour of karmic yoga for lying. But Arjun would pester her to describe the sound of a bottle opening, the slam of a door. "It's not *all* sounds," she would say, but he would push: "Just listen; just try and see it; just tell me how to do it." But she didn't know how. And, she assumes, Quinn doesn't either. It's just a part of her.

Simrin listens to the tang of the notes slowly start to become a pattern, then lengthen into an actual arrangement. It has been this way for the last year. Quinn will find an instrument and quickly master which keys or strings do what and what she needs to press or strum to make a recognizable melody. She can't play what you want her to play, is not one of those prodigy children who hears a Mozart piano sonata and then plays it right back, but still, people's eyes go wide when they hear her. They insist Quinn start music lessons. But Simrin is slow to do much of anything concerning Quinn, the two of them held in a stationary bubble of now.

"Wow, Quinn," is all she can say.

"Red, yellow, red, yellow, red," Quinn sings softly.

Simrin lies on the pallet and closes her eyes.

"Mama, I'm hungry," Quinn says.

They find their way to the closest town and eat hamburgers and sweet potato fries. After, they get cherry Slurpees from the 7-Eleven and sit on the curb and watch two crows fight over a sandwich. Simrin finds a weak signal and texts Tom that they'll be home by Tuesday. There is some kind of orientation on Monday, but it's kindergarten, for God's sake, and Quinn has already been for an interview, a class playdate, and finally a week of summer school to "ease the transition." What could they possibly be doing that is so essential?

"Are you excited about school, Quinn?" she asks.

"Am I going to have homework?"

"Maybe."

"I want homework! And I want to go on a school bus."

"Well, I think Papa and I will be taking you."

"Why?"

"I don't think Griffin has a bus." Simrin's phone whistles. Quinn needs to be there on Mon, Tom writes.

"What?" she says aloud. Why, she writes. His reply comes immediately. It's bloody school. It's another bloody practice run, she wants to write, and it's not about *you*. Tom often waxes poetic about his very British childhood boarding school. He was nicknamed Binks for reasons Simrin can't remember, and he will regale whoever will listen with tales of boarding school food ("The butter was almost always rancid, and we loved it!") and punishments ("Oh, the chair, the chair! You'd have to keep your knees even with your bum, or it was the paddle for you!"). It sounds horrible, and she wonders how one could remember such apparent agony with such fondness.

Fine, she writes back to Tom. Today is Saturday. JJ will have to get it together by Sunday, or Simrin will have to drop Quinn and come all the way back. Fucking school.

"Can we get a cookie?" Quinn asks.

"You just had a Slurpee."

"Please," Quinn begs.

Simrin looks at Quinn, so much a carbon copy of herself—fine brown hair and big brown eyes, skin so thin and white you can see the veins pulsing in her wrists and temples—that when Tom's son saw her at seven months, he couldn't help but joke that Tom's genes must have been too old to be passed down.

Simrin grabs Quinn's hand and squeezes, two squeezes. Quinn squeezes two back, then changes the pattern. It is their secret code, the way they say *I love you* without *love*, the word too shiny when sandwiched between *I* and *you*.

"One cookie," she says.

◆　◆　◆

The next day the cherry picker does not arrive. JJ is apologetic but unconcerned. And Quinn has the dogs to play with; and five chickens, each named after a Linux distribution; and a shed full of junk; and a soldering iron that JJ shows her how to use—"With help!" Simrin insists.

The property is charmingly rustic. Simrin has never been drawn to landscape photography, but the bright-orange lichen against the ashen boulders against the gray sky is strikingly beautiful, and she spends the day shooting a fish-eye series.

The next morning, she is framing Quinn and the dogs when JJ comes to find her.

"All set!" she says.

For a moment, Simrin is confused, so absorbed by how naturally they have slid into this life. "Oh, right," she says.

"Disappointed?" JJ asks.

Simrin blushes at her own transparency.

"I actually have to go up to Vancouver for a week," JJ says. "I was going to get the neighbors to look in on the dogs and chickens, but you're welcome to stay."

Simrin feels the thrill of another week, and then the sudden extreme weight of her body, her shoulders pushing her into the dirt. She can already hear Tom fuming in her head. "She's not a sociological experiment, Simone," he said when she bristled at Griffin. It was an allusion to Ananda, and she flushed and gritted her teeth. Now, she is sure he will pull no punches. He has a ferocious temper, and although it is rare, he is nasty when he feels justified. "Your views will always be suspect," he once said. "You were brainwashed by a fucking cult!" They rarely, thank God, fight about Quinn, but surely this is instigation, and she wonders if it's worth it, to have this empty, easy time with Quinn, to remember what it feels like to be "of the world but not in it," as the adults would joke at Ananda. Someone once told her ages three to five were the magic years, and Simrin can already feel the enchantment they have been under slowly draining as the summer slips away.

"We'd love to stay," she says to JJ.

"Excellent!" JJ says.

"Yes," Simrin says. Her heart is racing. "Excellent." She says it aloud, more to convince herself than to state her position.

The shoot is uneventful, but JJ is happy with the pics and leaves Simrin with a list of local attractions she and Quinn can explore—the glass beach, a botanical garden, the skunk train—but instead they do nothing, just climb rocks and chase chickens and eat cereal. The first day JJ is gone, Simrin hears a car on the dirt road. She is sure it is Tom, and she calls for Quinn to come inside and then makes her cry by yelling at her. But it is just one of the neighbors. Two days fly by, and Simrin is alternately anxious and more at ease than she's been in a long, long time. She has no phone signal, no TV, no computer, and she settles into their isolation, trying not to obsess about lost shares and likes, trying not to think about Tom's certain anger, trying not to count the days until she will have to bring Quinn back. And she thinks about Arjun. She emails him from town what she hopes is a breezy understanding email: Take your time. Hope it all goes smoothly. On their fourth day on their own, she locates Ravenna on a map JJ has in an old almanac, trying to glean something, anything, from the black dot that marks his spot.

That afternoon they go into town to buy bread, bananas, and milk from the elderly man at the 7-Eleven. There is a stack of *Mendocino*

*Beacon*s, and Simrin picks one up and—feeling friendly—waves it at the man. "I haven't read a real newspaper in years," she says.

"It's on me." The man smiles.

They dawdle in the store. Simrin agrees to another chocolate crunch cereal, and they make their way back to the car. "Is this home?" Quinn asks on the drive back.

Simrin laughs. "No, unfortunately we have to go back in two days."

She almost forgets the newspaper in the car, but Quinn remembers the comics. "Don't forget the drawings," she says, so they unfold the paper on the kitchen table and make a shared bowl of cereal. They read *Peanuts* (thumbs down from Quinn) and *Garfield* (thumbs-up), and Quinn colors the black-and-white pictures with her colored pencils while Simrin leafs through the local section. And then she comes upon a small article on the bottom of the third page: Local Family Involved in Escalating Nevada Tension. "Troy Carlson of Mendocino; his wife, Marsha; and their two children are involved in escalating tensions with the City of Ravenna police department. Six months ago, the family left Mendocino, where Carlson was born and raised, for Meadowlark, a community that describes itself as a self-sustaining cooperative."

Simrin pins the paper to the table with her elbows and reads: "There have been allegations of child abuse from someone formerly inside the commune, Child and Family Services has been sent and rebuked, the gates have been slammed. No one is getting in."

"No," Simrin says. Why would Arjun omit this in his email? Because he's afraid she'll think it's true? Because it is true? She can't help but think of the story here. It is a nauseating thought—both the possibility of this truth and her own thrill at the possibility.

Her phone has been drained of battery for two days, and she plugs it in and impatiently watches the charging icon fill and empty, fill and empty. They will have to drive to town to get enough service for her to email him, and then what? They'll stand there and wait for a reply? And even if he does reply, what will he say? "It's all lies" and "Please come" and

"I need you." Even the thought of him asking makes her heart pound. She spent a good two years after he left her alone at the hotel waiting for that call, that email. Every ring of her phone held the possibility; every knock at the door prompted ten seconds of full-blown anxiety. She would have to take deep *pranayamic* breaths just to answer. She hates him for this, but these surges of adrenaline are also comfortably familiar, her last tie to him—the same concentrated panic as when they left Ananda.

Their exodus, they called it, completely ignorant of the full weight of the allusion. Looking back, she thinks, it must have all begun a year before they actually left, the summer she was fourteen. The council had decided the teenagers needed more responsibility, so Jaishri was sent to the nursery, Simrin to the ambiguously named "community upkeep," and Arjun to the treasury, where he learned that Ananda had not paid property taxes in years. Within weeks he had negotiated partial payments and then a few days later found the money by selling off old stock options belonging to a longtime member. Outside of Ananda, he would have been given a scholarship to business school. Inside Ananda he began to look more and more like an unexpected guru to a small faction of community members. Arjun, the first child born at Ananda, with those penetrating eyes. Arjun, who, at only fifteen years of age, had saved Ananda. Arjun with his 100 percent accuracy of knowing the sexes of unborn babies and his uncanny ability to remember every community member's birthday. The golden child with the eye-shaped birthmark (a sign?), who in the months after the awesome tax-payment feat gained more and more adoration.

At first, the adulation was minor, funny even. Rupa made a joke about washing his feet, but then she had done it, with real jasmine-scented water. And Aarti, who playfully called him Arjun-ji, started oiling his hair every Sunday. He had always been able to meditate longer than the other kids, but now there was talk that his capabilities surpassed most of the adults', and didn't he seem to have a glow while he practiced? Soon there were casual requests for Arjun's opinion on the placement of furniture and what to name new babies, but when the questions on whether meditation was more effective in the morning or evening began and the inquiries about the benefits of *nadi sodhana* versus *kapalabhati* became more earnest, some members began to worry. Ananda had left that all behind. Gurus were dangerous, easily corrupted by power and adoration. There were still many who had seen it, founding members of Ananda who remembered seceding from Sambodhya to form Ananda.

The Ananda kids weren't told much about Sambodhya. As much as transparency was encouraged at Ananda, the most they ever got out of the grown-ups was that there had been a bad man. He thought he was a guru, "But any man that accepts the adoration of another is merely a worshipper of his own ego," Jyoti would say. Because of this, those truly dedicated to enlightenment formed Ananda, a place of liberation and freedom. Years later, for a freshman seminar, Simrin thought that if she had to research something, it might as well be something she was curious about, so she investigated Sambodhya. She was able to dig up old news stories about the group and their guru, a man named Hercules Shakir, who embezzled a bunch of money and ran away with two eighteen-year-old female disciples. Simrin found a picture of the three, a grainy image reproduced on microfiche. The two long-haired girls flanked an old bearded man, and all three smiled straight into the camera. Of course no one wanted the Ananda kids to know; of course members became concerned when Arjun began to appear more and more . . . well . . . divine.

But it was the "trying triumvirate," as Simrin, Arjun, and Jaishri called them, who were particularly bothered. Akshay, Gopal, and Lakshman had collectively served on the council for the past eleven years. They were three of the original thirty-six founders of Ananda, once devoted and vigorous young men who had slowly aged into stubborn, sedentary old men. Gopal was now fat, and when he had lectured a group of them on Ganesh's many names, Gopal being one, Jaishri, only seven, had naively piped in with, "Oh, that's why you're so fat." He had turned bright red and never returned for other lessons. Both Akshay and Lakshman rarely left their roost in Ambar's community room. It was the only house built on risers, and out the front room windows, you could see much of Ananda. When everything began to shift, Simrin would often look up and see them perched like vultures.

The changes came around soon after the miracle of the property taxes. The triumvirate cornered Arjun after dinner one night and left him pale. "What did they say?" Simrin asked.

"They said I couldn't run for children's representative again."

"That's not fair!" she said.

"They said life wasn't fair," he answered.

It was such a strange thing for them to say, to bring "life" into this place of liberation and enlightenment, and she thought he would protest, demand to take this to a council vote, but he didn't. Instead, he stayed still when it was time to nominate a new representative and watched Saachi tentatively raise her hand and break his five-year tenure.

Slowly, the council shifted, turned their moony faces to the triumvirate. And soon the council was worried that over the years meditation had been shaved of minutes, so minutes were added. Chicken had somehow sneaked into the kitchen rotation, and even though many abstained, meat had not been in the original Ananda charter; it was now cut. No one complained. In fact, there was near consensus. Everyone agreed Ananda needed a shot of discipline, needed a reminder that liberation required consistency. Enlightenment required restraint. Fast days, days of silence, full days of karmic yoga. It was all horrible but tolerable.

But then the incident with the camera occurred. Five months earlier, someone had pointed out that Ananda had no visual history. Arjun hadn't ceded his appointment as children's representative to Saachi yet, and so he had nominated Simrin for the position of photographer. She was apprenticed to community upkeep, he said. She was a natural observer, he said. So the treasury gave her forty dollars, and she found a Canon Super Sure Shot in Paula's Pawn. It had a fixed lens and autofocus, and it came with four rolls of 35 mm film. At first, she shot indiscriminately, going through all four rolls in a week. It was cheaper to send them away to be developed, so she had to wait for the prints. In the meantime, she found Sally Mann's *At Twelve: Portraits of Young Women*. She was afraid to check it out from the library, but she hid it in the philosophy section, thinking everyone in that hick town was checking out murder mysteries or cookbooks or pawing encyclopedias for class projects. The Mann pictures made her uncomfortable, the girls too close to her age, too confident in their hard stares, each detail hypnotic and troubling—the blood stain on the quilt, the discarded tennis shoe in the grass. She couldn't yet see the photographer behind the camera.

When her photos came in the mail, she was hugely disappointed— the colors were too bright, her framing awful, and her mother had to rescue the lot of them from the trash. But she begged the treasury for ten more dollars and was judicious with her film this time. She recorded Ananda cautiously, watching everything through the viewfinder and wishing she had subjects more interesting than dozens of pairs of shoes outside the great hall, the babies getting oil massages, the empty desert with Jaya and Saachi turning cartwheels.

Soon, she had figured out the rule of thirds and aspect ratio. And when the treasury refused to give her more money for film until next month, Arjun pawned a gold chain his mother had given him for his sixteenth birthday and left ten rolls on her pillow. She sneaked photos during meditation—Aditya's calloused hand scratching his ass, her own dirty feet on her zabuton. The color still seemed awful, but she was pleased with her composition (she called it display, then) and thrilled that Priya wanted the one of her combing her wet hair on her bed (the next shot had been her snapping at Simrin to get that "fucking camera out of my face!"). Simrin buzzed. She felt she was seeing in a way she never had before. She shot three-year-old Rohan sunburned and peeling from hours out in the hot desert, Karan spooning uneaten rice back into the dinner pot, Gopal pissing on a tree rather than walking all the way back to the house, Lakshman preventing six-year-old Deepika from using the bathroom during meditation until, eventually, she wet herself. It was dangerous and exciting, capturing the pieces of Ananda that no one wanted to look at, that no one was allowed to look at. Life at Ananda had always been just life, but the viewfinder gave her distance, allowed her to remove herself from the photo and look at it as if it was someone else's life. And the life she saw was becoming unsettling.

The more the triumvirate exerted their control, the more capturing the negative became resistance. Usually resistance was met with shame and silence. She had had plenty of talking-tos about the state of her heart, plenty of assignments of mantras that would help her mind catch up with those closer to liberation, plenty of silent karmic yoga cleaning, scrubbing toilets and shower drains, but then the council called her in for a meeting. The camera was distracting her from her studies. The camera was diverting energy from her spiritual pursuits. The camera was proving to be an unwanted disruption of Ananda's higher goals. Saachi, who was by then the children's representative, bit her lip, and Simrin glared at her. "I won't use it as much," Simrin said. "Please." Saachi stared at her feet, fingering her mala, and Simrin wanted to tear it from her hand, watch the 108 beads scatter to the dirty floor.

But Jyoti was the one who held out her hands for the camera, both together as if in offering. "Simrin," she said, "you must." The triumvirate sat, Gopal so big he only balanced on the chair, the vultures now busy thumbing through a stack of papers. The few others, even Saachi, nodded solemnly, no one paying much attention to equality for all while kindly, sympathetically, and firmly insisting that she return the camera immediately. And Simrin did, found herself handing it over, and afterward felt like she was rapidly collapsing, sand running through her like a broken hourglass.

A week later, Simrin broached the topic of their exodus. There was a group of them—not only Jaishri, Arjun, and Simrin but Priya and Saachi, Krish, and Gautam—huddled under the blanket of night, hiding half a bottle of vodka. There was no drinking at Ananda, but Priya

had delved into a flirtation with a townie, and he had presented it as
an offering. They took big gulps from the bottle, then cursed and spit
into the desert sand.

"Jesus Christ," Gautam said. "What the fuck is this made of?"

"Just drink it," Priya said.

None of them but Priya had ever had alcohol before, and Priya only
last week at lunch behind the bleachers. Simrin felt the warm rush of
it pulse through her body. "I'm hot," she said and took off her sweater.

"That's the booze," Priya said.

"The resident expert," Arjun said.

"Says the golden one." Priya reached over and socked him in the
shoulder, and Simrin felt the familiar urge to move closer to Arjun.

"If the shoe fits," he said and closed his eyes.

"Of course, he doesn't deny it," Priya said and took another slug.
"Okay, mahatma."

This talk of Arjun as divine always made Simrin nervous. Last week
she had heard whispers of what would happen if the group seceded again,
and the next day there was a mandatory forum on the dangers of elevat-
ing men to the height of gods. Yesterday, flowers had shown up in Arjun's
shoes, and today's forum had been about the benefits of sex segregation
during *darshan*. Simrin rarely listened, had become expert at scrapbooking
photos in her head instead, but that day she had fixed on what Lakshman
had said: "Men and women, boys and girls need to consider the impact the
opposite sex has on their consciousness. *Especially* boys and girls, who may
need some assistance in this matter." In previous days, it might not have
sounded so ominous, but with everything changing so quickly, with her
own mother choosing to cover her head ("Just during worship," she had
said when Simrin questioned her. "I'm not some browbeaten housewife"),
and others choosing silence during what had once been happily communal
mealtimes, Simrin heard the threat under the platitude.

"Leave him alone," Simrin said.

Priya sighed loudly and rolled onto her stomach. "Krish, give me a massage."

"Please?" said Krish.

"Pleeeeeeease."

Simrin lay on her back and looked at the stars, and Jaishri cuddled up next to her and put her head on Simrin's stomach.

"Let's stay here forever," Jaishri said.

Simrin ran her fingers through Jaishri's hair. "Or never go back," she said. She had meant it like Jaishri had: *Oh the stars, oh this moment.* But as soon as she said it, she felt the resonance of the statement. Arjun turned, and they locked eyes.

"I wish," Jaishri said.

"No, you don't," said Saachi, the resident follower of rules.

"Yes, I do." She was too loud, and Simrin clamped her hand over Jaishri's mouth.

They had made Saachi drink, one tiny sip, collateral against her tattling, but threatening to run away was something else. There had only been one runaway since Ananda had formed, a legendary boy named Aadi who sneaked away one night and was rumored to have been found dead the next morning. No one spoke directly about it, but the story passed between the kids was that he had either been hit by a train, killed while hitchhiking, or been the recipient of so much focused prayer that he had simply imploded.

There was no distinct punishment for threatening to run away, but the unspoken warning lay beneath every swallowed threat: once you leave, you can never come back. Sure, some kids went to college, many moved off-site, and some even moved out of state, but they kept the pretense: "I meditate before class; I've even taught my roommate!" "We've made the walk-in closet a prayer room!" But choosing to leave Ananda without the blessing of the community, without a clear plan on how to continue your path out of *samsara*—that was unthinkable. And lately the community seemed harder to convince. Jyoti's daughter had visited last month and been peppered with very specific questions about which mantras she was chanting and why, and Jason, Rupa and Dinesh's son, who had stopped using his Ananda name so long ago that Simrin couldn't even remember it, came to visit and was asked to leave. Rupa had stood in reception, trying to hide her tears, while Dinesh stared at his feet and quietly insisted Jason go. After he left, Rupa and Dinesh had been given hugs and blessings, and a rice-and-turmeric *mala* appeared on their doorstep. There was no shame in having a defected family member—it was their karma to answer to—but one did not invite that karma to stay, even if said karma had been visiting once a month for years. So running away, clearly saying namaste to everything Ananda stood for, was something one did not bring up without serious fear. The amount of silent karmic yoga that would be doled out for this crime seemed unimaginable.

Simrin looked at Arjun, who had propped himself up on his elbow.

"Jai," he said, "come get water with me." They had always been protective of Jaishri, who was tiny for her age and seemingly incapable of understanding subtlety.

Jaishri lifted herself and stumbled, and Arjun caught her by the elbow. Simrin watched her lean against him, their figures illuminated in the moonlight.

The next day, as they walked to school, hungover and spent, Arjun had held her back.

"Did you mean it?" he asked.

She waited a breath, knowing that things would be forever changed as soon as she spoke. "Yes."

He looked at her hard and long. "When?"

She didn't know the answer, thought this was the moment where he, like always, would take charge. "I don't know."

"Think about it," he said. And so she did. Ananda was becoming more and more restrictive, but it wasn't that long until she was eighteen, and they could all get the fuck out and then fake their way into visits if they wanted, and even if gender segregation was implemented, it would just be for meditation. Who cared about that? But then the talk of Arjun's divinity reached its crescendo.

Four-year-old Kavya almost drowned, and despite the fact that there were five of them there to pull her from the swollen river, Arjun had been the one who had seen her topple off the rocks and carried her back to Ananda. There were rumors that Kavya had actually died and Arjun brought her back to life by laying his hands on her head, that Arjun's skin seemed to be taking on a bluish tint, that Ananda would be foolish not to accept a guru that showed himself so certainly. The whispers of seceding were no longer whispers.

Twelve days later at a Saturday meeting, the council announced *samriddhi*, a high school exchange program in India. On turning sixteen, students would be given the opportunity to deepen their practice and fortify their commitment to their higher selves by spending a year at Jai Meenakshi Ashram. This year Arjun, Deva, and Krish would be allowed to go. Simrin heard Jaishri's cry clear across the room. "Ishwar iccha," all the adults said. Krish and Deva were being congratulated, accepting blessings with a wide-eyed confusion. "That will be you next year," Simrin's mother said delightedly. "No," was all she could say, her own voice, normally invisible, now blue and powdery around her.

Very quickly Simrin, Arjun, and Jaishri put together a preliminary plan—the secret meetings and stashing of resources in the nursery and six-week timetable. But then it happened. Eight days after the announcement, when even Arjun's mother, who had for years been immersed in a deep depression, seemed cheerful with the news of something new and wonderful on the horizon, there was a particularly spirited *satsang*. A group pulled Arjun to the front, dancing around him and swaying their arms, grazing his head with their hands and offering blessings, but then Jaishri joined in, too, and God knows why, she knelt in front of Arjun, placed her forehead on his feet. Priya snorted. Gautam doubled over in fake laughter, but suddenly Gopal was there, pushing into the circle and seizing Jaishri. It looked comical at first, a massive man dangling a miniature girl by the arm, but then Gopal roared. "We do not worship men," he snarled.

The following day, Jaishri was taken to an empty bedroom where she was instructed to meditate on her betrayal for three days. It was the worst punishment ever doled out. By the first afternoon Jaishri's quiet crying had turned to weeping, and by dinner, Simrin couldn't even recognize the sounds as sobs.

"You have to do something," she told Arjun. So he did. During *satsang* that night, he sneaked away and into the main office, expecting it to be empty. And it was. He found the master key and took two rolls of quarters while he was there, but as he was leaving, he heard Gopal close by. It was unusual for anyone to miss *satsang*, so he sneaked down the hall and lurked outside the room where years of Ananda paperwork was stored in large filing cabinets.

"The car's coming at seven tomorrow morning," Gopal said.

And then it was Karan speaking. Asking questions about layovers and luggage requirements and transportation from the airport, and then he said Arjun's name, asked if any documentation was required besides the passport.

"The notarized form with his mother's signature is in the envelope," Gopal said. "It's all been taken care of," and Arjun knew. They were sending him away. Tomorrow. They needed to leave. Today.

That night, he sneaked into Simrin's bedroom. "Now," he said. And she didn't even pause. Not to grab a bag, not to look one last time at the room she had slept in the last eleven years, not to mouth a goodbye to her mother. She simply slipped her shoes on and followed him. Past the bathrooms and the green common room, down the stairs, out into the night, and then back into Ambar and to the empty bedroom, where Arjun slipped the key into the lock and slid the door open. Jaishri was asleep, and Simrin covered her mouth, knowing she would scream. And she had. But Arjun scooped her up, and then they were outside, with the moon barely a crescent, stumbling in the dark, Simrin and Arjun fighting over who had forgotten to get Jaishri's key for the nursery. Yes, Arjun had told Simrin to grab Jaishri's backpack from her bedroom. Fine, she would go back. Yes, she would meet them at the nursery. So Simrin had sneaked back in, up the stairs, into Jaishri's room, and grabbed her backpack and, turning the corner, ran almost straight into Saachi. Saachi shrieked, and Simrin froze, waiting for what she was sure was inevitable. The anger. The silence. The constant monitoring. And Arjun sent away. A whole year without him and then a whole other year while Simrin and Jaishri languished in India, where who knew what suffering would have to be endured. Two years of liberation through sitting and chanting and nothing, nothing, nothing. Mindless nothing, her head and body and heart doing nothing nothing nothing. Just stillness. Just emptiness. Just . . . nothing. No Arjun to meld into. And no way to even document it.

And so she ran. If she had been relying on adrenaline before, now it was unadulterated panic. Thumping down the stairs and to the nursery, unable to say anything but *hurry* through her desperate catching breaths. They grabbed what they had collected and shot out into the center yard, past Rudraksh, and the housing units, and the dining hall, but when they sprinted past the information center, Arjun stopped them. "Wait," he said. He ran into the dark, ignoring Jaishri's pleas to go, go, go. They could barely see him, and then they heard a low crash, a window carefully broken, so quickly and quietly that he must have stashed the drum mallet there earlier in the evening. Then silence. Nothing. The crickets and her heartbeat the only pounding in Simrin's ears. And when Simrin thought she would surely fall dead to the ground if she didn't run, *now*, a towering crash. Then another. And another. And another. And then finally Arjun whispering "*Run, run, run*," and them running, into the desert night. Only miles later when a lone truck passed them on the highway could Simrin see the blood saturating Arjun's left shirtsleeve and the camera slung around his neck like a holy mala, just for her.

She still has that camera. It sits on a high shelf where Quinn can't reach it. A relic. A reminder of how far she's come. She shakes her head.

It seems such a long time ago, and yet she can feel her heart keeping the same explosive rhythm in her chest.

Her cell phone has 30 percent battery, enough to drive to town and send the email. "We need to go back to town," she says to Quinn and then, to ward off the whining, "You can get a Popsicle."

Simrin hurries Quinn into the car. It's fifteen minutes to town, and she steals glances at her phone as she's driving, looking for service. Finally, she sees two bars, but she forces herself to drive to the 7-Eleven, buy the orange Popsicle for Quinn, and get her settled with her iPad in the back seat. Then she refreshes her inbox and watches the emails come in. Five new texts from Tom interrupt her download, and she feels her panic build. She refreshes again. And again. Nothing from Arjun. "Come on," she begs. But there is nothing. She feels the tears gather behind her eyes. So long ago and still so much there. She rests her forehead on the steering wheel.

And then she hears her phone's whistle. She dials her voice mail, inputs the code. Two voice mails from Tom, Jeannie wanting a playdate, and then there he is. She closes her eyes and listens, his voice as soft and safe as ever. "Simrin"—her name like a warm kitten, the familiar copper ribbons dancing above her head—"we've had to close in. The town's come up with some crazy accusations against us." He sighs. "It's a long story, Sim. But now the cops want to get inside. It's definitely escalated. I thought maybe if you took some pictures, put them online, showed everyone how ridiculous this whole thing is . . ." He trails off. "I don't know . . . you could bring Quinn. If you both can come. That . . . that would be swimmy." She smiles. That word, their own private word, what it felt like to cuddle in on each other, smell his unwashed hair, rub his bitten cuticles—like swimming in and out of each other's warm selves. She tried to explain it to Tom once, the sheltered space they had shared and the swimmy feeling of it. "So what else happened between the two of you?" he had teased. "Nothing," she had snapped back.

But now he has said it—swimmy—and effortlessly angled up all her love. And fierce devotion. She googles *Meadowlark, Ravenna,* and *conflict.* All small stories in West Coast papers, syndicated and embedded—the iron gates of Meadowlark closed, a few curious kids peeping out from the yellow-and-blue-painted bars. There is no mention of anyone trying to forcibly break in, but at the bottom of the second results page is a blog post from Operation Cultwatch. The post is short and the comments long. "These kooks in Ravenna, Nevada, are accused of child abuse." She skims the dozens of comments, stops on one from a user named BalkBack: "I have a friend outside of Elko. They say these dudes are crazy. They don't let their kids go to school." "Cool," someone else writes. Followed by, "Not for the kids." "This time it's the hippies not the evangelicals." It is BalkBack again. "Watch out Waco."

"What the hell?" Simrin says aloud.

"Language!" Quinn says.

"Sorry." She had been ten when Waco happened, and they had been drilled to answer prying questions about their lifestyle with, "Ananda Nagar is not a cult. A cult maintains totalitarian control over its members and is led by a self-appointed leader who has complete authority." She can remember standing in the grocery store in her thrift store dress, defeated but repeating this over and over while three local boys in cowboy boots yelled, "Culty, culty," and pretended to hock loogies at her. There is no way Arjun has created a cult, and she feels her anger swell at the idea that anyone would think he has.

She clenches the phone and looks in the rearview mirror. Quinn is holding the Popsicle in one hand, the other swiping and pressing the iPad, her feet steadily kicking the back of the seat. She is happy. And Simrin is about to disrupt that. Or maybe Quinn will see this as another grand adventure. Soon enough she'll be wearing a crisp plaid jumper, white knee socks, and regulation hair bows. Maybe this is meant to be their last magical voyage.

"Quinn," she says, "we're going to visit a friend of mine for a few days. We'll get lots of Popsicles."

◆ ◆ ◆

Once they are on the road, the calls come in every few hours. She can hear the pointed irritation in Tom's voice mails, and she knows she probably has only another day before the brute emerges. And he'll be right to be irate. He never paid much attention to his first two children, but he is enamored of Quinn, and she is, after all, his daughter, his family. But isn't this visit also about family? Isn't Arjun the closest thing she has to a sibling?

Still, she'd be lying if she said this is just family obligation. If it were her mother, she'd have no problem dropping Quinn home, booking a plane ticket for the following day or the one after that. But Arjun has always exerted some kind of centripetal force on her. Even at his worst, when she caught him admiring himself in the mirror, arms widespread, dozens of *malas* around his naked chest, a caricature of others' expectations, she would roll her eyes but then find herself magnetized, unable to look away. "He has superpowers," Jaishri had once said, and Simrin had felt both the panic of it being true and the distress of it not.

The drive is long, but they make it two hundred miles, over half the way to Ravenna, when Quinn begins to get antsy. Quinn is a good traveler, and as long as she has endless hours of cartoons, she doesn't complain. But they have exhausted all ten hours of movies, so they stop at a Walmart and load up on Life Savers and dollar-bin toys. Back in the car, Simrin finds some old musical soundtracks to stream and sheepishly puts on *Bye Bye Birdie*.

They had listened to little music at Ananda. The kids could almost get a top forty station if they went close enough to the main road, but Gautam and Priya were really the only ones patient enough to sit through the static. Other than that, there were *satsang* CDs and, inexplicably, a weird collection of '40s and '50s musicals on tape in one of the common rooms. Jaishri and Simrin were the only ones interested in those, and sometimes they would lie head to head, listening and trying to work out the stories.

"I used to listen to *Bye Bye Birdie* when I was a little girl," Simrin says.

"*Birdie* tastes like feathers," Quinn says.

"When have you tasted feathers?"

Quinn sighs. "It just does." She is quiet for a minute. "Are we ever going home?"

Simrin feels her stomach seize. "Of course."

"I miss Papa."

Simrin takes a deep breath and murmurs supportively.

"Change the song, please," Quinn says.

Simrin is amazed at how quickly Quinn can switch topics without the least emotional residue. Even if Simrin probes, tries to get her to talk about how she is feeling, she is done, and Simrin is always left with the anxiety of Quinn's anxiety. "How about *Oliver*?" she asks.

"Which one is that?"

"The one that starts with them singing about food."

"Yeah. That one is super bluish."

They've listened to half the soundtrack when the car needs gas. They find a sleepy station, and Simrin gets out of the car and stretches. The air seems denser, definitely hotter. The temperature on the dash reads eighty-seven degrees at seven p.m. Quinn jumps out behind her.

"Let's get a treat," Quinn says.

"You just had a chocolate muffin." This road trip has been a near smorgasbord of sugar. Pure bribery. Although for what, Simrin isn't sure. Truancy? Kidnapping? The thought makes her cringe. It's a few days, she reasons with herself. She's just checking on a friend. She has a right to her past. And yet beneath the rationalization is the scratch of something harder to reason with, how electric she feels, Arjun's magnetism still working on her twenty years later and hundreds of miles away.

"Gum?" Quinn tries. She went through a pack of Fruit Stripe on the drive yesterday.

"Gum. Sure," Simrin says. She will revert to responsible mother when they get home, make sure Quinn eats extra carrot sticks, blend spinach into her smoothies.

They walk into the service station, and Quinn goes straight to the concessions racks.

"What does this say?" Quinn pushes the pack of gum into her hands.

"Strawberry Bubblicious."

Quinn laughs. "Fuzzy."

Simrin picks up a water and a bag of pretzels and puts them on the counter with the gum.

"How far to Ravenna?" she asks the boy behind the counter.

"Seventy-two miles."

She pays, and they climb back in the car. Her phone whistles. Tom again. She will inevitably have to talk to him, and the thought that this could be in any way construed as a kidnapping makes her wince.

"I'll be right back," she says to Quinn. She walks to the patchy island of grass on the border of the station, close enough to see Quinn but far enough so Quinn can't hear Tom's somewhat justified fury. She dials the number, and he answers on the first ring.

"Where the hell are you?" he demands.

"Tom. Just listen for a minute."

"Goddamn right, I'm going to listen. Orientation is Monday. Where the bloody hell are you?" He is more furious than she thought, and she feels her own panic set in.

"Jesus, just listen for a minute, will you? We're in Nevada. I have a gig." It is a lie. Not exactly a lie. Not exactly the truth. But there is not exactly a way to tell him the truth. And this is a good untruth. She knows, despite whatever has happened between them, he is unable to be impartial to her success. It is inevitably a reflection on him, the discerning mentor.

"With who?"

She can hear him simmer down considerably, and she stumbles over the possibilities. "A private client. From Nevada."

"Shooting what?"

"Portraits."

"What? You're in Nevada to shoot portraits? Simone, what the hell?"

"Look, it's a big client, a friend of JJ's—they have a working Leipzig glass plate that was passed down from some photographer relative, and they want to do long-exposure shots in the desert." She is completely out of her element, lying like this, and yet here it is, pouring out of her like syrup. Ananda drilled into her that truth was sacrosanct. There was no mark darker on your soul than a lie.

"Imagine thousands of tiny threads between us. When you lie, you cut them all," Jyoti explained to her the first time she was caught lying. Simrin had lied about something stupid, saying she could ride a two-wheeler or shoot a basket backward. "Snip," Jyoti said with a quick slice of her fingers. "All gone." Simrin had cried, and Jyoti had let her.

"What year is the camera?" Tom asks.

"1884."

"Well, when the hell will you be back?"

"I don't know." This is true. At least this.

"School starts in nine days. Be back by then. And answer your fucking phone."

"I will," she says. She looks at Quinn's feet propped out the unrolled window. "I'm sorry I didn't call."

He lets out an exasperated sigh. "Take digital too," he says and hangs up.

Her heart is racing, and she feels light headed. She sits and puts her head between her knees. It is too fucking hot. And she lied. Snip. Slice. That old well of shame creaks open. And then the heaviness. The impossible reminder that she has spent half her life a rabbit in a fucking snare of delusion. And the rest alternately trying to construct and deconstruct the truth. With a fucking camera.

She stands. The car is only a dozen yards away, but she runs. It isn't enough, but at least it jars her out of that horrible stillness.

Her camera bag is on the seat. Quinn is in her booster. "I'm ready," Simrin says.

"To take pictures?" Quinn asks.

"Yes. Let's go take a lot of pictures." She turns around in her seat. "And do stuff. Okay?"

"Yep," Quinn said. She kicks at her seat. "Music. That green bubble one."

◆ ◆ ◆

The highway lengthens into a stretch of gray. She can't see much in the dark, but she doesn't think there's much to see. A few dust-worn houses and battered fences, but mostly dirt and brush. Simrin knows Meadowlark is on the outskirts of Ravenna, but she doesn't know which direction on Highway 50. She has tried to call the number Arjun called from, but she gets a continual busy signal. And there have been no new news updates online. Even the Operation Cultwatch website has only two new comments, both about how you could earn thousands from the comfort of your own home.

Quinn is asleep when they drive into Ravenna. Google Maps shows a number of hotels on the 50, and she drives slowly down the main drag. It is a series of strip malls interrupted by an occasional old-timey building, some of which seem to be casinos made to look old and some carefully preserved city structures—city hall, a visitor's center, a county museum. There is a place called the Grady Motel that says it has free Wi-Fi, a swimming pool, and bingo barbecue on Friday nights. She can at least justify that this trip is a way for Quinn to see a glimpse of small-town life. And it's cheap. She finds it a few blocks off the 50, a U-shaped two-story building with a pool in the center. She pulls up in front of the glass doors and leaves the car windows open. There is no one inside, but she taps the old-fashioned bell on the counter and looks around. The requisite tourist brochures, a water cooler, and a tabby cat asleep on a torn pleather chair. Quinn will be excited about the cat. An older woman in a bright-pink rhinestone tank top comes out from a back room.

"How can I help you, honey?"

"I wanted to see about getting a room for me and my daughter."

"We have rooms," she says. "Just fill this out." She hands her a form, and Simrin writes her info—name, address, phone. Even after all this time, she still pauses at the signature, having to make the letters carefully—*Simone*. At the time it seemed a logical choice—its similar sound and powerful namesake. She sure as hell wasn't going back to her birth name. She wanted nothing to do with anything her mother had given her. But now she's tempted to write *Simrin*, to dip a toe in the past before throwing herself in. She hated the name when her mother first presented it to her. "Simrin is a meditation that frees one from attachment," her mother had said, bestowing it upon her like some kind of divine gift. But it wasn't a gift, and it sounded like snakes hissing in her mother's mouth, but then one Sunday morning, Arjun knocked on their bedroom door. "Is Simrin awake?" he asked, and in that moment, she saw the name curl around her in lovely warm copper ribbons. Just his voice. Just her name. It was easy to love after that. "Say it again," she would say, and he would. Again and again.

"Have you heard of Meadowlark?" Simrin asks.

"You a reporter?"

"No." She is taken aback. "I'm a photographer. Why?"

"We have a few reporters here to get a look at that commotion outside of town. Meadowlark. I don't mind that commune, to tell the truth. My daughter goes out there to give some of the kids piano lessons. They sent her home with honey at Christmastime. Nice people. Know how many nights?"

"No."

"That's all right. We got the room. How old's your little girl?"

"Five." Simrin checks the car again.

"Don't worry, honey. Ravenna's a safe little town. Even this . . . whatever it is . . . probably isn't anything to worry about. I'm sure it'll all blow over in a few days." She hands Simrin a wooden pig with a key dangling from the ring in his snout. "You're in room twelve. You can park right out front. We have a free continental breakfast in the morning."

"Thank you."

"Sure thing. I lock the lobby at eleven, but just pick up the phone if you need anything."

Simrin opens the glass door to a blast of heat and drops the keys. She bends down, and the air feels so heavy on her back she has to sit down on the curb. So this is real. And now she is a photojournalist here to capture the whole *mahabharata*. She digs in her purse for her phone. I'm here, she writes to Arjun. And I'm afraid. And I need you. The lump rises in her throat. She doesn't want to cry, sitting here on a curb in the middle of hot nowhere. But it has been so long, and she feels a fissure in her chest crack, then deepen, the unspoken longing for him. She puts her head on her knees and breathes.

◆ ◆ ◆

Quinn is still sleeping when Simrin wakes up the next morning. She plugs her computer in and tries to connect to the internet, but she can't find the signal, so she snaps a picture of sleeping Quinn on her phone and texts it to Tom. All well here, she writes. Thanks for understanding. And she *is* thankful. Tom despite his many (many) flaws is, as he would put it, "a good sort." Impulsive and immature but devoted to Quinn and, even now, devoted to Simrin.

The pregnancy happened quickly and in the clichéd way—early in their relationship when neither of them were thinking about consequences. They had waited to have sex until she graduated. Despite the many months of innuendo, Tom had been surprisingly appropriate, nurturing Simrin's rock star crush and delighting in her extraordinary talent but remaining the decorous thesis advisor. But at the afternoon graduation reception, Simrin sipped too much champagne and drunkenly let Tom in on what she called her "checkered past." It was, of course, all accurate, but in truth, Simrin knew how much Tom loved the curious. He had been the first photographer allowed inside the Downton when the story broke and had later gone on to win a Pulitzer for his work in Gaza. And here was the extraordinary right before him. And here was Tom fawning over the "rich and layered fabric" of her past, a past Simrin never, ever allowed others to glimpse. It had all conflated in an amalgamation of novelty for both of them.

Then Simrin got pregnant, and despite being twenty-nine, she felt completely unprepared to be a mother. But Tom wanted to keep the baby, and Simrin wanted Tom. Looking back, perhaps more accurately, Simrin had not known what she wanted. But Tom was excellent at marketing: their little family walking along the river boardwalk, going out for dim sum, taking sabbaticals in France. But when he casually threw out the image of her shooting gritty urban scenes with a baby on her back, she locked focus. That she could see. That she could move toward. And she had taken care of babies at Ananda. It hadn't been that difficult. But then Quinn was born a month early and required a NICU stay because her lungs weren't fully developed, and the reality of being responsible for someone besides herself set in. Tom was helpful, but Simrin was shocked at the fierce physicality of her need to care for Quinn, how her body tried to turn itself inside out to keep that baby safe—a baby she didn't even know, some barely developed mouse Tom named Quinn after his Irish grandmother. Simrin liked that the name meant *wisdom*, particularly rational wisdom, and having had her own name changed twice, she didn't put much stock in what someone else chose to call you. But soon "the baby" became Quinn. And when she took that itty-bitty five-pound Quinn home from the hospital, everything seemed to blur to the background, leaving Quinn in sharp and brilliant focus. It was exhausting and liberating. She had never before had to think of one, and only one, thing. It was its own form of meditation, this baby caring, and to her surprise, she liked it. So when Tom grew predictably restless, he had already slipped to the edge of Simrin's frame.

Now, she brushes the hair from Quinn's face. "Q," she whispers. "Time to get up."

Quinn sits up straight. "Where are we?"

"The hotel. Remember we drove here last night?"

"Why?" She is still half-asleep, and Simrin picks her up and puts her on her lap.

"How did you get to be such a giant?" she asks.

"I'm tired."

"I think they have doughnuts in the lobby."

"I'm ready," she says. "I want sprinkles or if they don't have that, chocolate. But no nuts."

They get dressed and walk down to the lobby. It is only seven but already a brilliant, bright day. The sky looks enormous, no mountains or tall buildings interrupting the horizon. There is a younger woman at the front desk now, and she points them to a small dining area.

"Do you know how to get to that commune, Meadowlark?" Simrin asks.

"It's just off Carson. Take Center South a ways, turn left on Carson, and you'll see an unpaved road that leads straight up to the gates. Don't know how far you can get, though."

They eat, take two extra doughnuts for later, and fill their water bottles. It is already hot, the familiar, assaultive hot of the desert, and Simrin blasts the air-conditioning and rolls down the windows to feel the pleasure of both. Quinn is used to tagging along on shoots. Despite Simrin's rehearsed explanations of where they are going and what they are doing, Quinn rarely asks questions. Simrin's own childhood was such a mishmash of "do this because we said so" and hyperexplanation that she is determined to make sure Quinn's interactions with adults are as straightforward and child appropriate as possible.

"So . . . this place we're going. There might be policemen there because they're making sure everyone stays safe." Quinn is quiet. "I'm not sure what will happen when we get there—"

"Mama, can we just listen to the music?" Quinn interrupts.

Simrin laughs. "Sure."

They drive about ten minutes out of town until they see a police cruiser at the head of an unpaved road. An officer with dark sunglasses sits in the front seat, but he doesn't try to stop them when they turn, and Simrin doesn't want to take any chances by asking any questions. It is a well-maintained road, and they wind their way through surprisingly dense trees and brush. Ananda was a true desert—cactus and tumbleweeds—but the outskirts of Ravenna seem more oasis than desert. In the distance, Simrin can see the road widen and the foliage become sparse. There are a number of cars and a police vehicle parked evenly in a dirt lot and behind them a lovely wall of tall poplars. She pulls in, and they sit in the car. No one seems to be paying much attention to either them or Meadowlark. Simrin can now make out the tall wooden fence that encloses the property and the sunny yellow-and-blue-painted iron gates at the entrance.

"Let's take a look," she says.

They get out of the car.

"Hot," Quinn says. "It makes my ears buzz. Like bugs, Mama. I don't like it." She presses her fingers in her ears and shakes her head.

Shit, Simrin thinks, now is not the time for Quinn to hear her temperature.

"Do you want to sit in the car?"

"I don't like it," Quinn whines louder. There are two cops in the cruiser. They look over at them, and Simrin quickly shuffles Quinn back into her seat.

"I'll leave the car running, but you have to promise not to touch anything." Is it legal to leave your kid in the car if you are in line of sight? Is it legal to take a kid to a location of "escalating tensions"? She hands Quinn the iPad. "Play whatever you want, but please, please don't touch anything or come out of the car without me." She looks out the window. The cops have gone back to their blank surveillance. "I'll be right here. You can see me. Okay?"

Quinn is already playing some puzzle game, so Simrin shuts the door gently, but the slam is loud enough to catch the cops' attention again, and they watch as she swings her camera bag over her shoulder and makes her way to the front gate. They don't move, and she tries to seem confident. There is another photographer lounging on a car and what she assumes are other media people. The gate has been backed with corrugated tin, a very recent addition if the picture in the newspaper is accurate, so there is no seeing in or out, and there is a high-tech intercom next to the gate, incongruous in the simple surroundings.

A woman with a large flowered sun hat sits on the ground, typing into her phone. "We need a fucking umbrella and lemonade stand out here," she says.

"Huh," Simrin says.

"I had to buy this god-awful hat because they had nothing else at that Krepp's or Kripp's—more like Krapp's." She looks up. "Where you from?"

"San Francisco," Simrin answers.

"The *Chronicle* financed this?"

"Oh, no . . . I'm freelance."

"Damn. Well, there's nothing to see—hasn't been for a whole day. I imagine the police will get a warrant soon, and we'll all be booted back, but for now, we can get a prime view of this fine piece of art." She flicks the gate, and the tin reverberates.

"Have you seen anyone?" Simrin asks.

"Nope."

"Or heard anything?"

"Nope. And the cops won't tell you anything other than that all they're doing right now is watching the situation carefully. No one even knows what the situation is exactly except that the cops want to get in, and they won't let them. So here we all are, until someone makes a move." The woman's phone pings, and she looks down. "There's service here, but it sucks."

Simrin wipes the sweat from her forehead and looks back at the car. The cops are still watching her, and she figures she should at least look professional. She pulls out a camera and shoots indiscriminately. The fence around the property is at least seven feet tall, and it goes, as far as she can tell, all the way around the property. You'd have to be worried about someone seeing something they shouldn't to build a fence that tall.

She walks over to the intercom and bends down to see if it has any buttons, and her phone rings. Tom, she thinks, and she lets it ring until it goes to voice mail. When it rings again, she digs it out of her bag and looks at the unfamiliar number—a bunch of nines and zeros.

"Hello?"

"Simrin." His voice pours out, thousands of coppery fibers warming their way through her, her body expanding and contracting like a pulsing sun.

"Sim?" he says.

This is what it's like to be Quinn, she thinks. Copper. Everywhere.

"Simrin," he says again.

"Yes," she says. "I'm here."

"I know." He laughs.

"No, I mean, I'm here."

"I know." He laughs again. "I can see you."

She looks up.

"Hi," he says.

"Where are you?" Her head feels heavy, dark, warm sand funneling through her scalp.

"There's a camera in the intercom."

She looks up again.

"And one in that big tree to the right of the gate. And one on the fence to the left."

She looks around. The woman who has been texting is staring at her now. "You okay?" she asks.

"Come inside, Sim," he says.

"What?"

"You okay," the woman says again. She is standing now and walking toward her.

"Yes, fine. No. What?"

"Sim. Listen. Please come in."

She holds on to the phone with two hands. "I can't come in. There are police out here. Don't you know what's going on?" The woman steps closer to her, quietly switches her phone to the camera setting.

"Sim. Don't say anything for a minute. Just listen. There's been no crime committed. No one has a warrant for any arrests."

"I thought you didn't have a phone," she interrupts.

"I don't, exactly. Just please, come in and I'll explain."

"I can't," she whispers. She leans her head against the hot iron gate. It is scorching, and she pulls away quickly. She touches her forehead and feels the warmth. "A warning," her mother would say. "The world reminding your body what the heart already knows." But knows what?

"You can," he says. "As long as no laws have been broken, the state can't dictate who we allow in or out."

"I have my daughter," she says. She looks over at the car and feels the distinctive buzz of everyone's attention slowly being shifted to her.

"I hoped you'd bring her."

"Are you crazy?" she says.

"No," he says. "Are you?"

Something inside her loosens. The familiar sibling quarrels. How instinctive it is with him. Arjun who loved her through her childhood, who drew pictures on his hands to make her smile while she endured some stupid silent assignment, who walked with her from class to class all throughout middle school because she was scared the townie girls would steal her lunch. And Arjun, who, when she woke up the morning after Jaishri had gone back to Ananda, had disappeared.

The pain of it is still fierce, and she has to back into the memory to look at it. The bright sun streaming in the slit of space between the black-out curtains. The *Full House* marathon she watched while waiting for him to return. The stale raisins she found in the bottom of her backpack and tried to savor like they were candy. And then finally, her tentative foray to the lobby to see if maybe he'd left her a note. But no, the greasy clerk had chuckled. "Sorry, honey, your cock paid and flew the coop." And then the shock, the denial, the self-talk that this was just some big misunderstanding, that the room really hadn't been cleared of all his stuff, that Arjun really hadn't left her only an envelope with forty dollars stuffed down in the bottom of her backpack, that she really, truly had no one left. And then she had cried. And then cried some more, not wanting to leave the room. The nasty motel room! And it was only the pitifulness of that thought, that a pay-by-the-day motel room was where she now felt most protected, that made her move. So she walked. From what she now knows is the Mission through the Tenderloin and finally to Nob Hill, where she found herself in front of an Andronico's, digging out the money he had left her, and then finding the note: the name Lawrence Heller and a phone number scrawled across the back of a flyer for a Chinese restaurant. And not knowing what else to do, she found a pay phone, called, and asked, "Do you have a daughter named Samantha?" the name foreign in her mouth and surrounded by a milky-white goo.

"Please," Arjun says now.

Her blood beats hard in her temples, and she can hear the thump of her heart turn the edges of her vision a blackberry tangle. This is crazy, she thinks. And yet here he is, almost twenty years and a few yards between them.

"Fine," she says. "Fine."

She hangs up, grabs her camera bag, and makes her way back to the car, where Quinn is sitting exactly where she left her. Simrin opens the door.

"Quinn," she says, "we're going to go inside my friend's house." She can barely get the words out; they sound so ridiculous. "It will be cooler inside."

"I'm playing."

"Come on, Quinn."

"Close the door. It's too hot." She stares down at the iPad screen.

"It's two seconds. I'll carry you."

Quinn says nothing, just swipes her finger over the cookies she is creating. "Hot!"

"Shhh!" The last thing she needs is to drag a screaming kid inside a police-patrolled compound. She feels her temper rise. "Quinn. We need to go now." In one swift movement, she undoes Quinn's seatbelt and hoists her into her arms. Quinn howls, and Simrin puts her hand over her mouth and wedges the two of them on the floor of the back seat.

"If you stop crying, I'll give you a chocolate chip cookie. I'll give you ten chocolate chip cookies."

Quinn thrashes and tries to yell.

"Please, Quinn, please." She feels the tears pool heavy in her own eyes. "Please, Quinn. A hundred chocolate chip cookies. I'll give you a hundred chocolate chip cookies."

Quinn flings herself onto the back seat, then sits up, straight. "Mama, you're crying."

"I'm okay. I'm fine, but please, can we go quietly? Can we just go?"

"A thousand chocolate chip cookies," Quinn says.

"Fine, fine." She wipes her eyes with her shirt. "I'll carry you." She shoulders her camera bag, picks up Quinn, and cradles her head against her shoulder.

"Two seconds," Quinn whines.

"Two seconds." Simrin's heart is pounding hard in her chest, revving itself up to run, again. She takes a deep breath and exhales into Quinn's dirty hair. "Two seconds." She walks, quickly, weaving her way through the cars, not looking to see who is watching. She doesn't stop, counting on the gate to open and swallow them up. And it does. Without even a creak, it opens, and they are inside, staring at Arjun's island.

It is a surprisingly lush landscape. There's no grass, but hedges of desert plants surround each of the five two-story houses, and a few dozen mature poplars ring the perimeter of the land. To the right and down a sloping hill, she can see what must be the top of the pirate ship and, at the top of the hill, a giant sycamore with at least four different swings attached. There are bikes and scooters and Hula-Hoops strewn around the property, a trampoline, a sandpit, and a giant spiderweb of a climbing structure. And then, at the center, a hexagonal-shaped pavilion, an exact replica of Rudraksh, the horrible, horrible Ananda meeting space. She takes a step back and bangs into the gate. Quinn shrieks, and Simrin spins around to see Arjun—his shaggy hair and skin as golden as ever, the green of his eyes so sharp and familiar that she feels the gauze of copper slip into sight before he even speaks.

"Let's go inside," he says. He places his hand on Simrin's back, and she feels as if she is falling, the world tilting clockwise as they hurry to one of the houses.

Quinn is crying now. She thrashes her head from side to side, and Simrin holds tighter and tries to take even, firm steps. "Two seconds," she says with every step. "Two seconds." Simrin's heart beats violently. She follows Arjun's flip-flopped feet, not daring to look up, to risk dropping Quinn, to risk tilting to the ground.

The door of a house opens, shuts behind them, and they are inside. Mismatched couches surround the perimeter of the front room, encircling a large play space, where two babies paw at some wooden blocks. Two women and a man sit on one of the couches, while two children read books on another. Simrin rocks Quinn and leans against the front door to keep from falling. The group stares at them; the man tries to smile. A woman stands: "I'll get some water," she says. Arjun takes her camera bag. Simrin feels the room tilt faster, feels the thick film of disconnection begin to slip over her eyes. She leans harder against the door and slides to the floor. Quinn tangles in her lap, and Simrin rests her forehead on Quinn's heaving back. She can feel Arjun's hand rubbing circles on her own back, his voice far, far away. "Simrin," he says. "Simrin. Simrin." It has been so long since she has heard the name spoken. Her name. She feels it weave through one ear and out the other, then back again, and again and again. She wants to lie down, to fall away, to melt into Quinn, and then she feels her stomach seize.

"I'm going to be sick," she says. She tumbles Quinn from her lap and vomits onto the floor. Immediately she feels better. And mortified.

"Mama," Quinn shrieks. "Mama!"

Simrin's skin is slick with sweat, and she slumps against the door. "Oh God," she says. Quinn is hysterical, and Simrin pulls her in and looks up at Arjun. "Jesus. Sorry," she says. He is sweating, too, and his face looks pale. She wants to simultaneously lean against his bare legs, reach up for his hands and feel them curl hers into a ball, and recoil through the door and out the gate. She can still taste bile in her mouth, and she spits on the floor. "And fuck you too."

A woman with short black hair brings her a cup of water, and Simrin slowly sips it and tries to console Quinn. "It's okay, baby. I'm fine. It's cool in here. You're okay."

Someone else is cleaning up her sick, and someone else is taking the other children out of the room. Another woman is trying to get her to lie down, but she is okay now. The world is straight. Even Quinn is calmer, still hiccuping and hiding her head in Simrin's chest but quieting.

"Come on, Q." Simrin stands carefully and carries Quinn to an empty couch. She closes her eyes and rocks. Her heart is steadying with Quinn's even breathing, but she keeps her eyes closed. She can feel Arjun in the room. She is here. They are here. Arjun and Quinn and Simrin. In one room. She feels him move closer, sit down near her couch. She keeps her eyes shut tight. Afraid. Of him. Of them.

She has felt this before, her most painful memory, even more terrible than waking up to find him gone. He had come back from dropping Jaishri at the bus terminal, looking defeated and lost, and she had peppered him with questions—"How could you let her? Why didn't you wait for me? How could she do this?"

"I tried to stop her," was all he could say, and the more he repeated this line, the angrier she became at him. It was his fault. Never mind that Jaishri slept with her shoes on, so afraid of a fire or other disaster. Never mind that she was barely eating, even saltines making her queasy; or that she would go to the bathroom only with one of them; or that she had chewed her fingernails down until they bled. Never mind that they both knew what neither would say—that they shouldn't have brought her. But how could they have not? How could they have left their beloved shadow, this fragile little girl?

Simrin had slammed the door, kicked Arjun's backpack out of her way, and thrown herself onto one of the queen beds, waiting for a reason—any reason—to lash out at him.

"Sim," he had said. "Sim, Sim," over and over, but she had ignored him until finally, he had stood right in front of her, put one hand gently on her shoulder, and said, "*Cakravat parivartante . . .*" But before he could get the next section out, before he could tell her to wait patiently for the pain to turn to pleasure, she was on her feet, shoving him back onto the other bed, looming over him and yelling—screaming—"It's your fault, Arjun. It's your fucking fault she's gone." Jaishri with her complete and utter adoration of Arjun. She couldn't believe that his arms around her, his assurance that he was here wouldn't have been enough to keep her with them. And even then—in that moment of unadulterated fury—she knew that this was what she wanted, to feel grounded by his body, to be assured that at least the two of them were here, together. She felt flushed with liquid current, anger and need whipping through her until she thought she would scratch her skin off if she didn't do something. So she did. She tried to slap him. With one hand and then the other, but he caught her wrists, and it was like they were back wrestling in the dirt, trying to see who could pin who and make it to the next round with the next kid, the final winner getting out of their karmic yoga chores for the day. But this time, as she tried to get leverage by pinning his hip with hers, she could feel him, suddenly hard under her, and despite the shock of it, the surprise of his body doing what she had been told boys' bodies could do, she felt the intoxication of being wanted, the sheer pleasure of knowing that he, too, needed her. And she kissed him.

His lips spread, and his tongue found hers, and at first they were clumsy—their teeth knocking, their lips losing traction—but soon they were moving together as if they could read each other's minds, and she almost wanted to stop, to marvel with him at how good at this they already were, but then he was tasting her neck, pulling her T-shirt up and revealing the undershirt she had put on that morning because her only bra had a broken clasp. And suddenly she felt shy, because it was Arjun. Arjun! Arjun who teased her for still picking her nose. Arjun who had stolen the wrong size underwear and a box of maxi pads from Kmart because she had bled through one of her three pairs of panties. But then he was kissing her belly, telling her she was beautiful, and she could feel the ache of desire flood her, and when he struggled with her jeans, it was Simrin who pulled them off, not even caring that she hadn't shaved in days (weeks?), wrapping her legs around his so she could push herself hard against his thigh. And then they were naked, and he was expertly lifting her hips like he knew what the fuck he was doing when he didn't. And she was shocked and embarrassed at how easily he slid inside her, but then it hurt. Badly. So she cried, and he was pulling out, and she was shaking her head no, pulling him in and eventually rolling on top of him because she understood that although it felt like he was breaking something inside of her, one day it wouldn't feel that way, and she wanted that day to be then, but if it couldn't, she would focus on the pain and, for once, know the pleasure would come: their sweat blending between them, her tongue on his shoulder blade tasting what their bodies could do together, the two of them swimming in and out of each other.

After, Simrin had been elated. "We did it," she said. "*Now* we're fucking liberated." But Arjun had been awkward. He had locked himself in the bathroom and showered until she banged on the door, desperate to pee. "What's wrong with you?" she said. "It's just sex." It felt exhilarating to be so bold, to try on a new persona.

There had been kissing at Ananda, but it had only happened once, and it seemed purely performative. After *satsang* one night, Priya had dared the girls to pick a boy to kiss, and when they had all ignored her, shuffled their feet in the dirt, and picked at nonexistent splinters in their hands, she had gone ahead and said, "Fine. I'll go first." Simrin was sure Priya would pick Gautam, but she hadn't. "I pick Arjun," she said, and Simrin had looked up just in time to catch the flash of satisfaction cross Arjun's face before Priya tilted her head up and closed her eyes. And Arjun had leaned in, pressed his lips to Priya's, and then opened his mouth. Simrin had stood watching, amazed that either of them knew what they were doing, and then outraged, first at Arjun and then at herself. Why did she care who he kissed? The day before she would have pretend gagged at the idea of kissing him. It wasn't disgust but the instinctual wrongness of the thought, like being told to go to school naked, but there she was, flushed with anger. So she had summoned all her courage and, to be honest, spite, and she had done it, picked Krish, then closed her eyes and tilted her head up, trying to look desirable. And then Krish's lips were on hers, and it felt . . . not bad . . . but weird, but when his tongue parted her lips and darted inside her mouth, Simrin opened her eyes, surprised, and caught Arjun staring daggers at her. It had felt good to see him angry. And then bad.

After, she had tried to get Arjun to walk back to the house with her, but he had put his arm around Jaishri (who refused to kiss anyone) and ignored Simrin until the next day, when he simply pretended nothing had happened. Simrin had been too grateful to question him, and they had gone back to their normal selves, pretending the electricity that surged between them in the desert had never happened. A month later they had run.

But there was no pretending that night in the motel. She'd made the invisible current between them real, and she felt bold and capable and then annoyed when he refused to acknowledge it. "Don't pretend nothing happened," she said, and this seemed to make it worse. He wouldn't look at her full on, and he just wanted to watch *Law & Order*, and when she went and bought him peanut M&M'S from the vending machine, he didn't even want them. And eventually, she couldn't think of anything to do but curl up next to him, bury her head in her knees, and squeeze herself tight, tighter, tightest. Eventually he put his hand on her back, but even then, she could feel the thin film that had sneakily oozed itself between them grow. And harden.

Now she knows what she hadn't then, that this was what it feels like to unplug yourself from someone, the feeling of connection only knowable with disconnect. In the morning he was gone, but it is that first slash of disconnection that she remembers most achingly, the deep and painful pull of separation, thousands of microscopic tears in a once-strong muscle.

It is fierce inside her, even now, and she keeps her eyes shut, focuses on Quinn, heavy in her lap, their bodies snug like puzzle pieces. She doesn't want to take a breath, doesn't want to see him, to risk not getting what she felt desperate for that day, what she suddenly feels desperate for now.

"Simrin," he says. It is the same as always. Heat in her head. Copper behind her eyes. She wants him to say it one more time, make her name a promise, and he does. "Simrin," he says, and she opens her eyes.

BETHANY

There is only one picture of Simrin on her blog, and although Bethany knows you can manipulate photographs to look however you want them, she's surprised at the difference between reality and her imagination. She's not as thin as Bethany expected, hair not as long, skin not as pale. Bethany's also surprised that there's only one photograph. It's a photography site, for God's sake. Shouldn't there be more photographs of the photographer?

A week ago, Aaron confessed that he emailed Simrin. Bethany hadn't even known about the blog, and when she questioned why he hadn't told her, he just shrugged and said, "I thought I had." Since then, she has been checking it daily. Looking for what she doesn't know. Meadowlark to appear? Old photos of Aaron and Simrin? But there is nothing. Not even any new posts. And by now, she has scrolled through three of the four years' worth of entries. Nothing on Aaron. Nothing even on Simrin. Just a lot of peeking into other people's lives.

What Bethany finds online about Simrin, she already knows—lived at Ananda, divorced, one kid, photographer. All info she gleans on various fan sites or unreliable Wikipedia pages. But she keeps returning to the blog, each time feeling a little more uneasy, a little less curiously voyeuristic, a little more aware that the more the media is directed to Meadowlark, the more guarded the community will become, and the more guarded they become, the more ripe Meadowlark's "dark corners" are for "unsecreting." Unsecreting. It is a horrible made-up word and a horrible thing to do to people. People keep secrets out of necessity. They aren't some luxury you go around exposing for others' entertainment. She feels her stomach sour, her anger turn physical inside her.

That this has even progressed to where it has baffles her. She knows what happened. Was actually there when it happened. Dana and Kevin were arguing. Again. It was their familiar fight over nudity and Marley. Mostly, the community agrees that the kids can be naked for as long as they're comfortable and that the adults should be clothed in public. In private, you can do whatever you want. But there are a few people that think this is just shaming of the adult body. Dana is one of them, and she had let Marley go in the hot tub with a group of naked adults. It isn't a big deal. Lots of people do it at Meadowlark, not to mention millions in Scandinavia and Japan, but Kevin is not one of them, and to be honest, neither is Bethany. There is something she finds fundamentally icky about all those bodies together, but she tries to breathe through it, reminds herself that what she knows of appropriate childhoods is not much. Since the blowup, there's been talk that Kevin was abused, that his overreaction could only be the result of past trauma. Which could be true. Bethany actually finds it comforting that her own anxieties might be explained away just by invoking her past. But the afternoon this all started, all Bethany knew was that Kevin was angry again, and anger was not well tolerated at Meadowlark.

She had heard the yelling from downstairs and gone up to help.

"Why not let Marley see what a real fight looks like?" Kevin had said when Bethany tried to coax Marley from the room. "Dana wants the kid to see everything else."

When that hadn't worked, Bethany had tried to scoop him up, but Marley cried and clung to the bed, and soon Dana and Kevin were screaming, Dana yelling up close in Kevin's face, Kevin escalating the fight, and then suddenly, Kevin pushing Dana back and hard onto the bed. Kevin looked shocked, spittle hanging from his mouth. Dana screamed. And then there were people. Kara, and Dylan, and Asia. And Candice. Of course. Candice, always scrutinizing a situation and jumping to quick conclusions. "Did he hit you?" she asked, and Dana had sobbed and nodded, and the rest was a whirlwind of Kevin throwing things into paper bags and being escorted from the property.

Then, four days later the cops showed up and insisted they produce Marley, but Marley had gone to Wayside with Dana and Marsha and her kids to buy shoes. If Marley had only been there, Bethany thinks, she is sure at least Star would have let the police in. The cops would have talked to Marley, had the whole story explained, and all of this would have evaporated. But that's not what happened. Instead people started to talk about the cops' visit as if it were a witch hunt, particularly Gavin, and if she is honest, Aaron. Why Aaron takes this nuisance as a threat she can't understand. DFCS has visited them before, insisting the homeschool paperwork be filed, and they filed it. Once there was a complaint from a neighbor that the dogs were terrorizing his chickens. They made sure the hole in the fence was fixed. Why this hitch seems so catastrophic she isn't sure, but she hasn't exactly asserted herself. She prefers to let Aaron take the spotlight. And she didn't think the cops would even come back. But they did. And then they came back again, each time escalating the rumors: they could force the kids to go to school; they could construct other false crimes; they could take the kids forever. And then Kevin went to the *Tri-City Tribune* and some fathers' rights group, and now there is a crowdsourcing fund-raiser.

Now the police will have to actually do something, no matter how unsubstantiated the rumors. But Bethany is less concerned with the police. There is nothing to find. But the media. She knows enough of the media to know the payday of child abuse allegations against some crazy commune. At least she imagines that's what it looks like from the outside. Crazy people doing crazy things with their crazy kids. Jesus, sometimes even she thinks that's what it looks like. At least lately. What they are doing with Meadowlark isn't crazy—anyone who took five minutes to talk to her would figure this out—but this whole refusing entrance to the police and locking themselves in? She's pretty sure that is crazy. Although what she knows from crazy is laughable. And Aaron, who she long ago gave the nickname Coo (as in *cuckoo*), *is* crazy, crazy enough to think they could create any life they wanted for themselves and their children. No one does that. People dig a rut for themselves (or have one dug for them) and then follow the furrow around and around and around until they die. You need to be crazy to be rut-less. And you definitely need to be crazy to think that dozens of other people will heave themselves and their families out of their well-dug ruts and follow you to a total unknown like Meadowlark. But that's what he did, her Coo, her crazy, crazy husband. It is one of the reasons she fell in love with him, his crazy coupled with his intense idealism and unquestionable determination. And his love, all that unadulterated devotion to Bethany. Bethany, who barely existed at that time.

She had met Aaron three years after leaving LA, when she was still barely known to herself and when she sometimes still forgot to respond to her new name. Which was stupid. She had chosen the name herself, chosen it because of the little girl who lived next door to her before *Angel Eyes* became prime time TV. Bethany Stephens was the most normal girl she could imagine. She had regular parents and played regular Barbies after regular school and went to regular swim lessons every Wednesday of every week and had regular brown eyes and regular brown hair and a regular, ordinary, normal life. She figured Penelope and Miranda were the kinds of name you chose when you were selecting a new identity to go along with your new illustrious life. Bethany, or the even more ordinary Beth, was the name you chose when what you wanted was the opposite of illustrious. So when she first moved to Portland, she became Bethany Jones, as normal and ordinary a girl as she could imagine.

Even Portland she chose for its lack of patina—a city but not *the* city, cold but not *too* cold, "real" America but still one of the coasts.

She knew better than to think she could easily blend into some small town in Kansas. But Portland, Portland fit all the requirements and was exactly midway down on the list of places people go to reinvent themselves. And it was gray. And rainy. Nothing to call up the visceral dread of relentless sunshine and ice-cold air-conditioning.

She grew to love Portland—the designated "bike boulevards" and artisanal doughnuts and copper-bottomed drinking fountains—but it took a while. Her first months there she did nothing but walk from her apartment to the cluster of shops on the corner—a grocery store, nail salon, coffee shop, and barely lingering Wi-Fi café—and back again. Every time she went out, it felt like a test. Could she pass for just another mixed-up eighteen-year-old trying to figure out her fucking life? Would the checkout guy with the purple hair finally place how he knew her? She dyed her hair brown and even bought fake tortoiseshell frames, but it was the eyes—the startling blue, the particular down-turn at the edges, the impossible-to-untrain way she looked up while keeping her chin down—that was the giveaway. Every week, tens of millions of people watched those eyes turn skyward as she explained to God what she had learned about humanity, and after eight years they watched them gently shut as she was finally called back to heaven. And then they watched them smeared in lilac eye shadow as her mother and her agent, "Uncle" Frank, tried to turn little Cassie Campbell into *Cassandra*. Italicized. It didn't work. No matter how much auto-tune you used, you couldn't make someone a pop singer through sheer will. Which Bethany knew. Of course. But it took a producer explaining to her mother that you couldn't teach a fish to walk on land for her mother to get it. And then Bethany had smirked and said, "No shit."

It was the only time her mother had hit her in public. She slapped her face. And even though it was the nineties, you didn't slap kids in public. Especially across the face. And especially when they were little money-making machines that needed to continue to function. "Jesus," the producer said, "you really want that handprint splashed across

Entertainment Weekly?" Her mother stormed out. The producer (one of the many Davids or Steves) put his headphones back on and sat down at the console. And Bethany sat in the corner and didn't cry. She never cried. Unless it was on cue. It was easy to pretend cry. She didn't even need to think of something sad to do it. She just set her face and willed the tears to come. And they did. It was harder if she was actually sad. That was trained out of her too. Her mother's fingernails on the fleshy part of her arm. The look that meant, If you cry, you will not only cost us tens of thousands of dollars, but I will not talk to you for days, and you will have to figure out how to get the milk down from the top shelf of the refrigerator for your goddamn Cheerios.

Her mother rarely hit her. Bethany saw parents who did it frequently. Davina, who played one of her school friends on *Angel Eyes*, was hauled off and smacked on a regular basis. Everyone knew, but Davina's mother did it behind the closed door of a trailer, so what could you do? Mostly Bethany's mother left her on the side of the road and pretended to drive away or bought only vegetables and tofu and rice cakes when she was mad. But she was also dazzlingly perfect. She was spontaneous and silly, and when times were good (which they often were), the two of them would ride up and down Pacific Coast Highway with the convertible top down (a convertible bought with Bethany's money) singing John Cougar Mellencamp hits. Or check themselves into the Beverly Hills Hotel for a week and spend all day at the pool. Or buy a puppy. Or three puppies. And then give them away when they peed all over the house and then buy a new house. She had actually done that.

Now, Bethany refreshes Simrin's blog and reloads the same photographs of the underage migrant workers picking strawberries somewhere in California. There is one picture that even Bethany admits is painfully striking. A baby strapped to his young mother's back, a handkerchief covering his nose and mouth to protect him from pesticides.

"What are you doing?" It is Aaron. Bethany has taken the laptop into their family bedroom, despite it being a no-technology zone, thinking no one will disturb her, but here he is, looking directly at the screen. She shuts the computer quickly and is then embarrassed.

"You should look at it," he says.

"I have," she snaps.

He is quiet, and she runs her thumbs over the laptop's ports.

"I know you're upset," he says.

She hates when he does this. States the obvious. It is the same tactic they use with the children. "I can see you're angry. I can see you want those crayons that River is using. I can see you're losing your mind over a damn cookie." She raises her eyebrows.

"Beth," he says. He is the only one who calls her this, and when she read *Little Women*, years after she chose her name, she cried when poor sick Beth died, imagining not her own loss but Aaron's. She closes her eyes and knows he will come to her. This time he bends down next to the bed and moves the laptop. He holds her hands in his, and she opens her eyes.

"Everything's going to be fine," he says.

She exhales. "You don't know that."

"I do." He squeezes her hands tightly. "It's always fine. Don't you know that? It's always just fine."

Nothing had ever been "fine" before Aaron. But the truth was that everything had been easily, unremarkably fine ever since. Not that there aren't problems. Not that Bethany's own mind doesn't trip over itself frequently, creating worst-case scenarios and potential catastrophes, but the reality is that day to day, month to month, year to year, everything with Aaron always turns out just fine. They bought the land Meadowlark sat on with no water rights, the reason the land was so cheap and had sat empty for so long. The real estate agent thought they were crazy. In fact, all five original Meadowlark families including Bethany thought it was crazy, all except Aaron, and although it was Bethany's money, she trusted him. And sure enough, a month after purchase, their water rights application was approved. Bethany knows that he hacked into the Division of Water Resources, pushed the application through with a mouse click, but there are dozens of other examples that have no easy explanation. When Blaze was born at home not breathing, Aaron puffed air into his lungs. When the storage unit went up in flames and everything was ruined by water and smoke, Aaron found Juniper's baby pictures perfectly preserved. "Aaron is special like that," Candice says, and despite Bethany's general distaste for Candice, Bethany has to agree.

Aaron *is* special like that. He is the most special person she's ever met. Even when she is angry with him, she can feel the special like some kind of voodoo. He radiates. It would be too much if he wasn't also so damn soothing. Bethany's known her fair share of illuminators. They flock to Hollywood with their "star quality." But with Aaron, she feels both set alight and quieted, hushed into the remarkable realization that everything will be okay, so different from the complete disarray of her childhood, so comfortingly just fine.

"Okay," she says.

He pulls her into him and holds her for a long moment. "I want to tell you something," he says.

"What?"

"I asked Simrin to come."

She feels the burst of something definitely not fine in her chest. She pulls away and presses her back against the bed. "Why?" She knows why. Of course she knows why.

"Just in case."

"In case of what?"

"Kevin's saying horrible stuff, Beth."

"Which isn't true."

"Of course it's not, but who knows how the cops will spin it. We need to present our truth."

"Or let the police talk to Marley."

He exhales and looks away. "Dana doesn't want that."

"*You* don't want that."

He closes his eyes.

"Why?" she asks.

"We talked about this."

"*You* talked about this."

He looks at her with those maddeningly earnest eyes. "If they get their hands on one kid, do you know how easy it is for them to just take the others?"

"That's ridiculous."

"They can spin the story however they want. Our kids, Beth. They could take our kids."

She feels the possibility deep in her chest. But it's impossible, isn't it? They've done nothing wrong. And how can pictures on some blog prove their innocence?

"If she comes, she can show the world the reality of Meadowlark. Everything we've built. The beauty of this world we've created. The beauty of our children."

And it is his last sentence—*beauty, our, children*—that makes whatever uneasiness she had before tornado ferociously through her body.

"No," she says. She pulls her legs away from him. "No way. No pictures of the kids."

"Beth . . ."

"Absolutely not."

"Have you seen Kevin's crowdsourcing site? Have you read what he's saying?"

Of course she has. Neglect. Emotional abuse. And the worst, the absolute craziest worst—sexual abuse. She hadn't been able to read beyond those two words. And even then, she had to go out in the yard. Breathe fresh air. And not see her children. Even the vision of them in her mind occupying the same space as those accusations makes her queasy. She hasn't been able to look at any of the other media, but she has heard the talk. And this morning, there were strangers poking around the property and this afternoon, talk of backing the front gate with corrugated tin so no one could see in.

"We need to tell our story whatever way we can, Beth."

"No."

"What are you afraid of?"

"What am *I* afraid of?" She says it louder than she means to, but she can't help it. Tension with the local police she can deal with. Protest against unreasonable search and seizure she will allow. But her children's photographs are nonnegotiable, particularly Juniper's. Juniper looks so much like Bethany as a child it is eerie. And people notice. It started even before Juniper turned five. At three, Juniper was regularly being noticed in the supermarket. "Has anyone ever told you . . . ," they would start, and immediately Bethany would steel herself for the comparison, trying to fiddle in her bag and avoid looking anyone in the eye. "Remember that cheesy show?" "No," she would say and search for some lip balm. But that was in Portland. Here in Ravenna, their exposure to the outside world is greatly reduced. It is one of the reasons she wanted this property. It was a chance to build their own world, a space that had never known Cassie Campbell and never would. That and, of course, a chance to raise their children in a world where nothing is dictated and everything is possible. But she can't pretend that the other isn't equally true. High protective fences, no exact address, not even a landline guarantee her complete and blissful anonymity. Sure, they go to town—they aren't hermits—but mostly people stare at them because they come from that weird commune off of Carson. And surprisingly, Gavin is the only one at Meadowlark who has ever noticed the similarities between Juniper and Cassie Campbell.

Of course it is Gavin. Bethany has disliked him from the moment she met him. He showed up a year and a half ago with Denise and the three kids and expected to move right in. Aaron explained about the trial period—the month of living in town and commuting daily to

Meadowlark, then the provisional two-month residency, and finally the official vote. But the family didn't have the cash to pay rent, so Gavin said they would just pitch a tent in the lot out front, which, everyone agreed, just seemed silly. So the family was given a room on a trial basis and then never left.

Aaron is charmed by Gavin. "He says whatever's on his mind," Aaron says. "He's totally authentic." An authentic idiot, Bethany thinks, a know-it-all who knows very little. He insists the government has classified information on hundreds of alien abductions, and he claims to know shamanic secrets for curing any illness. But he is an expert carpenter, and his wife loves to cook, and they were fierce devotees of Meadowlark from the day they came, so Gavin's "eccentricities" are overlooked. But he is also the one who noticed Juniper, and this Bethany finds harder to overlook. "She looks just like that kid on that show from the late eighties," he said last year.

"Hmm," Bethany said.

"*Angel Eyes*. You remember it?"

Bethany pretended to read a book and shook her head.

"I used to watch the reruns every day after school."

Reruns started in 1996, she calculated, which made him younger than she was. She assumed he was older. She shrugged, but he kept talking.

"That kid became a drug addict or something." She wanted to look up at this, to insist that was *not* what had happened, but she just gritted her teeth and nodded.

"I guess you look a little like her too," he said, and at this she went stiff. "Fucking Hollywood," he said and went to help with dinner.

Bethany sat there for a good long time, trying to convince herself that he was just Gavin being Gavin, spouting random info at whoever was in proximity. Still, it shook her, and later that night as she lay in bed with Aaron in the dark, she told him the story. "Huh," he said. "I always thought Juniper looked like me."

Sometimes his innocence is unbearable. Now, she looks at him and steels herself. "I will not have them photographed," Bethany says. She has spent way too much of her life under a fucking telephoto camera lens and then an equally long time erasing all traces to just wave a photographer on in.

He is quiet and stares at her for a long time. He is good at this. Whatever bizarre training he survived as a kid has made him irritatingly attentive and exasperatingly patient.

"No!" she says again.

He sighs. "I don't even know if she's coming."

"Good. But if she does, there are twenty-eight other children available to photograph."

They sit in silence, Bethany trying to pull as far away as possible without the statement that physically moving would make.

"All right," he finally says.

"Promise."

He is silent for a minute, but then he stands and kisses her head. "Promise," he says and closes the door gently behind him.

She lays her head down on the bed and closes her eyes. How he cannot see the danger of bringing a photographer here she doesn't know. She's shown him the tabloids. Once when he asked her why she ran away from LA, she skipped right over her crazy mother and searched the internet for old pics and sensationalist stories: "Little Cassie Campbell ALL Grown Up" with zoomed-in pictures of her looking uncomfortable in a bikini on Jack Karin's boat; dozens of Google images that showed her at ten, twelve, sixteen—her underwear showing or someone else's cigarette in close proximity to her hand; and the most cringe inducing, the studio-thrown thirteenth birthday party, where photographers were invited to take pictures of her getting a cart full of "teen" presents—Wet n Wild lipsticks, a pink Discman, signed posters of the Backstreet Boys. Her mother had even sneaked a bra in there, wrapped to look like a shoebox, but Bethany had slammed the lid before anyone saw, only her deep-red face a reminder of her mortification. There are dozens of pages of results like this, all evidence of the constant crush of observation, like being a dancing goldfish in a relentlessly watched fishbowl.

This was what happened when you were accidentally thrust into the spotlight by a mother who thought it was her birthright. Her mother was the epitome of '70s beauty—a profusion of blonde feathered hair and those same blue eyes as Bethany's. She had come to Hollywood to be famous, but at twenty-three, when her body should have been at the peak of its casting couch career, she got pregnant. And no matter how far she had come from the small-town notions of Malinta, Ohio, abortion seemed out of the question.

So on April 11, 1980, after a six-pack of Tab and eight hours of morphine-heavy labor, little Cassandra Arielle Campbell was born. Five months later, her mother was back to auditions. With no child-care, little Cassie Campbell was towed along, and, as with nearly all other child actors, she caught the eye of a casting director. He was also casting a bubble bath commercial, and could the baby sit up in a tub yet? Of course she could. And she could also wave shyly. And blow kisses on command. And babble in an adorable singsongy way that was straight out of some cartoon rendition of cherubic perfection. So there was the Luxom bubble bath commercial, and then the Riga's restaurant commercial, then Wright's Moving Company, then some West Coast car dealership, a bunch of print ads, and then the mother of all moneymakers—a national Pampers commercial. By then Bethany had Uncle Frank as her agent, monthly headshots, and a résumé longer than her mother's. The transition to theatrical casting was easy. She booked the first three auditions she went on, then landed young Tabitha on *The Beautiful City*, and suddenly she was six and able to work eight hours a day and audition for *Angel Eyes*.

She knew the audition for *Angel Eyes* was a big deal, even then. They didn't shoot *Beautiful City* on Mondays, and her mother had woken her early with chocolate chip pancakes—the *homemade* kind—and curled her already curly hair with a curling iron and bought her a new white dress—itchy at the seams. But even when Bethany complained and scratched at her legs, her mother just gritted her teeth and gave her another pancake. They drove to the Valley, to a lot she had never been to before, and parked in a special space with a special permit. Her mother allowed her not to wear her seat belt to avoid wrinkling her dress, and Bethany jumped out while the car was not yet stopped and fell and skinned her knees. One knee had a hole in the white tights, the other a sprinkling of red leaching through. She sat on the oil-stained lot and looked up at her mother, who looked at her with an indecipherable mix of horror, panic, and something else. Usually Bethany could read her mother before her mother could read herself. Bethany knew when to make herself invisible, when to be shy and hide demurely behind her mother's legs, when to crawl into her lap and tell her she loved her most-est. But this was a look she couldn't read. And then her mother forced her teeth into a concerned smile and whispered, "Cry. Quietly." Bethany had been confused, but she knew better than to second-guess her mother, so she set her mouth in a trembling pout and imagined the individual tears marching up the staircase of her brain and down the slide of her eyelids. She sucked in her bottom lip, closed her eyes, and softly (and beautifully) whimpered. When she opened them again, what she saw first was her mother, beaming, and then a man in a white V-neck sweater, white pants, and impossibly white tennis shoes. Later she knew him as Roge, Roger Fiorello, executive producer of a hit list of '70s and '80s television shows and what would soon be his crowning glory, *Angel Eyes*. He originally envisioned the show with an older girl—prepubescent, able to command an hour-long drama—but then he saw Cassie Campbell with those majestic blonde curls and those beatific blue eyes full of tender tears. This was the story he repeated in countless interviews. He knew he had a star. And a multimillion-dollar fortune. There were Cassie Campbell dolls (they kept her utterly charming name; why mess with perfection?), and lunch boxes, and chapter books, and posters, and commemorative plates, and snow globes, and even brilliant-blue contact lenses. Eight seasons of Cassie Campbell bringing the town of Harksville together one hour-long episode at a time.

Even then she thought the premise was problematic. Why would a six-year-old be sent down to earth to help one small town? Why not the whole world? Why not send an adult who could do things like drive (and save the Wilkinson boy from jumping off the water tower rather than just help the town see that they needed to rally behind rights for the disabled)? Or send God himself, who could just command the black folks and the white folks to get along rather than having Cassie spend two episodes almost dying in a car accident and then receiving a blood transfusion from little black Leroy Williams? And why didn't the town catch on after the twentieth time she helped someone "look from other eyes" that she wasn't just some human child found in a basket on the church steps and adopted by the childless pastor and his wife? But the fans loved it. That's literally what every review said, "A critical cringe fest, but the fans love it!" And the fans. They called themselves Cass-els, and they weren't just in the eight-to-eighteen demographic. There were grown-ups (lots of them) who wrote her regular fan mail. And there were a number of people who thought Cassie was *actually* an angel. They had to court order one woman in New Jersey to stop sending miracle requests after she threatened to come to Los Angeles and "collect a relic." After that, they stopped letting Bethany see her mail. And they only occasionally let her visit sick children in the hospital, preventing too much confusion over her divine abilities. And they always had a bodyguard at press events.

By the time Bethany was nine years old, she was raking in $100,000 an episode, 10 percent of merchandising, and five-figure sums for appearances (Peter Delaney, the supermarket billionaire, had paid her $11,000 to simply show up at his daughter's seventh birthday party). There were new cars, a condo in Hawaii and one in Aspen (although neither she nor her mother skied), and endless bags of new clothes. The year she turned ten, she grossed $3 million, 15 percent of which was put in a Coogan account to be given to her when she turned eighteen. Except that it wasn't. At least not all of it.

There are too many lawyers and managers, each with a different story depending on the length of time they slept with her mother, to ever really know how much money there should have been. She knows millions were spent the last year and a half she was in LA. *Angel Eyes* ended, *Cassandra* was an embarrassing two-year failure, and then the work pretty much dried up. There was a guest spot here, a hosting gig on MTV there, but mostly Bethany spent a year and a half waiting for her eighteenth birthday. A year and a half of plotting and planning. A year and a half watching her mother slowly come to the stark realization that there would be no more big money coming in. So they lived in a precarious state of attack and contrition, her mother alternately telling her what a hateful, selfish bitch she was for not landing a role and then trying to smother her with cuddles, compliments, and gifts—a turquoise BMW convertible, a Nokia 5110 in red and another in blue, a Chihuahua puppy with a customized wardrobe. And drugs. When she was little, there was a revolving door of people coming to the house to deliver a nonsensical amount of takeout, and forgotten keys, and "papers," but when Bethany was sixteen, her mother completely dropped the charade.

The offerings started casually, a line of cocaine left out in the bathroom, a joint and matches on the kitchen table, but when Bethany didn't bite, her mother was more overt. For Bethany's seventeenth birthday, her mother gave her an oval compact with her name etched into the mirror, a chain with a telescopic spoon/straw combo, and a silver vial filled with cocaine. Bethany held the package, and her mother, already high on the stuff and eating away at her cuticles, impatiently pulled it from her and did a line in demonstration. "It's lab-grade Peruvian fluff, Cassie," she said. "It doesn't get better than this."

Bethany didn't do the coke then, but that night, when the house was filled with over two hundred people, and she was tipsy on champagne, and Toby Santos was flirting with *her*, she couldn't remember why she shouldn't. Gorgeous Toby with his ice-blue eyes and black hair and sweet-smelling neck. He told her she was beautiful; but she knew that, he said. But she didn't. She had been a beautiful little girl, of course, but then prepubescence hit. When they tried to sell her as Cassandra, the chub of hormones hadn't melted yet. No one said she was beautiful then. They cut her hair short on one side and pierced three holes in one ear and stuffed her into a crop top and miniskirt. And the press called her a doughy puppy, said she had too many cheeks and not enough talent, renamed her Cassie Cakes-a-Lot. But at seventeen, she had lost all the pudge. And she wasn't little Cassie Campbell anymore. Toby noticed, and in that moment, Bethany noticed too.

She felt the power of beauty, the pleasure of being desired, and it was exhilarating. So she mustered her courage, tossed her hair, and said, "Want to do some blow?" He smiled a crooked half grin and grabbed a bottle of champagne, and they made their way through the crowd, Bethany gulping swigs along the way, until they arrived at her bedroom, her mother's gift still out on her nightstand, four lines that she didn't remember before laid out in four bright rows. She froze, but he eased the transition, patting the space on the bed next to him, handling the paraphernalia like a rock star, helping maintain the illusion that she knew exactly what she was doing.

The first line stung. She gripped her nose hard and pinched her eyes closed, and he laughed affectionately and stroked her hair, and as he did, the flush of the drug hit her hard. And his hand in her hair and her head full of exploding stars made her lean into his chest, tilt her face to his, and open her mouth like she was receiving the host on *Angel Eyes*. And then his lips were on hers, and they were kissing—her first kiss!—the bitter drip of the cocaine mixing with his tongue, his hands holding fistfuls of her hair, his mouth on her neck, and then a break for him to do a line and another for her, Bethany so in love already, with the drug and him, and feeling what it felt like to be alive and have the world at your disposal.

Later, she thought that she had seen Uncle Frank hand Toby the bottle of champagne, her mother gently close her bedroom door. But in those first moments all she felt was overwhelming joy. And the shame of that naive joy, even now, makes her reel with disgust. But then, the moment coursed through her body, the future through her brain—moonlit walks on the beach, flower bouquets for every date—and she let him take her shirt, bra, jeans off. But when he shoved his hand in her underwear, thrust a finger inside her, she grabbed his wrist. "That hurts," she managed, but all this did was make him stab harder, her hands atop his, seemingly helping him go deeper inside her. "Please," she said, but he shushed her, called her baby, pulled his finger out and rubbed her roughly, then thrust it back in again and again until she cried. Real tears. Real sobs. And finally, he stopped. "What the hell is wrong with you?" he said, and Bethany, so accustomed to doing what was asked of her, felt the guilt like a pinch from her mother. She shook her head and willed her hands to stay by her sides. But when he pulled her underwear down, spat on his fingers, and stabbed again, she felt the pain lightning through her. "Stop," she begged. "I'm sorry. Stop." And he did. He cursed something under his breath, but he sat up. He put on his shirt. He did two more lines. And then he stood up, ran his hands through his hair, and said, "You can tell your mother I don't rape little girls." What? she wanted to say. What? What? But the pathetic truth was that even in the fog of cocaine and fear and alcohol, she knew exactly what he meant. She didn't need her mother's hungover disappointment, her "Jesus, Cassie, he's the head of that new teen network" to explain what she already knew, that the complete and total commodification of Cassie Campbell had been achieved.

And so, exactly one year later, she fled Los Angeles and took whatever money was left. And it was a lot. Enough to later buy Meadowlark.

Enough for an apartment and food and enrollment at Portland Community College, which was where she met Aaron. She arrived at her human development class twenty minutes early, expecting to wait and read, but Aaron was sitting front and center, working on a laptop. She tried to slink silently into a back desk, but he turned around and started talking to her—how long had she been at PCC, how did she like it, was she from Portland, what did she do now? He was everything she dreaded embodied in an incredibly attractive package. She answered—politely—and prayed someone else would come in, and eventually someone did, but that class and every one after, he made it a point of saying goodbye to her.

He was both strange and magnetic. He asked the teacher pointed, sharp questions but interrupted without raising his hand. He had a head full of shaggy curls and wore old jeans and T-shirts but spoke with such precision and grace that if she closed her eyes, Bethany could imagine him in some presidential office. He was the first person she met that she wanted to find out about more than she wanted to be left unfound. And so after their final exam, as he said his usual goodbye, she asked him if he wanted to get coffee, blurted it out in such a ridiculously awkward way that he laughed at her. She was mortified, which made him laugh more, but then he covered his mouth, his smile clearly on display under his hands, and nodded enthusiastically. So they went to the student union, where she played with her paper coffee cup and listened to him talk. And talk. He was open about his past, and frankly, she thought it sounded so much like an episode of *Angel Eyes* (the one where the boy runs away from the weird apocalyptic cult and is taken in by the pastor and his wife before finding a permanent home with a lovely family) that she wondered if he was pranking her. But he was so earnest. And he asked so many questions (most of which she answered deftly but honestly) that she just couldn't believe that anyone could put on such sincerity. And he wanted to see her the next day (they went up and down the river walk, and then up and down again), and the next day (to the rose garden where, because it was December, there were literally no roses blooming), and the next day (this time to his apartment, which was packed with computer parts).

That third date she had sat on the couch and tallied what she knew about him with what he knew of her. It seemed grossly unfair, so she opened a tiny window. She grew up not just in Los Angeles, she told him, but in Hollywood. She watched him carefully, looking for some flash of recognition, but there was none. "Huh," he said. "You must have watched a lot of movies." It was such a childlike thing to say, and that was the perfect explanation of him. He seemed an incredibly smart and mature child peeking out from this lovely man's body. It charmed her, and she leaned over and, summoning up all her courage, kissed him.

Soon she was staying the night regularly, then spending full weeks at his place. He was a self-taught computer programmer and made big chunks of money in unpredictable intervals, and at the beginning he had lots of time to want to know everything about her. And slowly, she let things slip. Bits and pieces about people she grew up with (Mary-Kate and Ashley? He never heard of them) and sets she visited (*Blossom*? *Growing Pains*? He hadn't even watched a television until health class in middle school) until one morning, she sat him down, her heart pounding, and googled *Angel Eyes*. She brought up the clips on YouTube, then chose the one where little Cassie Campbell helps a blind girl meet the puppy that later becomes her guide dog. "Well?" she said when he said nothing. "Well what?" he asked. "Don't you notice anything about her?" He looked at the still image on the screen and said, "She looks kind of like you?" By then she was light headed and sweating through his borrowed T-shirt, and she blurted, "She *is* me!" He looked back at the screen. Looked at her. Then smiled. "Cool," he said. And they went out to breakfast.

Sure, he asked questions, but it seemed to him a past like any other. He grew up in a cult, for fuck's sake—how could a TV show be any weirder? But it was exactly this that made telling him, and only him, possible. He had been completely unfamiliar with the concept of celebrity as a child, and no matter how much media he consumed as an adult, nothing could lay those tracks of starry-eyed awe almost every other American had had pounded into their TV-riddled childhood heads. But this lack of awareness of fame as a nefarious, assaultive force was exactly why the thought of his children linked and retweeted across the planet didn't fill him with unrelenting dread.

She reopens the laptop again and refreshes the screen. Still the migrant workers. Still that little boy's big brown eyes beaming down at her from some server in the sky. She can imagine Juniper flickering to life on millions of screens across America. How many hours would it take for TMZ and Extra and Celebrity Today to be flying drones around the grounds? How many hours before shots of Bethany with a baseball cap and sunglasses were populating the sidebars of every social media site across the country?

It is selfish, she knows, this terror of discovery. And probably ridiculous. How many children are replicas of her childhood self? Some? Maybe. And does anyone really care about the kid of some has-been TV star? Maybe Aaron is right and it is the pictures of the children that will save them all. Maybe she needs to put aside self-preservation in service of the greater good. What they are doing at Meadowlark is important. It deserves to be protected. But doesn't she also deserve this? Don't the children?

Of course she worries about all the children, but she can't pretend it's not really about Juniper. Juniper is eleven. When Bethany was ten, *Angel Eyes* was at its height of popularity. Bethany was carted all over the world doing press junkets and promotional tours and private dinners. She knew how to code shift from person to person depending on importance and nationality and gender. She isn't sure Juniper even knows how to eat with a knife and fork. She's still such a baby, and yet Juniper seems to be skipping right over that awkward chubby body that Bethany inherited at eleven. She is growing longer and leaner, and

Bethany can see the few silky hairs under her arms when she wears a tank top. She imagines she will get her period soon, and although Bethany has always tried to normalize puberty, buy the books about how it's all perfectly natural, there's something about Juniper's eagerness that scares her.

Juniper bought herself Teen Dream deodorant with her own money, and she has a little purse full of pink tampons that she keeps expectantly on her shelf, and when Bethany tries to talk to her about how this new chapter in her life will be exciting but maybe a little bit scary, Juniper just sighs and rolls her eyes. It's not scary to Juniper. At all. And that's what scares Bethany, how quickly and easily Juniper might saunter into adolescence, which seems just an oblique way of saying the completion of childhood. Bethany isn't ready for childhood to be over, but Juniper is. Bring in the photographers, and Juniper's sure to get a whiff of possibility, the promise of a world unable to get enough of your newly minted teen self. And why wouldn't the world want her? Or if not the world, some third-rate producer hoping to cash in on an *Angel Eyes* remake? At eleven, Bethany wanted nothing more than to escape from all those fake fuckers, but Juniper knows none of this. And Bethany won't allow her to. No. No pictures. It doesn't even matter that Aaron can't understand her reasons. He promised, and she has to believe that this is enough.

◆ ◆ ◆

For two days, there are no police, and then the sheriff comes with "his minions," as Candice calls them, and tries to sweet-talk Candice and David into opening the gate. When that fails, he announces he will be back the next day with an order to produce, which Candice brushes off like it is some census poll they can all just refuse to take. But Bethany talks to Star, and Star, who used to be a lawyer, is worried. An order to produce is a court-mandated document, she says. You can't defy an order and not be held in contempt of court. And if you are held in contempt, the judge will impose sanctions—fines, maybe jail time. They'd have to be stupid to ignore the real danger.

So Aaron calls a community meeting, and they try to come to a consensus on what should be done. At first, Dana refuses to allow Marley to talk to the police, but that night, Bethany and Star come to Dana's room and talk to her, assuage her, persuade her to at least let Star talk to the sheriff. She will gather information and then proceed. Star went through a long custody battle with her ex, and it was the police who helped prove that her ex was abusive. The sheriff might work with Dana; they might resolve this within hours. Finally, Dana agrees, but only if Bethany goes too. "He likes you," Dana says to Bethany. "You're not just some lawyer. Sorry, Star," and it's true. Bethany met the sheriff once at a Fourth of July parade. He gave all the kids mini chocolate bars and joked that she certainly had her hands full, and later that day, when River fell and broke her finger, he gave the two of them a ride to the hospital, siren and all. Now, when Bethany sees him in town, he still remembers her. It used to make her nervous, but he calls her "River's mama" and only asks about the kids, so she agrees to do it. She doesn't like being the center of attention, but if it will put an end to all this, she will. "Okay," she says to Dana, and Aaron sets his jaw but says nothing.

At eight the next morning, the police buzz the gate. The computer pings, and Bethany rushes to turn the sound off. Blaze and River are still asleep. Juniper is already awake and out somewhere.

"I'll go," Aaron says.

"Aaron, please," Bethany says. "Let us go alone."

Bethany is still in her pajama bottoms and T-shirt, and she pulls on jeans and tries to wrestle her hair into a ponytail.

Star opens the door to their family room. "Ready?" she whispers.

Blaze stirs but stays asleep, his mouth slung open, baby teeth strikingly white in the hazy sunlight.

"I'll wait on the porch," Aaron says.

"Fine, fine," Bethany whispers.

The three of them creep downstairs. Much of Meadowlark sleeps late, but there are a few people up. Surprisingly, Gavin is awake. He is a night owl, often roaming, or "patrolling" as he calls it, late into the night and then not waking up until noon the next day. Now he is making coffee in the kitchen. Anthony is preparing breakfast for the babies, and Kara is trying to talk Dana into having some tea instead of pacing the length of the common room.

"Finally!" Dana says. She grabs Bethany's arm. "Come right back and tell me exactly what they say," Dana says.

"Of course," Star says.

"And don't let them in." It is Gavin. He has come in from the kitchen and is hovering, mug in hand.

"She won't," Aaron says. It is a strange thing for Aaron to say, to speak for her. It is something the community firmly opposes, and Bethany catches Star's look of mild surprise.

The police buzz the gate again.

"I'm going," Gavin says.

"No," Bethany says and almost spits it.

Aaron shoots Gavin a look and then hugs Bethany tight. "Beth," he murmurs. It is what he says for everything—his term of endearment, the way he soothes her. Embarrassingly, it is even how she calms herself—a reminder of the life she has constructed with this devoted, constant man.

"We'll be right back," Star says.

The walk to the gate feels endless, and Bethany forces herself not to look back at the porch, at the crowd she knows has gathered. She can see the cops through the blue bars. There are three of them, the sheriff towering over the two others. He is a huge Goliath of a man with a soft demeanor, and she tries to remember this as she approaches.

"Good morning," the sheriff says.

Bethany feels awkward and uneasy, and she tries to convince herself that this is no different than a performance.

"We need to talk to Marley," the sheriff says.

"I'm Star Carter. I'm an attorney, and we have a few questions."

One of the officers smirks, but the sheriff nods.

"I'm assuming no charges are being levied at this point?"

"No," the sheriff says.

"And you'll allow the mother to be present at the interview?"

"Well, we can't do that, but we have a very competent social worker. She's just right here waiting in the car, or if you'd prefer, you can bring Marley down to the station."

"And are you aware that the father has been abusive in the past?" Star asks.

"We'd be very interested in discussing that."

Star is good at this, and Bethany feels the tension she has been holding for the last twenty-four hours start to ease.

"If Marley's mother concedes, she'll want an attorney present."

"That can be arranged."

"And the mother will need an emergency temporary-custody order until the father is proven fit."

Bethany sees the officers slowly work their hands to their guns, sees them shift their bodies to their left, and then she sees Gavin.

"Good morning, gentlemen," he says.

Bethany bristles, and Star tries to ignore him. "You understand the mother will not negotiate temporary custody?" Star continues.

"I'm assuming you have some kind of paperwork?" Gavin interrupts.

The sheriff slides the order to produce through the bars, and Gavin snatches it.

"This is an order to produce," the sheriff says. "You are legally required to produce the child within twenty-four hours—"

"And where's the warrant?" Gavin interrupts.

"We don't need a warrant to question a child."

"You do if he's on our property."

"You understand this is a court order?"

"I understand you don't have a warrant." Gavin smiles, and Bethany feels dizzy. She clutches the fence with one hand and watches the sheriff smile right back at Gavin.

"But we can get one," the sheriff says.

And that's when Bethany understands that she and Star have lost. And Gavin must know this, too, because with his mouth set in that furious grin, he walks to one side of the iron gate and uncoils a long roll of corrugated tin Bethany hadn't even noticed was there.

"And you can go fuck yourselves because you're not coming in," he says. "Even with a search warrant." The metal is already pierced and bound to one edge of the gate, and the sound of it unfurling shatters whatever's left of the calm Star has negotiated. Gavin pushes in front of the women and attaches this new barrier to the other side of the gate so that Bethany cannot see the police get in their cars, cannot see the sheriff follow the children's "Come back soon!" signs down the driveway, cannot watch as the possibility of a peaceful resolution completely disappears.

"We're not letting them in," Gavin says.

Star is livid. "Do you have any idea what you've done?"

Gavin wraps the wire tightly around the bars. "I've protected my children."

And at this, Bethany feels her anger cyclone up and out of her. "This isn't protecting them!"

He stops and looks up at her. And then he laughs. "Okay. Beth." He spits the name, and she takes a step back, that name in his mouth making her prick with an inconceivable thought. This is Aaron's idea. But as soon as the thought arrives, Aaron is there, running hard and breathless.

"We're screwed," Star says.

Gavin dismisses them with his hand and keeps working with the wire.

"Let's go inside," Aaron says.

"They're coming with a warrant," Bethany says. "We have to let them in."

"Let's go inside," Aaron says again. He reaches for Bethany's hand, and she pulls away.

"Did you tell him to do this?" Bethany asks.

Gavin laughs, and then Aaron is slamming his hand against the metal, the sound like thunder, reverberating in the dense air. The noise is shocking, but more so is Aaron's rage. It is fierce and uncharacteristic, but just as quickly, he looks stricken, and Bethany immediately regrets asking the question.

"Why would you think that?" he says.

She opens her mouth but has nothing to say. Because of Gavin? Gavin, who weighs the kids' dessert to make sure his kids aren't cheated? Gavin, who demands written IOU notes for any amount borrowed that's over a dollar? Gavin, who rushes to judgment and action on any perceived injustice?

"I'm sorry . . . ," she says, but she can see his hurt turn into irritation and then into anger. Still, it is the calm, even anger that she is familiar with. It is rare that he is angry, but it lasts, and now she has brought it on herself, confused her fear of exposure with her husband's betrayal.

"I'm sorry . . . ," she tries again, but he has turned and is walking toward the house. He nods but keeps walking.

"Fuck," she says to herself and holds her head in her hands. Of course it is all Gavin. He has only been here eighteen months, but he's made everyone feel as if he's one of the founding families, spouting child-development statistics and quoting Aaron as if Aaron were some kind of modern-day Piaget. Yes, Meadowlark was Aaron's vision, but it's not just some godforsaken hideout to Bethany. She's been right beside him this whole time, viscerally knowing that a childhood devoted to learner-led activities and child-initiated education within a natural environment would produce profoundly different children. They created Meadowlark together. And Bethany, *Bethany*, is the one who paid for it. She spent nearly all that was left of her money on these four acres and the buildings that now sit atop them. And Gavin—Gavin is threatening all that. And now he has not only unfurled a tin wall between Meadowlark and the rest of the world but between her and Aaron. Aaron is angry at her now, and this anger will last. He is quick to forgive, but the anger can still smolder for days, and it leaves Bethany feeling something close to panic.

Once, when Juniper was three and they were first talking about the idea of Meadowlark, they had met a family at the park and talked about parenting. Bethany had been so excited about the idea of Meadowlark that she had talked on and on. They envisioned a place where children could listen to their heads and their hearts, she said. Children would be confident, curious, and unburdened by society's expectations. Children would know their truth.

Later, when she looked back at that day, she could see herself dominating the conversation, but she was so eager to make Meadowlark a go, and it was so rare that she took center stage. After years of attention, she gladly withdrew from the spotlight, happy to have Aaron shine enough for both of them. But that day, her excitement seemed to spill out of her. And yes, she had talked over him, and yes, she hadn't let him get a word in, but his reaction had been excessive. He hadn't raged, had barely even raised his voice, but she could feel the anger emanating from him like a fever. "You made me look like I was nothing," was all he could manage, and when she cried (real tears!) and told him she was sorry, that she never wanted him to feel that way, he nodded and told her it was okay, but he was still angry. And it lasted. Two days? Three days? She felt herself coming apart, begged him to forgive her. "Of course I forgive you," was all he would say. "Just give me time."

She hadn't known then whether his distance was punishment for her angering him. But each time it happened (four times in all these years? Five?), she came closer to believing that no, it was not punishment, that the smoldering twine of his anger just unwound slower than most. All that love and devotion so generously given took longer to let back out. But—and it is a but she only allows herself to consider fleetingly—she isn't sure. She read for a movie when she was ten in which the father said to the mother, "You threaten my authority, I threaten your life." For some reason, the line carved into her, and now, when Aaron is angry, it sometimes pops up uninvited. A ridiculous fusion of two completely contrary things. Aaron hates violence. But still, she hears it now—the threatening voice of the man playing the father, the way the words burrowed deep into her.

◆ ◆ ◆

The next day the media begins to arrive, and the next a police cruiser parks openly in the dirt lot in front. Bethany watches the world begin to descend. The whole time, Aaron silently circling her, his anger still palpable.

On the third day Aaron calls a community meeting, at night, when most of the kids are asleep. This is unusual in itself, but what is even more unusual is that Bethany doesn't know what he is going to say. She sits there with the rest of Meadowlark waiting for him to speak, feeling dumb and embarrassed, trying to tamp down the humiliation of his distance.

"Simrin is coming," he finally says.

Bethany feels the balloon of fear that's sat in the pit of her stomach since she understood this was a possibility begin to inflate. Simrin can help them tell their story the way they want, he says. She can help make whatever bullshit the cops are going to concoct refutable. If the world sees Meadowlark, the world will be on their side, and the cops will have their work cut out for them. This will all pass if they stay unified and deal with the problem calmly and diplomatically. But the problem is, Bethany thinks, there is no way to be calm and diplomatic when some stranger wants to upload your children's pictures to a site that gets three thousand views a day. And it is even harder when the person who keeps you calm and diplomatic has barricaded himself away from you.

"And what are we supposed to do while we're waiting?" Candice asks.

"Stay focused on why we're here," he says. Then pauses. "And why is that?"

"For the kids," Dan says.

"Exactly," Aaron says. "These kids were born with magic inside of them. We're just here to help them retain it."

There are the usual murmurs of affirmation. Bethany's heard this speech many times before. Normally, she feels the thrill of his words, but there's something about the word *magic* that pricks her this time, the same puncture of dread she's felt a few times before. Once, right after Juniper was born, she found him holding the baby and crying. "What's the matter?" she had asked, and he had looked up at her, tears streaming down his cheeks, and said, "I can see the divine in her."

Bethany had cried too. Juniper was divine. But then he had looked at her with all the fierce intensity she so admired and said, "We will shape her future, and she will shape the world," and she had felt that same trepidation stab through her. Does it have to be the world? she had wanted to ask, but she was awash in hormones and leaky milk and her own adoration. So what if he was overcome by the thought of his daughter's future? So what if he gifted her a touch of his grandiosity?

"Don't lose track of our mission," he says now.

"Preach!" someone says, and they all laugh. Bethany tries to fake it, but her acting chops seem long abandoned.

"All right," he says. "Let's call it a night."

People get up to leave, and Bethany waits to see if he will come to her, but he doesn't, just crosses the room, receiving pats on the back on his way up the stairs.

◆　◆　◆

The next day Simrin arrives.

The police cruiser is still out front and has been joined by a number of other cars and people hanging around, mostly checking their phones and occasionally shooting a picture. Everyone inside Meadowlark can watch everyone outside from any of the four community computers in the house, and although they are trying to keep the full truth from the kids without overtly lying, River and Darcy and Micah like to switch between the cameras on the computers and try to catch people picking their noses or scratching their butts.

Bethany is in the upstairs playroom with the kids, pretending to eat Blaze's plastic ice cream when River yells. "There's someone new at the gate!"

"She's looking right at the camera!" Darcy adds.

Bethany gets up and looks at the screen. She knows it is Simrin immediately. She is pacing in front of their once-beautiful and now boarded-up gate.

"Go get Daddy," Bethany says to River. "He might be outside hanging laundry."

River races through the house, and Darcy and Micah stand and press their fingers to the computer screen.

"Who is she?" Darcy says.

"You can make her head disappear with your thumb," Micah says.

"Touching the screen can make it not function," Bethany says. She wills them to stop and bites the inside of her lip to keep from demanding it.

"She has a camera," Darcy says.

91

She looks very much like the photo on her blog. Although Bethany expected her to be smaller or maybe not smaller but more reticent? She is pacing, moving a lot, throwing her head down on her forearms, turning around one way. She isn't a nervous little thing, but maybe she is mixing them up. Jaishri is the timid one, Simrin the firecracker, but that isn't the word Aaron used either. Fiery? Maybe. Or fierce. Yes. Quietly fierce. She does look a little fierce, but more agitated than fierce. Although Bethany supposes she would be agitated, too, showing up in the middle of Nevada to find that her long-lost "brother" has locked himself inside another commune.

What Bethany knows of Aaron's past isn't limited. Aaron, who grew up Arjun in his own bizarro world. He has told her all about the hours of forced meditation and chanting; their seclusion inside Ananda; his friends who were more like siblings, especially Simrin and Jaishri, who he helped escape when they were teenagers. Still, it seems a fairy-tale past with bad grown-ups and good children that eventually run away. But isn't that her story too? Their lives seem to parallel and conflict in equal measure. Except Bethany doesn't want a reunion, not with her mother and not for her husband. And maybe that's what is pricking at her. This woman on the screen has followed the bread crumbs to Bethany's husband, not some make-believe Hansel.

It seems a long time before Aaron arrives, but he must have run hard because when he hurries into the room, he is out of breath. "That's her," he says. He bends down at the computer and clicks and types. Bethany hears the long unanswered rings and then Simrin's voice mail. She catches the first few words, the predictable "You've reached," before Aaron hangs up and tries again. She sounds just perfectly . . . normal. It rings again, four, five, six times, and then she picks up.

"Simrin," Aaron says.

Bethany feels a sudden stab of bitterness.

"I can see her talking!" River says.

"Can we try and be quiet?" Bethany asks.

"Simrin," Aaron says again. He grabs for some headphones and plugs them into the port.

"Who is it? Who is it?" Darcy yells.

Allison is reading a book to Sage and looks up. "Is it her?" she asks.

Bethany nods, and Allison quickly picks up Sage and Blaze and lures the bigger kids away with promises of lemonade. "I'll take them to the TV room." TV. It is still one of her and Aaron's major conflicts. She wants none. He doesn't want his children growing up completely unacquainted with the outside world. They have settled on animation. A gauzy peek into the lion's den.

Bethany strains to hear, but the headphones muffle Simrin's voice, and the children are loud. She hears Aaron say "Please," then nothing, and then he slams the headphones to the desk. He kisses River's head and then hurries out, and Bethany turns back to the screen. It is blank now—just the dirt out front visible. Bethany feels the sweat collect at her hairline and begin to slide down her temples—not just the heat, but the waiting, the anticipation of something wholly unwanted. And then Simrin appears on the screen, holding a child against one shoulder, a bulky bag on the other. She knows Simrin has a daughter, but why did she bring her here? To this? "Stupid," she says aloud, and hearing it, outside her head, makes her inhale sharply. If you can't bring a kid to Meadowlark, things are very, very wrong. She tries to think of something that makes her happy—Blaze's hot sleepy head, Juniper's endless flips on the trampoline, Aaron's palm on the small of her back. She turns from the computer and takes the stairs. She reaches the landing halfway down when the front door opens.

And then, there they are. Simrin holding a tiny dark-haired girl. Aaron standing beside Simrin, one hand on her back. Bethany feels her breath quicken, and she sits down on the landing and tries to steady her inhales and exhales. Peace begins with me, she thinks and counts the words on her fingers. It is something they teach the children. She had always found it personally unhelpful until Juniper totally lost it one day

93

and declared that "peace begins with me" was stupid, just grown-ups making kids pretend everything was okay. And suddenly, the idea of *pretending* your way into serenity made complete sense.

Aaron shuts the door behind them, and Simrin looks around the room. She is pale and sweaty, and she leans uneasily against the door and lets her bag sag to the ground.

"I'll get some water," Aaron says.

"I can get it." It is someone in the living room. Candice? Bethany looks. Yes, Candice. Kara and Dan have also somehow sneaked in, and now everyone is paying rapt attention. She counts on her fingers again, peace begins with me, takes a final deep breath, and then looks back at Simrin. She sees it before anyone else, knows what is going to happen, and it does. Bethany stands and watches Simrin as she slides to the floor.

"I'm going to be sick," Simrin says. She tumbles the little girl from her lap, her head swaying atop her neck, and vomits. The little girl is crying now, and Bethany takes the stairs quickly. Someone is getting towels, and Candice is there with the water. Aaron is kneeling next to Simrin. And Bethany, heart racing, can only stand stupidly on the bottom step.

Simrin retches again.

"Oh, God," Simrin says. "Jesus, I'm sorry."

Aaron puts his hand on Simrin's back, and Bethany bristles.

"And fuck you too," Simrin says.

Bethany catches it before Aaron can recover, the wounding and the subsequent cover-up. She grips the banister tighter. Candice hands Simrin a cup of water, and she sips it and tries to console the little girl. Kara is cleaning up the sick on the floor, and then Aaron is helping Simrin stand and carry the girl to a couch. Bethany watches it all, feeling suddenly like she is back on set, a scene playing out before her that she has no part in. She watches them, keeping her back against the banister, and slowly inches her way into the living room.

The little girl has stopped crying, but she is hiding her face in Simrin's chest, her body wrapped up like a squirrel in her mother's lap. None of

Bethany's children has ever done this. Yes, they sit on her lap and cuddle on the couch, but not this animal instinct to burrow up into her. She reasons that it is Meadowlark that allows them the strength to not cling like this, but she sees other children at Meadowlark do this, feels the same pinprick of loss she does now. She wants Blaze, her baby, needs to feel his warm body close to her. She feels her milk let down, and she wraps her arms around her chest and squeezes so she doesn't feel the sting.

Aaron sits on a stool in front of Simrin. He is talking, softly, but Bethany can't make out the words. The little girl looks up and says something. Aaron smiles, and then he is looking around the room.

"Bethany," he calls. "Can you get Quinn some cookies?"

Bethany. Not Beth. Even now, with this chaos erupting around them, he's perfectly fine affirming his anger.

"I'll get them." It is Candice again. And suddenly Bethany isn't even sure if she is visible. She takes a few steps, and Simrin looks at her, then looks away.

"I'm Bethany," she says. She speaks too loudly. Both Aaron and Simrin turn and look at her, and the world suddenly feels very uneven. It has been a long time since she routinely introduced herself. "It makes you seem down to earth," her mother told her. "Of course everyone knows who you are, but you don't want them to think *you* think that." So she spent her childhood introducing herself like some late-night talk show host. "Hi, I'm Cassie Campbell!" But she is a grown-up now. A totally different person, in fact. One who doesn't remember the last time she said her own name. Now, she wants to add, "Aaron's wife," but she knows how that will sound, both to Simrin and Aaron. Juniper, River, and Blaze's mother? But why would this woman care about her children? She has her own child to keep safe.

"This is my wife, Bethany," Aaron says. "And this is Simrin."

She doesn't like Simrin's name in his mouth. Doesn't like her here at all. She crosses her arms, and Aaron looks deliberately away.

"Cookies." It is Candice. There is a plate of them—way more than any one kid needs—and Quinn stares at them excitedly.

"Where can we talk?" Simrin says.

"Here is fine," Aaron answers.

Simrin gestures toward Quinn, and Aaron looks confused. They are so accustomed to talking in front of the children that it doesn't even occur to him that this might not be an appropriate conversation for a child.

"We don't like to hide things from the children," Bethany says.

There is silence. Simrin stares at her and then turns to Aaron, and Bethany suddenly feels that sour wash flood through her body. Anger. But also something else, the unmistakable burn of exclusion. Simrin's eyes lock with Aaron's, their history woven not only between but within them. She feels the shock of it scald through her chest, and she lets out an involuntary sound. Not a cry, exactly. Not a gasp, but something reflexive and accidental and completely foreign.

And then Candice is interceding, placing her hand on Quinn's shoulder. "Your mama has a lot of boring grown-up stuff to talk about," she says. "Do you want to eat your cookies and watch a show with some of the other kids? They're just in the next room."

Quinn hides her face in Simrin's shoulder and shakes her head.

"Maybe they're watching something you like," Simrin tries.

Bethany stares at the girl's long brown braids and tries to calm herself. Here is a child, just like any child, she thinks. Here is a mother, just like she is a mother.

"They're either watching *Radiobots* or *Bird Girl*," Candice says.

Quinn peeks at Candice.

"*Bird Girl?*" Simrin says.

"Come with me, Mama."

The almighty power of TV, Bethany thinks.

"I'll walk with you," Simrin says.

Quinn nods, and Simrin lifts Quinn from her lap and holds her hand. They follow Candice around the corner, and Bethany watches the empty space they leave before turning to Aaron. He is scowling at the floor, refusing to look at her. She feels the distance between them increase, the room stretched long. She wants to say his name, to feel the warm sound of it in her mouth, but then they are back, Candice leading Simrin and explaining the floorplan like she is a real estate agent.

"Quinn's all settled in," Candice says. Simrin stops next to Candice, her arms tight around herself. The four of them stand awkwardly around one couch. Kara and Dan are hovering nearby, everyone else gone with the children, she guesses.

"Sim," Aaron says, all anger flushed from him. He reaches for her hand, but she pulls it away.

"It's Simone now." She lets out a deep breath. "Or Simrin . . . I don't care. Jesus. Where are my cameras? And why are you all so calm?"

We're not, Bethany thinks.

"There's not much happening right now," Aaron says. He sits down on the couch in front of Simrin, and Bethany can feel how badly he wants to touch her. Dan and Kara are sitting on an adjoining couch, and Bethany wishes she had something solid behind her, something to push against.

"There are a bunch of cops outside your front gate," Simrin says.

"There are two," Aaron says.

"And media people."

"No one's broken any laws," Candice says.

"Then what the hell is going on?" Simrin asks.

Aaron sighs.

"Why don't you sit down?" Candice asks.

"No," Simrin says, and for the first time Bethany feels both anger and admiration. Candice is one of her least favorite people at Meadowlark, so insistent on "having a voice," always the first one to extol her twins and what Meadowlark has allowed them to "see."

"One of our former community members was kicked out," Aaron begins.

"Encouraged to leave," Kara adds.

"He pushed his girlfriend," Aaron says.

"That's an understatement," Candice says. She has pulled a stool over and is perched on the edge, closing the circle.

"I read child abuse in the paper," Simrin says.

"It's ridiculous, just retribution," Candice says.

"And we don't really even know what the charges are," Kara says.

"There *are* no charges," Aaron says. "That's the point. They have no reason to come in."

"But . . . if there's no abuse, why not just let them in?" Simrin asks.

"Because there's no abuse!" Candice says. They are all quiet for a moment, and Bethany feels the awkwardness permeate the space between them.

The front door opens, and Bethany is grateful for the interruption. Marsha and Troy come in with Sammi and Drew, and Kenny carries West.

"Is this the photographer?" Troy asks.

Aaron colors, and Bethany understands that Simrin doesn't know she was expected. "I told them you might come and take some pictures."

Kara brings Simrin her camera bag, as if seeing her with the camera will confirm Simrin's status.

"Should we get the children?" Marsha asks.

"There's a bunch of kids in Hawthorne," Kenny says.

"And the twins are with Ocean in Willow," Troy says.

"We could bring a bunch of them down to the ship."

Bethany keeps her focus on Simrin, watches her holding her camera bag like it might be stolen.

"Hold on, hold on," Aaron says. "She just got here."

"I don't think this is a good idea," Simrin says. She stands, and Aaron grabs her arm.

"Please, Sim. Just wait. Just wait."

"I didn't agree to any of this," Simrin says and pulls away.

"I know. I know. Just take a walk with me at least. Just listen. Just wait. Please." He is struggling. Bethany doesn't think she has ever seen him this agitated. Normally he is such a beacon of composure. And it hurts her to watch him like this.

"Please," he says again. "Please."

"Where?" Simrin says.

"Rudraksh."

"Jesus, Arjun!"

"It's the name of a tree! All the buildings are named after trees. Hawthorne, Willow, Bodhi, Tule, Cedar." He is counting them off on his fingertips, desperate.

"I want to leave," Simrin says.

"Please, just a walk," he begs.

"I don't like it here," she says.

"You don't have to," he shoots back.

There is silence, and Bethany understands there is something unspoken going on between the two of them, something vital and cryptic. Simrin looks stricken.

"Fine," she finally says. "Let's go."

Aaron says nothing. He walks to the front door, and Simrin follows. The door opens and shuts. And then they are gone.

Bethany feels the fear flush through her. It is the familiar strain of dread over Aaron's anger and disconnection, but there is something else. Not just disconnection this time, but connection. Fierce, instinctive connection. But between Aaron and Simrin. It has charged Bethany's fear with something more nauseating. Jealousy. She can feel it in the hollow of her stomach like a living thing, growing as the threads of Aaron and Simrin's past yank together like the tightening of a shoelace, swift and sudden and long awaited.

JUNIPER

These are the things that Juniper knows about herself: that she would be in sixth grade if she went to real school, that she can do more trampoline tricks than anyone at Meadowlark, that she loves dogs, and that she wants to be able to ride her bike to town by herself. This last one she finds particularly annoying, not because there is anything particularly interesting in town but because she is eleven, and when you're eleven (and the oldest kid at Meadowlark), you should have privileges that others don't. But this is the problem. No one is privileged based on age, which Juniper argues is *exactly* the reason that she should be allowed to ride her bike to town by herself. The latest installment of this saga is that she took the time to write (missing a trip to Candy Emporium) a well-thought-out letter explaining this to her parents, who then took the issue to a house meeting where the community came to the decision that if Juniper felt this strongly about it, she should be able to ride her bike to town . . . on her twelfth birthday. Which is six months away. Which is basically an eternity. In six months, she will probably be able to backflip off the trampoline and stick the landing. She tries it now and again doesn't get enough momentum, lands on her knees, and gets a nasty scrape on her elbow. She wipes the blood on her shirt and lies down in the dust.

Even though the trampoline is at the back of their property, every now and then she can hear the muffled scratches of the police scanner from outside the front gate. Yesterday she lay on her stomach and peeked out the bottom of the barred-up gate for a while, but eventually someone bent down and tried to shove a camera through the gap, and Jennifer encouraged her to come inside.

She spreads her arms and legs and makes a dust angel. She can hear someone coming, so she scrambles up and gets back on the trampoline before anyone can lay claim. She jumps lazily and watches River, Darcy, and a kid she doesn't know approach.

"We want to jump," River says.

"One kid at a time," Juniper says.

"No, two kids," Darcy says.

"Who's that?" Juniper asks. There is a dark-haired little girl with them that she has never seen before.

"Quinn," River says.

"And?" Juniper says.

"And what?" River says.

Juniper rolls her eyes. She is the oldest kid at Meadowlark, and sometimes it is trying to deal with all these babies. "*Who* is Quinn?"

River shrugs. This new kid, Quinn, has long brown braids and is wearing a pink tank top and purple leggings, and she has shoes that light up when she walks. For a moment, Juniper is amazed that such shoes exist, but quickly after, she is annoyed. Every time she goes to town, she finds something else she's never seen. It's mostly stuff she couldn't care less about: coffee pods at Target, T-shirts that say "Sassy and I know it!" at Krepp's, but every now and then there's something she really, really wants: a make-your-own-lip-balm kit, or the Furlicious lounging beanbag chair, or a purple bra with a tiny gold heart at the center. Stuff that no way in a million years anyone will ever buy her.

She jumps, jumps, jumps, then does a front flip and lands on her feet but can't stick the ending and has to do a seat drop. They'll think she meant to do it, and she's waiting for some kind of admiration, at least from Darcy, who is six and not her sister and usually pretty devoted to her, but Darcy pops her thumb in her mouth.

"That's gross," Juniper says. Immediately there are tears in Darcy's eyes, and Juniper feels bad. It's not like she's learned nothing at Meadowlark. She does another seat drop on the trampoline and then jumps off. She takes Darcy's free hand. "Hey, I'm sorry. It's not gross. Don't cry." They are encouraged to feel their emotions, to go get the peace path if they need to resolve something, but there are no grown-ups around right now, and Juniper wants her trampoline back, but River has already climbed up on it, and she and the new girl are bouncing away.

"No fair," Juniper yells, but River just giggles, which makes the new girl giggle, and now Juniper is back to wondering who this kid is. She is jumping and holding her hands over her eyes.

"You're gonna fall," Juniper says.

The new girl doesn't say anything, just jumps and giggles, her hands held tightly to her face. Juniper sighs. She kicks the dirt. Darcy is sitting under the trampoline now, trying to punch up and onto the little girls' feet.

"What's everyone else doing?" Juniper asks.

"Watching TV," River says. "And I don't know."

"My mama is taking pictures," Quinn says.

"Why?" River asks.

Quinn shrugs.

Juniper doesn't say anything, but she knows something. The other night Juniper overheard her father in the Bodhi community space talking with the other grown-ups about a photographer who would come and introduce Meadowlark to the world.

A bunch of kids were asleep in the kids' loft, and another bunch had decided to camp out in the TV room, but because there is no official bedtime at Meadowlark, Juniper was awake, trying to figure out if she should cut bangs into her long blonde hair. She had stood motionless in the bathroom, trying to hear more. It was so weird to have something that seemed so important discussed in the middle of the night. Normally there were house meetings and community gatherings with everyone there, but things had, *obviously*, not been normal lately with the police and the other people out front and the gate closed and now sealed up with metal.

She heard someone else say something about needing it done quickly, but she couldn't hear anything else, and then she remembered she had seen Sammi passed out on her mother's lap. *Supposedly* passed out because spying is what Sammi does best. If Juniper does have a best friend, it is Sammi, who is ten and at least close to Juniper's age. But more than friends they are comrades-in-arms, or that's what Sammi's father, Troy, calls them. Juniper likes the military sound of it, the two of them steeling themselves through their days together. Now she remembers that she had meant to ask Sammi if she had heard any more of this conversation, if she had any covert intelligence.

The two of them have notebooks full of Meadowlark covert intelligence, a tribute to the Crow Seekers books that Sammi is obsessed with. Juniper has read only the last one, but she likes looking at the long list of tribal trees detailing the characters and their powers, and she likes amassing Meadowlark intelligence. Her handwriting sucks, but Sammi doesn't care, and between the two of them, they have already filled a whole spiral notebook with *top secret* information. Last night, she wanted to steal up to their family room and grab the notebook, but Blaze was asleep in there, and even more so, she was afraid of missing something important. Like, really important. The stuff they have written so far is all pretty lame. She is pretty sure even Sammi knows this, but Juniper doesn't want to be the kid who ruins the game. She stopped being that kid last year when the little ones had grown old enough to look at her blankly when she told them fairies weren't real or unicorns couldn't fly. She quickly realized that she wasn't proving herself smarter than anyone, and instead she was becoming the kid who was intentionally excluded from the wide world of kid-dom. And that's what Meadowlark is all about. Kids, kids, kids. It isn't that Juniper *isn't* a kid, or that she doesn't want to be a kid; it's just that she is eleven now, and to be honest, she has felt eleven for quite some time. Sometimes it is depressing to think about.

"Where's Sammi?" she asks River.

The Quinn kid shakes her head and spits on the trampoline.

"Hey, don't do that," River says.

"That tastes like mud," Quinn says.

"What?" River asks.

Quinn has stopped jumping and is wiping her mouth on her shirtsleeve. "That name."

"Sammi?" Juniper asks.

"Stop it!" Quinn yells. She spits a big glob of spit into the dirt. When she yells, Juniper feels the kick of something in her chest.

"Don't spit," River says.

"Your words taste like things?" Juniper asks.

"Sometimes." She spits again and jumps off the trampoline. "I want my mama."

River shrugs and jumps down beside her.

"Wait," Juniper says. She can feel the kick in her chest speed up. Can this girl really taste words, and if so, what else can she do? Her heart feels like it's drumming her from the inside. Juniper catches hold of Quinn's wrist. She is trying to be super gentle, but she thinks Quinn must sense her need.

"Let me go," Quinn says and starts to cry.

Juniper lets go and starts to apologize. She is actually really good at being the big sister. "It's okay. Really. We can just jump or play in the pirate ship?" She really, *really* doesn't want to bring Quinn back to her mother yet. "Or make fairy houses?" At this Quinn quiets a little—she blinks her eyes a number of times and scowls, but something has shifted.

"You want to make fairy houses?" Juniper says.

"Real fairies?" Quinn asks.

River looks at her, and even Darcy, who is still below the trampoline, turns over.

"Sure," Juniper says.

"We've seen them!" Darcy adds.

"When you talk, it's golden with purple zigzags on the edges," Quinn says to Darcy.

"Does it taste like anything?" Juniper asks.

"No," Quinn says, as if she's answering the most obvious question in the world. "But fairies do." She crinkles her nose and smiles.

"What do they taste like?" Darcy asks.

"Minty, but not like toothpaste—like those Christmas sucky things."

"Candy canes?" River says.

Quinn nods. "Can we make the houses?"

"Sure, sure," Juniper says. She holds Quinn's hand gently, and although Quinn pulls away at first, by the time they've trekked halfway over to the back fence, she's sneaked her hand back into Juniper's.

Juniper knows she needs to be very careful now. This Quinn girl shows up, out of nowhere, when there haven't been any new families in almost a year, claiming she can taste words and see voices, something Juniper is (mostly) convinced is total make-believe and only a tiny bit worried is real. A lot of the littlest kids can "taste" words, but their answers change all the time: *purple* tastes like grapes one day and pancakes the next; *moon* might taste like chocolate, but Marley and Ocean really need to check the taste of chocolate to make sure. Often River goes along with it—pink *always* tastes like bubble gum, she'll say—but once, in the dark when the two of them were almost asleep, Juniper asked her if she could really taste words. "I don't know," she said and then a whole lot later, "I don't think so, but don't tell Daddy."

There are other things the adults try to get the kids to do that "cross senses": draw the music they hear or watch someone's arm stroked and feel it on their own arm. The music thing is the easiest for Juniper. She can close her eyes and see patterns, but she hates to draw. So no one really makes her. Which is the best thing about Meadowlark. No one really makes the kids do anything, which Juniper knows is not how it is in the "real" world. The Meadowlark kids watch TV; they go to town. They know that grown-ups out there are always making kids do things they don't want to do, which is why there are so many books and shows about kid superheroes. "Kids who don't have any power need to pretend to feel empowered," her dad says. "But Meadowlark kids already have that power. The power to do anything." It's this last part that makes Juniper the most uncomfortable, the intensity of the *anything*. She knows what he means: the crossing senses, the sensory perception, the world wisdom. *Anything* doesn't really mean anything, and power is only power when you actually have it, but she would never tell the grown-ups this—and definitely not her father, *especially* not her father. He is giving them what he never had. "I wasn't allowed to discover my power," he says, "but you, *you've* been given that." And the thing is, even though she's pretty sure she doesn't have the power to do anything, she's not sure the other kids don't: Devon and Micah and particularly the twins, Jessie and Kai. Jessie can play that card game and guess the shape more times than not, and there was that thing with Kai and the rattlesnake. And now this girl Quinn.

She wants Sammi here to help with the questions, to see if this kid is the real deal, but she knows that even Sammi pretends sometimes. She's seen her flutter her eyes upward when a grown-up leads them on a nature vision walk and then pick her underwear out of her butt the second she thinks no one's watching. She's not sure Sammi even knows she's pretending. And that's where it gets complicated. And confusing.

It's hard to know if what people *say* is real is real, or if there's actually a *real* real, or if one makes the other one. It's a lot to think about.

Lately she's been doing a lot of thinking. And when she thinks, she has to go *secret* herself somewhere. *Secret* is her new favorite verb. It's the opposite of *unsecret*, which is a word she heard her mother say to Star. She had never heard it before, so she looked it up in the dictionary. But the word hadn't been there. Secreting isn't hiding (which you do when you're scared) or spying (which you do when you're trying to find out something you're not supposed to). It's just secreting, nestling yourself into the corners so no one can see you and you can't see anyone. She secrets herself in the gulley beneath the trampoline or in the space above the refrigerators and lets Meadowlark swirl on without her.

But her favorite place to secret herself is on the roof of Hawthorne. The door to the roof is locked so no toddlers can drown themselves in the rain barrels, but she knows that the grown-ups hide the key on the sill above the door. If she gets a good foothold, she can boost herself up on the railing of the external staircase and feel for the key. Yesterday she spent a long time up there. But yesterday she wasn't just secreting. She was watching. At the bottom of the stucco walls surrounding the roof, there are holes, each the size of a tennis ball. Most are connected to plastic drainpipes that funnel rain so the roof won't flood, but there is one that is open, its pipe lying broken with the other irrigation junk. Yesterday, she lay flat against the roof floor and looked out over all of Meadowlark and beyond the front gate.

When the kids finally reach the back fence, Quinn is still holding Juniper's hand, and they find Justice and Blaze playing in the dirt while Jennifer writes in a diary. Jennifer looks up when she sees them approaching.

"Hey there," Jennifer says.

Blaze holds up two handfuls of dirt to show Juniper and garbles something.

"Hi, Blazey," Juniper says and pushes his long curls out of his eyes. She's disappointed a grown-up is here because there's sure to be a long explanation about who Quinn is, and then questions, and Quinn might decide she wants her mom again, but Jennifer just smiles at Quinn and says, "I'm Jennifer. I'm a friend of your mama's friend Aaron."

Quinn lets go of Juniper's hand, and Juniper is sure Quinn's about to say she wants her mom, so Juniper says to Jennifer, "I'll watch Blaze and Justice if you want to go inside."

Jennifer looks at the babies. Justice is three and Jennifer's kid with David, but there's something weird about him. No one ever says anything about it, and even last year when River, who says just about whatever she wants, asked what was wrong with him, their mother just cradled River's face in her hands, smiled, and said, "Absolutely nothing." Jennifer and David do a lot of circle dancing with him, and often a bunch of grown-ups will watch like they're waiting for something special to happen. And Jennifer calls him her "shining Lark." All the children are Larks. The lark is the symbol of dawn, and Meadowlark's Larks are children who have been awakened. They are children who are finding their gifts. At least they're supposed to be, but Justice shines "on and on and on, just like the song," Jennifer says.

"I can take him inside," Jennifer says. "He needs a bath. Don't you, my baby Juju?" Justice is plowing his hands through a pile of dirt Blaze is building—over and over and over.

"Bath time?" Jennifer says again, but he keeps up the plowing, and just like all the grown-ups do, she lets him be. "Guess he needs some more dirt time," she says. "Can you call me if he needs something?"

"Sure," Juniper says. She's inwardly thrilled. She wants Quinn to herself, and the babies won't matter, but she wants River and Darcy out of the way.

"Why don't you go watch TV?" Juniper says to them.

"We just watched," River says.

Darcy is poking tiny sticks in the crevices of the back fence. "This is how you build the fairy staircase," she says to Quinn.

"I'll get water," River says.

"Well. Okay," Jennifer says. "See you in a bit."

Half the time Juniper feels the grown-ups are waiting for the kids to tell them what to do, so she adds, "I got it," and smiles.

Quinn is watching Darcy carefully poking sticks. Juniper twists her arm around and checks out her elbow. The blood is gone, and it's already starting to scab, another *wonder* of childhood. The adults marvel how fast their little bodies heal. And this is why, her father says, it's so important to see what else their bodies can do, what else their *minds* can do. "We built Meadowlark for all of you," her father says. He makes sure to include the *all of* and not just the *you*, which is what he really means. Juniper has heard the story enough times of three-year-old Juniper visiting Daisy Preschool with her parents and literally bolting out the front door and down the sidewalk when the teacher called the children for circle time. "And that's when we knew," her mother says, "if we followed your lead, you would guide us." Her father always laughs, then says, "And guide us, you did." Down the street, around the corner, and into Wren's front yard, where her parents met Wren's parents and they all became friends and they all discussed child-led learning and found a community of like-minded people and blah blah blah. That was Portland. This is Ravenna. Where they're playing in the dirt. And making fairy houses. And ignoring the brouhaha that's going on outside.

Brouhaha. That's the word her father is using. If any word tasted like something, it should be *brouhaha*, and it should taste like soup. Stone soup with the carrots and the squash and the random stuff they pile in it once a year with that "magic" stone that they keep in the kitchen on the top shelf. But *brouhaha* doesn't taste like anything. And Juniper gets the feeling that there's some debate about the use of the word *brouhaha* anyway. She's seen her mother turn her back on her father when he uses it.

"Want to make a fairy bed?" Juniper asks Quinn.

"Sure."

Juniper shows her how to find the heart-shaped poplar leaves and fasten the stems to make a little hammock. She's dying to say *Sammi* again, to see her reaction, but instead she says, "I guess elves could sleep here too." She sneaks a look at Quinn, and there it is, that slight pucker of her mouth, the twitch of her eyebrows. "Or gnomes." She looks at Quinn, but there's nothing. "Or sprites." She looks, and Quinn is staring straight at her.

"None of those things taste like anything," Quinn says.

Juniper blushes. This tiny girl can see right through her.

"How old are you?"

"Almost six."

"And you can . . ." Juniper doesn't want to say it. It feels too precarious. If she says yes. If she says no.

"I got the water." River is back with a bucket to fill the fairy swimming pool. Juniper wonders what her sister sounds like. River's always had that scratchy-voice thing, and she imagines it would look like the pencil scribbles the toddlers draw on the walls.

River was two when they moved to Meadowlark, but it wasn't really Meadowlark then. Juniper remembers because she was five, almost six, like this Quinn girl. It was all dirt and trees and bushes and just five families, including Wren's, but they left even before Rudraksh was built. Then, they all lived in three trailers and two tents, and Wren and Juniper would basically spend the whole day just playing owls or fox families. And the grown-ups were building or taking care of babies (there were *a lot* of babies then), and no one talked that much about how to be a Lark in a Larkless world. Most of that came a little later. At least that's the way Juniper remembers it, but it's possible she was just too little or oblivious. Oblivious is entirely possible. In fact, she thinks she was pretty oblivious until she figured out what *oblivious* meant and decided—no, determined—she was *not* going to be it. That was when she was seven. When Marsha's baby died. Except, as they told her, it wasn't a baby, just clumps of cells, but she *saw* it. It might not have been a baby, but it was *not* a clump of cells. She saw her mother scoop it out of the toilet, and there it was, like a little bloody newt, right before her eyes. Her mother wrapped it in a washcloth and then tucked it between two dirty towels. This was in Bodhi, where the upstairs bathroom leads right out to the stairs. Juniper had tucked herself down in the stairwell and then slithered back down, and her mother had never seen her. But Juniper *had* seen. And Juniper had heard, heard her mother say, "Thank God the kids are oblivious," and her father say, "I wouldn't say oblivious," and her mother say, "I'm not in the mood for semantics." And so Juniper had found the paperback dictionary in the library and brought it to David, who she knew would not ask questions, and asked him to read her the definitions of *oblivious* and *semantics*, and when he did, she had for once agreed with her father. But at the time, that probably wasn't that unusual. Because her father didn't care if she could read when her mother did. And her father was fine with her eating three bowls of ice cream when her mother wasn't. And her father let her watch as much (appropriate) TV as she wanted when her mother pursed her lips and walked away when she found her on her third hour of *Toy Mania*.

But after the newt baby, Juniper had copied the words from the dictionary on a piece of yellow construction paper: "Oblivious: *adj.* 1. Lacking awareness. 2. *Archaic* Lacking all memory," and taped it to the underside of their family bed and memorized and looked at the letters until she could read the words by herself and swore to herself (made herself say it aloud) that she was *not* lacking awareness, that she was *not* lacking memory. No one would ever be able to say she wasn't completely sure of who and where she was ever again. Which is why she isn't sure if all the other stuff at Meadowlark came later or was always there from the beginning. But either way, she knows that soon after, she became *very* aware that she could totally, definitely, positively (she is pretty sure) not taste words, or see music, or sense other people's bodies, or feel people's thoughts, or heal people's injuries, or any of the other gifts she's supposed to be discovering within herself.

Juniper watches the girls fill in the fairy swimming pool, watches the water seep slowly into the ground, and then watches them fill it up again. They try lining it with small rocks, then leaves, then Quinn's socks. Finally, Juniper says, "It's not going to hold water."

"You don't *know* that," River says, but she does, and even River knows because she sits down on the ground and starts pushing her toes into Blaze's dirt pile.

"Bury my feet, Blazey," River says.

Quinn's feet are very clean. Juniper thinks she hasn't seen feet that clean since winter. In the summer, they mostly go barefoot. Even if she tried, Juniper doesn't think she'd be able to get the thin black line of dirt out from under her toenails. Quinn's feet are spookily white. Juniper can see the fine blue veins running along the tops and around her ankles. She wants to reach out and trace them. Instead she says, "Where do you live?"

"America," Quinn says.

"Yeah, but where?" Juniper asks.

"A-*mer*-ica," Quinn says again.

Juniper nods and wonders if she's a little bit dumb. "River, where do you live?"

"Meadowlark," River answers. They're both dumb, she decides. But not really. River is, in fact, one of the smartest people she knows, mostly because she asks questions. *All. The. Time.* And half the time she answers them. The adults love River because of this. It falls right into their Socratic method of inquiry. There is a mission statement framed and posted in every house. At the top is a black line drawing of a lark holding these copper swirly things in its mouth, and below it is a long paragraph of words. Juniper has read it before, blah blah raising a community of people unburdened by expectations, blah blah blah child initiated, blah blah children who know their truth, blah blah, but there is a line in there about the Socratic method. She noticed it even before she could read because of the big *S* in the middle of the sentence. The rest of the sentences had no big letters in their middles.

Socratic. It's another word she taped to the underside of the bed, another word she looked up: "the use of questions, as employed by Socrates, to develop a latent idea." "You have the answers," her father says. "Ask the questions." It's another idea that makes her nervous. Are there actual answers to questions, or are there a lot of answers that are all actual? How does she know if she has the actual answer or if there *is* even an actual answer? Her head is going in circles again. The easiest way to stop it is to jump, but she can't leave the babies here. Which isn't exactly true. No one would get mad at her if she did. The truth is she doesn't want to leave this Quinn kid here. Instead, she wants to ask her questions. Have her answer them in Q and A format, just like the author has in the back of the Crow Seekers books. But she knows people require more than just the question. Answers can actually be very, very hard to get unless you talk around a question and then eventually maybe ask a question sideways and then wait, and wait, and wait some more, maybe wait a full week until the person being questioned is doing dishes or distracted by a hungry baby. But even then, you never really know if the answer is *the* actual answer or one of many possible actual answers.

She lies facedown, then turns her head to rest her cheek on the warm dirt. "Sometimes I can see colors when someone sings," she says.

"Me too!" Quinn says.

"Me three," River says.

"Me too," Darcy adds.

"It's actually 'me four,'" River says.

"What colors do you see?" Juniper means this as a question for Quinn, but Darcy answers instead.

"I see rainbows."

Juniper ignores her. She wishes they would go away. River and Darcy argue over the order of colors in a rainbow. River insists that indigo and purple are two different colors. Darcy says there's only one indigo-purple color in the rainbow.

Eventually, Quinn says, "That's kind of a bad question."

Juniper looks at her. Quinn is drawing in the dirt with a stick.

"What do you mean?" Juniper asks.

"There's not one color for all songs, and there's not even one color for each song, and there's no colors for some songs, and some songs have colors, but it's the words that have the colors, like the ABC song—each letter has the colors, so it's not really even the *song* that has the colors."

Juniper looks at her. This is more information than she could have hoped for.

"And it's not really just colors anyway. It's like patterns and stuff."

River and Darcy look as surprised as Juniper must.

"What kind of patterns?" River says.

Quinn starts scratching a hole into the dirt. "Like when you talk," she says to River. "It's yellow lines, but there's pink lines, too, underneath the yellow lines." She sighs. "It's hard to explain."

So she was wrong, Juniper thinks. River's voice is nothing like she thought. Now she wonders what she sounds like, but she is afraid to ask. What if it's brown with black splotches or just dirty gray?

"What about Blaze?" Darcy says.

Quinn tilts her head. "Make him talk," she says.

"What's this, Blaze? What's this?" River says and holds up Quinn's shoe.

"Shuu," Blaze says.

"Blue, but . . . talk some more," Quinn says.

"What's this," River says and points to her nose.

"Nosey," Blaze says and smiles.

They turn to Quinn.

"Super light blue and some of the blue is, like, coming out in circles," she says.

River and Darcy are sitting up now, totally fascinated. "What about Justice?" Darcy asks. "Justice, say *Quinn, Quinn.*"

Justice ignores them and pounds the dirt.

"Say *dirt*," River says.

"Da," Justice says and keeps pounding.

"I don't know." Quinn laughs.

"Da, da, da," Justice says.

"Reddish?" Quinn says. "Like hiccups." The little girls laugh. They are making themselves hiccup now, and laughing, and Juniper works up the courage to ask about herself.

"What about me?" she says.

They all stop, and Quinn tilts her head. "Talk again," Quinn says.

"What should I say?" Her voice cracks, and she feels stupid. "Blah, blah, blah," she says.

They are quiet, waiting for Quinn. She shakes her head. "Nothing," she says.

Juniper feels her heart pause, her throat make a lump like she's about to cry. She pushes it down, but Quinn knows.

"Not everyone's voice looks like something," Quinn says.

"Whatever," Juniper says.

"Lots of people don't look like anything," Quinn says.

"It's fine," Juniper says. But she is hugely disappointed. How can she be so hurt by something so stupid? And probably not even real. Quinn's mother probably told her to lie, to say she could do these things that Larks are supposed to do.

"You're lying," Juniper says. She puts her head back down on the dirt, but she can feel the change in Quinn.

"No, I'm not," Quinn says. But her voice is small and uneasy.

"Yes, you are," Juniper says. She keeps her cheek on the ground but steals a peek at Quinn, sees the big fat tears fill her eyes. Juniper feels the lump return to her throat. You're not lying, she wants to say; I know, but she can't. She's too angry. And sad. And embarrassed. Juniper is invisible. And it hurts.

"Let's go play somewhere else," River says, but it's too late. Juniper can hear the little hiccupy sobs from Quinn. Juniper grits her teeth to keep from crying too. It's all a mess. Everything.

"I want my mama," Quinn says, crying for real now. Juniper feels like the most horrible person alive. She pushes her forehead hard into the soft dirt. Blaze thinks she's playing and pounds his flat palms on the small of her back. She tries to shake him off, but he pounds harder.

"Stop it!" she yells, and then he starts to cry.

"Juniper!" River says. "Why are you so mean?"

Both Quinn and Blaze are crying. Darcy has run to find Quinn's mom. And now Justice has started in with the crying. They're all making so much noise, and Juniper just wants to run and find a place to hide away. Instead, River stands up and grabs at the babies' hands. "Come on," River says. "Let's go inside."

Juniper stays flat on the ground, still and nearly choking on dust, until she's sure everyone is far, far away. Then she turns her head, puts her ear to the ground. When she was little, she used to imagine she could hear people speaking through the ground, as if there were tubes beneath all of Meadowlark, everyone's conversations amplified for her to hear. Now she hears nothing. Absolutely nothing. And she feels even more invisible. She wants to cry, but she's too tired. This is a horrible new feeling, like every part of her body is being suctioned into the earth. She lies there a long, long time. So long that she thinks she falls asleep because the next thing she sees is her father bending down beside her. She's confused and then embarrassed because there's someone else with him, and she's fallen asleep on the ground, like a baby.

"Did you fall asleep?" her father asks.

"No," she says. She sits up quickly and wipes the drool from her chin. She has dirt in her mouth, and it feels gritty on her teeth and disgusting. She wants to spit or ask for water, but she's still not completely sure where she is and when it is, and she looks around and sees a woman she's never met before. But she knows this woman. This is Quinn's mother. This is Simrin. She has seen her picture, the only one her father has from when he was a kid. It is a snapshot, and it hangs in the hallway of Bodhi, held up using the same thumbtack that pins a messily drawn picture by one of the kids, maybe even herself when she was little. In the photograph, her father is sixteen. He is wearing a red flannel shirt, one hand resting on the shoulder of a much smaller girl, the other arm pulling Simrin to him as she laughs and tries to pull away. As long as Juniper remembers, it has hung there, and as long as she remembers, she has known that the small girl with the handfuls of black hair is Jaishri and the laughing pale girl is Simrin.

She has stared at that picture enough to know that this woman standing in front of her now is Simrin, her face just thinner, her hair just shorter. Juniper has heard lots and lots of stories about the three of them—her father's sort-of-sisters. So many fragments of stories, so well animated in her head that when Simrin bundles Quinn, who Juniper now realizes has been standing behind her, up in her arms, Juniper wants to reach out and pull the little girl away, so awkward is the transition from Juniper's imagination to real life.

"You okay, Junie?" her father asks.

She nods and looks down at the ground.

"This is Simrin," her father says. "And you met Quinn."

Juniper tries to read her father's voice. Did Darcy tell them she made Quinn cry? Did Quinn?

"This is Juniper," her father continues.

"Hi," Simrin says.

Juniper steals another look. Quinn is resting her head on her mother's other shoulder, looking at Juniper warily. Juniper looks down again, feels the guilt seep back to the surface.

"You sure you're okay, Junie?" her father says. He puts his hand on her back, and it feels so comforting, like she should be a baby, and he should be about to carry her around the house singing "Goodnight, My Someone," like her parents tell her he did when she asks for stories about when she was little. She imagines it was pretty great then, before she turned into a plain old normal girl, an invisible person. It feels good to feel sorry for herself, and she tries to see herself as the one who got her feelings hurt. It's Quinn's fault for even "seeing voices." It's weird, not normal. But this thought feels even worse. And suddenly it feels all too heavy to carry—she's not special, and there's nothing she can do about it.

"Quinn sees voices," she blurts out. If she can't be special, she can at least bring this maybe real gift to her father.

Her father looks at her.

"She says she can see colors, and taste words, and probably other stuff," she says. She looks over at Quinn and Simrin, who has turned red.

"It's just this thing," Simrin says, "the colors . . ." She stumbles through some explanation about sensory integration and how it's nothing to worry about, but her father interrupts her.

"A synesthete," he says.

"Yes," Simrin says.

Juniper has never heard this word before, but clearly Simrin has. It sounds like a real word, and she wants to ask them to spell it so she can look it up later, see if it's there in the dictionary—a real, true thing.

Her father smiles at Simrin. "A mini-me," he says.

"Well . . . it's a lot more . . ."

"A lot more than blue finger paint?"

Simrin looks startled, and Juniper is completely confused now. She thinks they are speaking a language she doesn't know, and then she is sure they are.

"*Om Dum Durgayei Namaha,*" her father says.

Simrin inhales loudly, then tucks her chin tightly down to her chest.

He says it again, but this time he sings it, just like Juniper imagines him singing to her, and she feels something swell up through her belly and expand in her chest. She wants her father to hold her tight, but she is embarrassed to even think this.

"Stop," Simrin says. Her voice is crackly, but Juniper can't see her face to see what she's feeling. But she can see her father's face. He is looking at Quinn, trying to suppress a smile. Juniper can see the wheels spinning in his head. What does my voice look like? he wants to ask her. Do the colors tell you anything? Juniper wants these answers, too, but she can feel the itch of something else. She wants to say something, remind him she found Quinn for him, but he looks back at Simrin.

"Everyone here is loved," he says. "Everyone is happy. Did you ever feel like that when you were her age?" He gestures to Juniper. "Look at this *amazing* kid." He puts his hands on her shoulders, and Juniper almost turns around to see who's behind her, but Simrin is watching, her jaw moving side to side.

"Can you imagine who we could have become if we were allowed to just be?" he says. It is quiet for a long time, and Juniper wants to say something, but she doesn't know what they are talking about.

"Fine," Simrin finally says. "Fine." She takes a deep breath, exhales. "I need my cameras."

"Yes," her father says. He stands up quickly and starts walking toward the houses. He is happy, and Juniper thinks this should make her happy, but it doesn't. She sits there a moment, but he turns back to them. "Come on," he says, smiling. "Let's go take some pictures!"

Then time seems to pass very slowly. Simrin takes a lot of pictures, but none of Juniper, none of River, and none of Blaze. Juniper watches Simrin from afar. She has two cameras hanging from a belt-like thing that crisscrosses her chest, and she shifts from one to the other without even looking. Juniper remembers the story her father told her about how the people at the place he grew up took Simrin's camera away from her and how he rescued it. Even though everyone at Meadowlark rolls their eyes at fairy tales, Juniper always imagined him with a sword, triumphing over the bad guys. It's a stupid thing to believe, she thinks now. Of course he didn't have a sword. But he did triumph; that's the word he uses—*triumph*.

Most of the stories he tells are about Jaishri, Simrin, and him triumphing over the people at the place he grew up. Those are the other words he uses: *the people at the place I grew up*. She's never thought about it before, but now she does. Who were those people? And what was the place? She knows it was a bad place for kids. There were a lot of rules and things they had to do, but was it a bunch of houses on a street like in town or a place like Meadowlark? Juniper looks at Quinn and tries to imagine her as a young Simrin, tries to imagine what her father would look like standing next to her, but she's never seen a picture of him when he was younger than sixteen, and Blaze is too much a baby to be a stand-in.

And then she thinks about something else. If Quinn can really do all this cross-sensing stuff, how did she learn to do it if she didn't grow up at a place like Meadowlark? The thought is so surprising that she actually says "yeah" out loud. Was Quinn just born this way? And what is "this way" anyway? Juniper wonders if Quinn can do the other stuff, too, the stuff that only some of the grown-ups talk about, like call on the oncoming. Ever since this brouhaha started, there have been way more adults than usual trying to get the kids to call up their world wisdom and call on the oncoming, which is just a sideways way of saying what she heard Brandon say much more clearly when he asked Gavin, "What the fuck is going to happen?" And it makes her think her mother is right. That this brouhaha is in fact not just a brouhaha. It is bigger and badder than a "noisy and overexcited reaction to something unimportant." It is something important. Very important. So important that there are now a number of adults (her mother definitely *not* included) who think that the kids should be able to see the future. But no one can do that, she thinks. At least she can't. And she's pretty sure none of the other Meadowlark kids can. But what if Quinn can? She doubts it, but . . . she's not sure.

Juniper looks for Quinn now. She is hovering around Simrin, turning something over and over in her hands. Quinn keeps it held tightly to her stomach, and it's only when she drops it that Juniper can see it's the worry eater they've had forever. It's this knitted blue, green, and red thing with eyes and a zippered mouth. Their mother tries to get them to write down their worries and feed them to the worry eater. It has a name, she thinks. Hershel? Hans? Something weird that she can't remember because she never liked it. It's ugly with its mismatched eyes and a half-working zipper, but Blaze loves that thing. He likes to chew on its one remaining leg when he goes to sleep. It's ratty and horrible, but Juniper feels a pang of irritation that Quinn has snatched her brother's lovey. But that's not really fair. His loveys are his boo duck and River's old blanket that Juniper made into strips and braided for him. This thing is just a chew toy. If Quinn wants to adopt ugly Hans, why should she care? Maybe it *can* help Quinn call on the oncoming. Maybe it just makes her feel better. Juniper wants her to feel better. Poor kid. She's really, really small, like Marley small, and she's almost six. And where's her dad? Small with no dad and some big kid is picking on her and making her cry. Juniper feels bad about this, and she wants to do something nice for Quinn. She's wondering if Quinn would like to check out the secret hatch in the gate between their property and Mr. Turner's.

Mr. Turner is their grumpy neighbor, his property behind and to the side of Meadowlark. All the kids know the story of how Mr. Turner called them all hippies when they first moved in, how he watched them build Bodhi, and Hawthorne, and Cedar from the deck of his second-story bedroom, and then, when they finally built the fence, Mr. Turner stormed down and ordered his own fence. It went all the way around his land and butted up against Meadowlark's fence in one small rectangular chunk, a four-board shared space that they're encouraged to avoid. But River thinks that one spot is an entryway to some made-up place called Purple Land, so last year, Micah, who's super good with building stuff, sawed a hole in the fence and covered it with leftover corrugated plastic so River could have her portal. Mr. Turner has chickens, and sometimes they come right up to the fence and you can slide the plastic to the side and sneak the babies right into their yard, at least for a few minutes.

But before she can say anything, River is jumping up and down demanding to finally be photographed.

"It is definitely *my* turn now," River says.

"Sure," Simrin says. She is smiling, and Juniper can see that Simrin likes River. Everyone likes River. Even Juniper. But it's complicated. Juniper knows that Juniper, herself, is harder to like. She would not be "popular" if they went to real school. She knows what popular is because it's in all the comic books they get from the library. But Juniper is beautiful. She knows this despite the fact that no one at Meadowlark talks about what you look like on the outside. It's her hair. And her eyes. She knows her eyes are unusual because people often comment on them. People like Gavin say things like, "I've never seen that color on a human being before," but people outside Meadowlark use words like *stunning* and *gorgeous*. Juniper's not exactly sure how she feels about being beautiful. Of course she'd rather be beautiful than ugly, but she's not sure if she likes all that attention. Sometimes yes (like the time she got her hair cut by a real hairstylist who insisted all the other ladies come look at her) and sometimes no (like the time an old man tried to give her a peppermint candy for having the face of an angel, and her mom threw it in the trash). She knows it makes her different, but she can't decide if, in this case, being different is good or bad.

Simrin changes the lens on one of the cameras and turns it to River, who is standing on a couch, arms and legs spread out like a starfish.

"Why don't we take some in the bedroom?" her father says.

"Yes!" River says. "I can show you my rock collection!" She bounds up the stairs.

"Come on, Junie," her father says. "Can you get Blaze?"

Juniper finds him in a basket of laundry. "Me Mama," he says. He has one of their mother's shirts draped around his neck, and she picks him up and kisses him on the forehead.

"Okay," she says. "Let's go upstairs and find the other mama."

It's only when she says this that she realizes she hasn't seen her mother this whole time. She expects she's in the bedroom, but when they go upstairs and open the bedroom door, their mother isn't there either. The bed is unmade, as usual, the sheets crumpled and balled up on the floor. It feels weird for them all to be in here without their mother also there, and Juniper is about to ask where she is, when her father speaks.

"Let's close the door," he says. This is a weird thing to say because they almost never close their door, but Simrin shuts it behind her, and the room immediately feels not only smaller but thicker, like they're each taking up twice as much space. It doesn't feel good to her, but Juniper notices Quinn's body seems to soften. Quinn has stuck close to her mother the whole time Simrin's been taking pictures, only inches away, but when Simrin closes the door, something changes, and Quinn goes to look through Blaze's basket of dolls in the corner. Juniper watches her take the dolls out one by one and lay them side by side on the floor, their different-size heads each lined up against the wall. She keeps ugly Hans tucked under her armpit and presses each doll's chest with one finger. When she finishes, she goes back and starts again.

"What are you doing?" River asks her and bounces on one of the beds. Quinn shrugs and turns to watch River bounce.

"You should bounce," River says. "It's fun."

Quinn doesn't say anything and goes back to the dolls.

Juniper feels jammed up in a corner, like the room has shrunk even though it's the same as always. There are two mattresses, one on the floor, one on a proper bed, under which are Juniper's definitions of words—but you have to crawl way under, almost up against the wall, to see them. Then there is a dresser. The dresser drawers hold their clothes, or some of them. Mostly they pull whatever they can find from the piles in the laundry room, each separated by age. Then there is a long low bookshelf thing with lots of cubbies. Each of them has two cubbies for themselves.

Juniper's cubbies hold her spy notebooks markered with "DO NOT OPEN" warnings, all hidden behind a piece of burlap she glued to the outside. She also has a bunch of Sharpies she doesn't let anyone else use and the dictionary she took from the communal library and a picture River drew of their whole family and her penny collection and a book she checked out from the Ravenna library, *The Big Book of Hoaxes: True Tales of the Greatest Lies Ever Told!* This is the second in the *Big Book of . . .* series. The first, *The Big Book of Cons*, she's read twice, but she thinks she likes this one better, particularly the story about the Cottingley Fairies and how the two girls made the whole world think they discovered fairies with just some lame cardboard cutouts. She wonders if it's really that easy to trick people or if those people were just stupid. Oblivious. Her other cubby is empty. Usually she likes it that way, just in case she needs it for something, but now it looks sad and lonely.

Simrin is holding the camera up to her eye, pushing buttons, then looking at the screen and pushing more buttons, then holding it up to her eye again. Juniper realizes that before today, she has never seen an actual camera in real life. She's taken pictures on phones, silly photos that she mostly deletes and deletes and deletes so she can take more, but this thing is a real machine. It's big and makes noises.

Her father is standing very still, but he is gripping his hands firmly against each other, watching everything Simrin does. Simrin shoots quickly, moving around the room with the camera covering her face. She clicks River—lots of fast, quick clicks as River bounces and then hides her head in the bedcovers. She clicks Blaze, who tries to put his face up against the camera. He wrinkles his nose, watching himself in the glass of the lens.

Then it is Juniper's turn. Simrin turns the camera on her, and Juniper stays still. Like they're playing statues. Juniper stares into the lens. She can see it open and close. There are a few clicks. Then quiet. She looks for Simrin's brown eye through the opening but only sees the sun strike and bounce against the glass. Simrin lowers the camera slightly. Juniper stares at her, this lady who is her father's "sister." Was she like River is to her? Or like Sammi? Juniper imagines herself grown and staring at her sister. Or is she the one with the camera? She raises her chin, puts her hands on her hips, and looks out the window. She thinks it makes her look grown up, and Simrin must think so, too, because she raises the camera and starts clicking again. Juniper turns her head the other way. More clicking. Juniper likes the rapid tick, tick, tick. She turns one more time and looks straight into the camera. People will see these pictures. People in town. Or maybe in New York. She imagines the public mesmerized by her blue, blue eyes. They are special, and she knows whoever is looking at these pictures will think this. They will see her beauty and imagine how special she must be. She is tilting her head down and looking up at the camera, when her father interrupts.

"Why don't we go outside?" he says.

Simrin ignores him and keeps clicking. The sun is lower in the sky now, and Juniper imagines she looks outlined and glowy.

"Let's get some with the pirate ship," her father says, but Simrin isn't listening to him. This makes Juniper smile, just a little bit. Juniper turns her head, and Simrin clicks. She turns again so she's looking over her shoulder like she's seen the women in the magazines at the grocery store checkout do. She lowers one shoulder, and her tank top, which used to be her mother's and is really still too big for her, dips low so her shoulder is bare.

"That's enough of Juniper," her father says. His voice is not *not* calm, but it's not calm either. Simrin must hear it, too, because she turns the camera on him. Juniper hears a beep and a click, and she looks at him. For a split second he is somehow different, but before she can figure out how, he is back.

"Let's go outside," he says.

There is silence, like they're all one beat behind her father and can't quite catch up, but then Juniper understands that he is telling Simrin to stop taking her picture; he is telling Juniper to stop getting her picture taken.

"No," Juniper whines. She is too old to whine, but she's outraged. Why is she allowed only a certain amount of shots? And why is her father telling her what to do? Grown-ups don't do that here. Her *father* doesn't do that. And it makes her mad. She stomps her foot. "Why?"

Simrin brings the camera down and turns to Juniper, and suddenly Juniper is embarrassed to be acting like a little kid, to have Simrin look full at her, without the camera in between.

"Let's take pictures of the fairy houses!" River says.

"Yes, Mama," Quinn says. "There are fairies here!"

Instantly the focus turns from Juniper, and everyone is set in motion. Quinn is pulling at her mother's jeans, River is back to bouncing on the bed, Simrin is trying to pay attention to both Quinn and her cameras, and her father has picked up Blaze and is leading them out of the room.

Juniper sulks for a minute, but there's really no point. She doesn't even want any more stupid pictures. They'll just end up on some wall, sharing a tack with some three-year-old's artwork. She follows them down the stairs, through the common room, and out the side door. She wishes they were done with all this picture-taking stuff, that Simrin and Quinn would just leave already. But this thought makes her breath catch. She doesn't really want them to leave. Not yet. She wants Quinn to know she's sorry. And she wants to know what else Quinn can do.

She catches up with them and speaks too loudly. "Quinn's very good at building fairy houses," she tries. She's talking to Simrin, but she hopes Quinn is listening. She tells Simrin about how Quinn learned to make hats out of acorn caps and tablecloths out of spiderwebs and how artistic Quinn was in the design of her triple bunk beds. She wants Quinn to accept this as an apology, but Quinn doesn't say anything, and when the little girls see the back fence, they break into a run.

"Wait," Simrin says, but Quinn doesn't. Blaze wants to run, too, and her father puts him down, and Juniper watches him try to run after the girls. She can think of nothing else to say about dumb fairies, so they walk in silence until they reach the fence, and River takes over.

River gives them a tour of the latest additions, the staircase leading to a loft bed, the barn for the fairy animals. Simrin picks up her camera and click, click, clicks. She is aiming at both girls, but Juniper can see the lens lengthen, tilt toward River. Quinn is quiet but watches River intently. Quinn mouths a few words to herself and scratches her toes into the dirt.

And then River says it. "Sammi."

"Sammi can build the staircase higher," she says, and Quinn, just like on the trampoline, flinches and spits. One time, two times, three times—the third right on River's feet.

"Hey! Don't do that!" River yells.

"I told you not to say that," Quinn says.

"You spit on me," River says.

Simrin drops the camera around her neck. "Quinn, it's okay." She is talking softly, trying to not let them all hear. "Just think *Go-Go's*. Or *swing set*. Please don't spit."

"I don't like it," Quinn whines.

"Like what?" This is her father speaking. He has bent down and is looking at Quinn and suddenly smiling his very normal Daddy smile.

"She spit on me," River says.

"It's that thing . . . ," Simrin says, trying to explain.

"I know," her father says.

"Quinn," her father says. "That thing you can do. Tasting words, hearing colors. That's special. You're special."

Quinn is looking at him but pushing herself against her mother's legs.

"We try and find that in ourselves here at Meadowlark," he says.

"What's Meadowlark?" Quinn asks.

"That's what we call where we live." He extends his arms. "All around you. It's a special place where kids can grow and see all the amazing things they can do."

"What kinds of things?" Quinn asks.

Juniper watches her father's eyes; they shine bright, but she wants him to be quiet. Don't tell her, she wants to say. Juniper needs to know what Quinn has inside her. Not what was wedged there by some grown-up.

"Well, everyone's different. Everyone has their own gift to discover," he says. "Some kids might see music—"

"I can do that!" Quinn interrupts. She seems to grow taller in that moment, and Juniper can see her father's eyes almost on fire.

"And taste words," he says.

"Yep. I can do that too." She's super proud of herself, and it's feeding her father, making him burn brightly. And the glow is multiplying between them—something big, and warm, and lovely—spilling all over the place. It is breaking Juniper's heart to watch this. She feels it like a physical pain, a ripping in her chest—everything her father wants her to be, but she isn't, in this one little girl. But she also wants to know if all these things are actually possible, if she is, after all, a great disappointment of a girl.

"And maybe even see what's ahead of us," her father says. "We call it calling on the oncoming."

Juniper looks at Quinn, then quickly at her father. Not all grown-ups talk about this. Her mother doesn't. Her father does.

"I think it's time to go," Simrin says, and just like that, Simrin smothers whatever was intensifying between her father and Quinn. Juniper can see the fear—or is it disgust?—flash across Simrin's face. Simrin doesn't believe it is possible. She is only one person, but if she—the mother of the kid who can do all this other stuff—doesn't believe kids can see what's going to happen, then maybe Juniper is right about something.

"I want to stay!" Quinn says.

Juniper looks at her father. He is still bent down, looking intently at Quinn, and Simrin must notice, too, because she pulls Quinn to her. Simrin is afraid, Juniper thinks. And now Juniper is just confused, because Simrin's fear makes her want to say mean things again, tell these two to leave her home.

"I got everything I need," Simrin says.

Her father stands up. "Are you sure?"

Simrin looks down at her cameras, fiddles with something while keeping one hand firmly on Quinn. "I can upload tonight or tomorrow," she says.

"Why not now?" he says.

"I can't do it now," she says and looks at him. "I need to go through hundreds of images, process the ones I choose."

"Can't you do that here?"

"No." She scoffs. "They aren't going on Snapchat."

Her father doesn't like this. He is silent, but Juniper can see his jaw clench. Quinn pleads with her mother to stay, and River has joined in. They want to go down to the pirate ship. They want to make a marble run.

"No," Simrin says. There is more pleading, and then her father interrupts.

"We'll get you set up here. You can have dinner."

"My computer is at the hotel," Simrin says. "I need Lightroom."

"Go back and get it."

"No."

Their voices have both tightened. Something is wrong. The little girls don't notice. They are still begging for more time. But Juniper does.

"Why not?"

"These are *my* pictures, Arjun." She says it too loud, and everyone goes quiet. Even Blaze is still, like the silence has frozen them all in time. Then River interrupts.

"Who's Arjun," she says, but no one answers her. Juniper knows who he is because it says it on the back of that picture in the hall: "Arjun, Simrin, Jaishri. *Raksha Bandhan*."

"You don't get to decide," Simrin hisses. Her shoulders are squared, and Juniper almost thinks she's going to hit him, but she is waiting— waiting for him to hit first? Her father is silent, but there is something being said beneath the silence. The grown-ups are back to their foreign language, talking about things Juniper can't translate.

"Do you understand?" Simrin says.

"Yes," her father says. Instantly.

And Simrin is taken aback because she looks down. And in that moment, Juniper can see her father's anger—clear and unmissable—so thick that Juniper wonders if it's not the kids who have the power to do anything, but him. But Simrin doesn't see it. She is staring at the ground. And like before, her father is back a second later. He softens before he speaks, lowers his voice. "It's not just the pictures."

Simrin takes her time, but then she looks up.

"One more visit," her father says.

It is not only a request but a plea. This is how grown-ups beg, Juniper realizes, without the actual begging.

"Come back, show us the pictures, and then go," her father says. "Just once more."

Juniper watches Simrin, tries to imagine the conversation she's having in her head, but then Blaze is on Juniper, trying to climb her like a tree. He reaches up, snags her tank top, and claws her stomach. She jumps back instinctively, which makes him cry, and then she has to comfort him, so she misses what comes next. All she knows is that Quinn is jumping around River, and then the four of them are going back toward Bodhi. And then Blaze is fine and running after the grown-ups, and she is once again alone with the fairy houses, all tangled up over what is happening.

She is trying to decide if she wants to lie back down on the warm dirt or jump on the trampoline and get all this stuff out of her head when she sees her mother. And the fear that pulses through her is like an alarm telling her to run. She doesn't know why, but she does know her mother is far enough away that she will not know she has been seen. So Juniper runs, unsure of why, just that this brouhaha seems to be expanding, at least inside of her, and that her mother shouldn't know.

SIMRIN

She has to wait until Quinn falls asleep to look at the shots, and then she makes herself wait even longer, wanting the sun to be completely down, the bright laptop screen the only light in the darkness. It is frustrating enough that she'll have to work with only one screen, not to mention that it's a laptop screen. It's extremely difficult to see detail on such a small monitor, and balancing adjustments even with a full-screen image is impossible, but she figures she'll do the best she can, and the darkness will help.

In the meantime, she sits near the window and pulls the drape back. There is still a sliver of sun on the horizon. She can't see it, but she can see the rosy hue softening the edges on the cars and making the teenage couple in the parking lot glow. The magic hour. If she were smart, she would see what she could shoot through the scratched windowpane, see if she could catch the boy's tongue flick against the girl's upper lip. But she doesn't feel like taking pictures.

She watches the boy sneak his hands into the back pockets of the girl's jeans. He is sitting on the hood of Simrin's car, the girl leaned up tight against the boy's crotch. They are so unabashed, as if they run the world and the grown-ups just don't know it yet. She wonders if this is the thrill of being a teenager, to feel the world as yours. She never felt that. From inside Ananda, the world seemed to brim with possibility and expectation. And then they arrived in it.

And the world felt huge and menacing. A girl wearing thick black eyeliner stole forty-eight dollars from Arjun's back pocket. A guy in a van asked Jaishri to suck his dick. Simrin cut herself on a broken bottle, and the manager yelled at her for leaving blood on the sheets. There was nothing luminous about that world, and there was nothing any of them could do about it. Not even Arjun.

She wonders if it would have been a smoother transition to real life if Arjun and Jaishri had been there with her. They would have done it together, like baby ducks out for the first time without their mother. But that's not what happened. Jaishri had cowered back to Ananda, and Arjun had fucked her and left. At least that's the spin she puts on it when she's angry. "We fucked, and then he left" is more accurate. She hadn't felt taken or conquered. She had felt exhilarated. Until he had disappeared. Then she had felt angry.

She's not angry right now, but she was earlier today. Standing in Arjun's new and improved Rudraksh, she had been very angry. They had stood there, neither of them speaking, the only sound a bunch of children's flags flapping in the background. Simrin had tried to breathe and focus on the fabric cutting the air, make him speak first and then demand explanations and apologies, but her anger had toppled all attempts at composure, and the rage had tumbled out.

"You abandoned me," she had spit.

"I know," he said, and it wasn't what she expected, but what *did* she expect? For him to beg for forgiveness? She couldn't remember a time he had ever apologized, ever even admitted he was wrong. Once, Priya had kidded that if Arjun ever admitted he wasn't perfect, the world would implode. But yes, that's what she wanted. An apology.

"You left me with a father I didn't even know," she said. She had waited in that Andronico's parking lot, looking for a white Toyota Corolla. It was embarrassing to not know what a Toyota Corolla was, but it was even more embarrassing to not know who your father was. She vaguely remembered he was very tall with brown bushy hair, but the man who showed up was neither, and she had to take it on faith that he was indeed Lawrence Heller. She clutched her paper bag tightly in her lap and was thankful that he drove her first to the Fountain for lunch, then to Golden Gate Park, then to Target so she could buy a toothbrush and (mortifyingly) a new bra, and then finally back to his apartment, where they sat awkwardly, not talking about Ananda, and petted his cats.

It wasn't until the next night that she finally consented to let him call her mother. Simrin was here with him, her father told her mother. She could stay if she wanted. It was barely a conversation. No discussion of logistics or emotional damage. And when her father told her mother he would put Simrin on the phone, her mother said no. She needed "space." But she gave her father a message to relay: "Jaishri is safe. To want is both to desire and to lack." Her father repeated it, looking embarrassed, but Simrin felt no more than a quick sliver of hurt, then gratefulness that Jaishri was okay, then worry over the word *safe*. Why wouldn't she be safe? But she had stuffed the worry down. Along with the embarrassment that her mother didn't even want to talk to her and the great devastation of Arjun's desertion. Because that's what it was, a desertion.

"You deserted me," she said today.

"I know," he said.

"I was fifteen."

"I know."

He met every accusation with "I know." I know I left. I know you were devastated. And then, "I don't know." I don't know why I did it. I don't know what I was thinking. And the more "I knows" and "I don't knows" he offered, the more her anger grew. She could see the tears start in his eyes, the twitch of his eyebrows, his sorrow on display, but she wanted to wound him, pull the apology from a place of suffering.

"You fucked me and left," she finally spit. He recoiled at the word, and she was glad.

"Please," he said, his voice cracking. And then finally, "I'm sorry." And again, "I'm sorry. I'm sorry."

She felt her anger blur to pain. And then that damn mantra looped through her head: Pain and pleasure revolve like a wheel. The last moments they'd been together, he'd refused to look at her, and she'd felt the pain of separation flush through every neuron. It had been excruciating, this severing of connection. But now here he was, his eyes full of tears and trained on hers, the apologies pouring from his mouth. What was the point of idling there in pain, and what did pleasure look like if not him finally standing there, the connection so intense she felt it singe though her?

And then he said her name and reached for her hands, and this time she let him take them, let him snake his arms around her back, feeling the strangeness of his grown-up self and the ease of their bodies together. "Swimmy," he said, and behind her eyes, the burst of opalescent confetti. She had forgotten. Only his voice, only that word—the shimmery splinters of pearl covering her vision. He had said it often, just to let her see the shimmer, to enjoy the flash of pleasure. And then after, made her describe it, made her try to dissect the magic her brain was constructing, both awed and sullen at his own inability.

"Let's stay like this forever," Jaishri had said before they escaped. And the prick of her name in Simrin's mind today made her heart catch, her shoulders tense. Jaishri, she thought, but she selfishly pushed back the memory. Just Arjun and her, for just another minute. Pleasure first. Pain later.

They had stayed that way a long, long time, the tears disappearing and the warmth of each other's bodies growing more and more familiar, and there had been a moment—a split second of time—where she had wondered what it would be like to be back in that motel room, their grown-up selves naked on that bed. But then River had burst in with Quinn, and Arjun had let go of Simrin so quickly that she had almost lost her balance. And then there were crying children and stories to untangle, and finally, when everyone was calm and River was showing Quinn the giant wood blocks in the corner, Arjun had become all business, explaining how important her pictures would be, how essential they were. Then he paused. And added, "And I'm giving you exclusive access to a story you know is going to go viral. Your following is large now, but it's going to multiply."

She was surprised not only at his change of tone but his knowledge of her world. How long had he been lurking? But he was right. Of course. And she knew that she had to admit this. That the possibility of watching the shares and comments and likes explode into the millions was part of the pull. There was no guarantee, but kids in jeopardy coupled with the chance of government misconduct were internet gold. It was painful to admit this, to acknowledge that they had grown beyond the purely visceral need for each other, and he must have sensed this because he followed up quickly with, "And who else could possibly do it?" A kid with a camera phone, she wanted to say. If everything progressed the way he thought it would, the media would be clamoring for these shots. But she understood what lay beneath the question. Who else understood where he had come from? Who else could grasp the enormity of what he had built? Who else knew him like she did? So she agreed first to the tour of Meadowlark and then to taking the pictures.

It is finally dark, the streetlights barely illuminating the couple who are still perched on Simrin's car. She closes the drape and boots up the computer. It takes a while to import the pictures, but when they are finally all transferred, she clicks through slowly. It's usually the shots that in the moment seem most ordinary that in postproduction reveal their power. And there are many of those. In the shot of the two bare-chested boys showing their muscles, there's a little girl in the back corner she didn't notice. She is sucking her right thumb, her left thumb in her ear, fingers twirling her hair. Such a picture of universal childhood. There is always a thumb sucker, always a hair twirler. And there is one of River and Darcy she thought was cute in the moment, a portrait-type photo, but when she looks at it on the screen, she sees their feet on top of each other—brown, then white; brown, then white—and knows it will be someone's lead. Lots of pictures of happy kids and doting parents doing totally normal family things for Arjun to be pleased with.

But it's the ones of Juniper that are the most striking. She knew there would be at least one stunner in the series of her, but there are so many. Her favorite is a long shot. Juniper pushed into a corner, her shoulders pressed in by the two walls. Her head is slightly turned, the slant of a smile performed for the camera. Her blonde hair is tied back in a messy ponytail, but she has tossed her head, made the loose curls pour down one shoulder. And those eyes. Of course there is the color, but there's something in the shape, something in the angle. Even with a black-and-white filter, those eyes demand focus.

Simrin noticed them immediately, knew she could shoot anything of this kid and have it come out well, and in the moment of that shot, Simrin leaned back and tilted the camera up instinctively, and what she caught was this eleven-year-old beauty, a great expanse of wall and ceiling above her. She knew this shot would be one of her favorites, but it isn't until she is looking at it on her laptop screen that she notices two things. One, how seamlessly this photo would fit into Mann's *At Twelve* series, how transfixed she would have been to open it in the library at fourteen and see Juniper's stare arresting her from the page. And two, how familiar this girl is. She opens a shot of Arjun next to the one of Juniper, zooms in on the eyes, thinking she is seeing Arjun's eyes, all that Ananda propaganda, but no. It isn't just that the color is different—it is the shape, and something else. Arjun's eyes penetrate you; Juniper's pull you in.

She backs up all the images to the cloud, then burns everything to a flash drive. She is paranoid about losing images. She has flash drives hidden in the house and car. She even makes Tom keep an encrypted stash of them. She double-checks that the files have copied to the drive, then chooses twenty-two shots and moves them to a separate folder on the same flash drive so she can find them easily when she shows him tomorrow. She figures he can choose ten he wants posted immediately, and they can use the remaining shots for a second blitz, when (she hopes) they have the media's full attention. She checks the drive once more and then attaches it to her key chain. She likes that she can hold it in her hand and know her work is safe.

Now she goes back to the computer, googles *Meadowlark*. There are no new stories, but she finds the crowdsourcing site of the guy making the child-abuse claims. He has raised $370, not much in terms of crowdsourcing, but there are twenty-one donors, some donating as little as a dollar with comments like, "Give them what they deserve!" and "Kill those pedos." Her stomach turns, and she feels the flip-flop of wondering if it could be true, then knowing it couldn't, then wondering again. She searches for Kevin Lowery until she finds his Facebook page, then finds the page for his cause: "Saving Marley." There are lots of pictures of him with his son, a kid with a too-closely shaved crew cut and beady eyes. And lots of wall posts. Most are in the "keep on fighting" vein, but there are a number that are clearly antagonistic, ordering him to leave those people alone and stop making up lies. She assumes some of them come from inside Meadowlark, but she doesn't recognize any of the names as people she met today. And there is a post from Jim Acoste, a self-identified retired police officer of Stevin County, who writes, "Kester knows you're lying. Get a good lawyer, get your visitation, and get out of town." She googles Kester—the sheriff—then scrolls through the replies to Acoste's post: a number of people who have relatives in the police department, someone who went to school with Kevin, and the anonymous PFunk all agreeing with Jim Acoste and proclaiming this a waste of taxpayers' money.

Then, as she is scrolling, a new post appears on the page. Someone named Tatiana Culver writes, "I'm a journalist and very interested in talking to anyone involved in this story." Simrin clicks on Tatiana's page—purely professional, lots of links to articles she wrote, some traditional news outlets, but a whole lot more online media—Nowbot, and FeedMe, and ShipKey. ShipKey has made more than one of Simrin's blog posts go viral. They claim to know the news before it is made, a statement Tom says proves his disdain for online media is warranted. She clicks back to the Saving Marley page. Someone is typing, answering Tatiana Culver's post. PFunk: "You need to talk to this guy Aaron. Good guy, but some crazy ideas. Google 'Ananda Nagar.' He grew up there."

Simrin feels the blood drain and pool in her legs. Who the hell is PFunk? Has Arjun told this person about Ananda? It isn't a secret . . . exactly. But it isn't something she thinks he would advertise. She certainly doesn't. When asked about it in interviews, she always gives the same one-line answer: "Oh, it's not very interesting. Just a bunch of old hippies who liked to meditate. We left when I was fifteen." She leaves the "we" unspecified.

She waits to see if anyone replies to PFunk, and soon there is Tatiana, a brief message, "PMing you" and then nothing. She waits for something more to appear, even opens a chat box, first for PFunk, then Tatiana. Then shuts both boxes. And then the phone rings. She scrambles to get it before it wakes Quinn. It is Tom, and she wants to send it to voice mail, but while struggling for the mute button, she accidentally presses talk instead.

"Shit," she says, then realizes he can hear her and holds the phone to her ear. "Quinn's sleeping," she says.

"Well, that's a relief," he says. "I hope she's eating too."

She sighs.

"How was the shoot?"

There is silence, and she has to remember the details of the lie she's told him. Were there details? It seems forever ago. "Long," she says. "The Leipzig is a pain." She closes her eyes and grinds her teeth. More lies.

"Quinn's fine?"

"Yes. Good. She made friends." This is true, and she's glad she can give him some happy, honest news. It is not always easy for Quinn to make friends—all that spitting and feeling—and she knows this will please him.

"That's our girl," he says.

She can hear the pleasure in his voice but also the relief, and she feels the sting of how little it takes to lessen their worry when it comes to Quinn.

"All right, then," he says, and she knows he wants to get off the phone with this small comfort in mind. "I'll call tomorrow."

She says goodbye, hangs up, and looks at Quinn. She is sleeping, covers thrown off, sweaty despite the air-conditioning. So much worry over one perfectly imperfect little girl. But at least she is worried, she tells herself. At least she is one up on her own mother. No one will say this child was unseen, this child unknown. Quinn will know, if nothing else, that Simrin witnessed her daughter's full and glorious self. It is the blanket she wraps her in.

She can't imagine how Quinn would have fared at Ananda. All those demands. All that freedom. Although Quinn did well with freedom today. She can't see that there are any demands at Meadowlark, but there seems to be a hell of a lot of freedom. And Quinn had loved it, running around with River and Darcy, only that one little conflict with Juniper. And that was smoothed over quickly. Quinn, she realizes, felt completely comfortable there, and Simrin, for just a moment, wonders what it would be like to stay. The thought is embarrassing, but there it is. If nothing else, Arjun is right about these kids. The Meadowlark kids possess an ease the Ananda kids never had, or at least Simrin never had. Nor did Jaishri. Nor Krish, nor Priya, nor Gautam, nor any of the others really, except maybe Arjun. He seemed to exist in his own hyper-self-possessed domain, the same then as now. Even today, she could see the boy flare within the man.

But the boy would not have apologized. The man had. In fact, he had apologized again and again, reached inside and gripped her heart in a nearly assaultive plea. It had felt intoxicating, their past made clean, a tether still fixed between them, and she had felt an almost embarrassing thrill at his pleading. It wasn't the supplication itself but the fact that *she* was the recipient. Even now, the idea of being chosen by him is worthy of elation. But now it all strikes her as so out of character that she wonders if it was connection or manipulation, if she was being "handled." It was another one of Jaishri's terms. "Arjun will handle it," Jaishri always said, and Simrin never knew if Jaishri fully understood that if Arjun had superpowers, one of them was certainly the almost imperceptible way he was able to sway favor and opinion. But never with them.

Or almost never. There was one time—was she twelve? She had tried not to think about it then, but now, it's not so easy to push away. The council had discussed changing their publicity materials, replacing Arjun's eyes with something more contemporary. People were receptive. There was talk of Ananda getting a little bit of spiffing up. But Arjun, all thirteen years of him, firmly resisted. Puja teased him, saying he just wanted his own eyes on everything, but he vehemently denied this.

"What better symbol than eyes to sum up who we are?" he said. "And the eyes of a child," he continued, "the closest beings to enlightenment."

"Of course *you're* the child," Gautam mumbled during the children's meeting.

"Then choose another child!" Arjun said. But that just seemed petty. And Arjun made a convincing argument. So Arjun went to the council meeting, representing the children's desire to have the eyes stay. There was arguing, and in the end, the council decided to put it to a community vote. Lalit designed a lovely lotus blossom with *Ananda Nagar* threaded through the leaves, and Diya came up with a very abstract *A*, the *Cakravat parivartante duḥkhāni ca sukhāni ca* mantra hidden in the lines. Simrin quite liked Lalit's design, but of course she voted for

Arjun's eyes. Everyone cast ballots, and ten members of the council were appointed to count them, each ten creating tallies, then giving those tallies to Gopal to tally. It was a lot of steps to go through, but it was supposed to guarantee impartiality.

Gopal began the count at the end of morning meditation, people at first sitting patiently, then circling out and back in again. Finally, he called Arjun, annoyed at both his own pitiful math skills and Arjun's natural affinity for numbers. So Arjun counted, scribbling numbers quickly until he had a final vote within minutes—seventy-seven votes for Lalit's lotus, thirty-six for Diya's *A*, eighty-nine for his eyes. No one was much surprised or really cared that much. But Simrin watched Arjun smash the paperwork down into the dirty napkins of leftover *prasad*, and after everyone left, she shook the wet scraps of *halwa* off the tally sheet. It took her a minute to figure out his scribbles, but then she saw the numbers so clearly. Lalit—89, Diya—36, Arjun—77. He had switched his numbers with Lalit's. He had lied. She read it three times more, trying to figure out how she was misreading, but she wasn't. And when she was absolutely sure she wasn't, she ran to him.

"You made a mistake," she said, hoping this would help him save face. She held the soggy paper out to him, and he took it and stared like he had never seen it before.

"Lalit won," she said.

He squinted at the paper, then looked up at her and smiled. "I see. Yeah, I put the numbers next to the wrong names."

"No, you didn't." She had never doubted him, but he had never lied, at least not to her, and she felt his denial like a slap to the face.

"I did," he said.

She stared back at him, waiting for his smile to fade, but it didn't.

"You're lying," she said and reached for the paper, but he snatched it away from her.

"I won," he said. His eyes blazed, the furrows between his eyebrows turned deep and angry, and she took a step back. He shoved the paper in his pocket and turned, but she had seen the half second of rage, had felt his fury at being discovered. It had left her shaken. And sickened by how effortlessly he had lied to everyone, but especially to her. But the next evening, he had tackled her before *satsang*, tickling her until she agreed to sit with him. And she had. And then half-heartedly convinced herself that she had been wrong.

Then it was too terrible to imagine her life without him woven through her. But now. Now, she thinks about whether she saw him handle anyone at Meadowlark today, whether he was any different than who she thought he was, but she can think of nothing. Meadowlark had revealed itself to be exactly as he had portrayed it, eighteen families committed to raising incredible children with Arjun at the helm. Nothing concerning at all. He had said that one thing about "calling on the oncoming," which was odd, but mostly it was talk of allowing children to discover their gifts, how society tainted a child's ability to uncover their own power. If he wanted to think you could create a Quinn just by raising kids in an incubated kid haven, he could. It wasn't hurting anyone.

She looks at the clock. Only ten, but she is exhausted. It has been a long day, and she needs to sleep. In the morning she will show him the photos. And then what? Then she will go home, of course. How can she even ask herself the question? She needs to get Quinn to school, get back in Tom's good graces, shoot the Mutineer ad. She takes a shot of the motel sign through the window, just the *otel* in red neon with the moon behind it, posts it #somethingscoming.

◆ ◆ ◆

The next morning Quinn wants doughnuts again, so they pack the car, then sit in the motel dining room and eat while Simrin looks on her phone for anything new on Meadowlark. There are a few new posts on the Save Marley page, but none from Tatiana and none from PFunk.

Quinn insists on putting her bathing suit on under her clothes because River promised her they could swim in the lake. You're definitely not swimming, Simrin wants to say, but she doesn't need a battle this morning. She wants to get in and out of Meadowlark with as little conflict as possible.

"Let's get going," Simrin says.

"I want another doughnut," Quinn says.

"Get it to go."

Quinn jumps up and clumsily wraps a plain glazed in a napkin. Simrin watches as one of the hotel staff helps her put it in a to-go bag.

"That man is kind of blue, purple," Quinn says. She has spent the morning bouncing around the dining room declaring what everyone's voice looks like. "But he has, like, silver slippy things also."

"Okay," Simrin says.

"He is!" Quinn insists.

Arjun told her she was special, and she, of course, believes him. Fucking Arjun. Quinn is special, but not because Arjun says it. Tom is going to just love this new-and-improved Quinn. He already grits, "Yes, darling," to just about anything Quinn says about what she sees and thinks and tastes, but this self-assured synesthete will push him over the edge.

They check out of the motel and drive the ten miles to Meadowlark. Both police cruisers are still there, but there are fewer civilian cars in the lot. She parks in the same spot as yesterday and looks around. She can't tell if the two guys in the cop car are the same ones as yesterday. They have their windows down, arms hanging out, and she wonders how they will be able to bear the heat in a few hours. She gives a mechanical smile and then pretends to gather her stuff. She planned to take only her keys with the attached flash drive and her phone—get in and out—but the idea of leaving her cameras in the hot car while she crosses what is arguably a barricade with police presence surrounding her is almost physically painful. And why not take the cameras? Because then there is an opening for more pictures. Then there is a chance that she can be seduced into covering this fiasco. Which she can't do. She has already crossed the line from balanced and unbiased to fully enmeshed. But even more so, there is Quinn. Simrin is willing to push boundaries with Quinn, but she isn't willing to risk her safety. Still, there was a moment yesterday, with Arjun pleading with her to come in, when Simrin felt Quinn slip from focus. And it scared her. That need to get to Arjun, it was drunk-like. How intoxicating it was to forget you were a mother of someone.

"We can't stay long," Simrin says.

"Why?" Quinn whines.

"Because we just can't." She can feel her patience fray.

"River said I could go swimming." She has already taken her T-shirt off and tied it around her shoulders like a cape.

"Put your shoes on."

Quinn slips her sneakers on and jumps from the car. Simrin watches the cops turn and inspect them. She locks the car and stuffs the keys and phone down into her camera bag. She told Arjun she would be there at nine, and as promised, the gates swing open as soon as they walk up.

Even though she saw him yesterday, the reality of him in front of her produces the same response. She feels her knees wobble, her body vibrate.

The gate slams shut, and Quinn takes off. The little girls are waiting in front of one of the houses, jumping up and down.

"River's been awake since six," he says. "She loves Quinn."

"I think it's mutual."

They walk toward the girls in silence. It is uncomfortable, and she tries to focus on the girls, to pretend they are both waiting for them to do something worth watching, something worth talking about. He has always been better at silence, never bothered by the endless hours of meditation. Once, during a brief period of devotion, he had stayed silent for five whole days. They were around ten and convinced they were saved from death by divine intervention. It was summer, and five of them decided to trek to town one Sunday morning, hoping to find enough spare change on the road to buy a few sodas, which they had. Jaishri and Simrin shared a 7 Up; Arjun, Gautam, and Krish a Dr Pepper. They drank their sodas and wandered through the air-conditioning of Safeway for an hour until they got bored and decided to head home. But by then it was noon and the sun was beating down a fierce 103-degree heat. They should have called someone at Ananda to pick them up and risked the extra karmic yoga they'd be given, but they were dumb kids, and so what if they didn't have water or even hats; they'd get back tired and hot.

A mile and a half out, they knew they were in trouble. Jaishri began to cry, and even Gautam, who never allowed himself even a minute of looking uncool, hunched down with his head on his knees. But Arjun, in typical Arjun form, announced they should breathe into the heat, chant *Cakravat parivartante duḥkhāni ca sukhāni ca*. And because there was nothing else to do, they did, sat by the side of the road and chanted, feeling stupid and even more like complete weirdos than usual. They chanted and chanted and chanted until Jaishri opened her eyes and said, "Where's the car?" "Nowhere," Gautam said, not having the energy, for once, for sarcasm. But then Arjun saw something, a glint across the road none of them had seen before, a bottle of water—unopened! The divine had heard their chanting. Or the bottle had fallen from someone's flatbed. But they hadn't even *seen* it before! They opened it and drank and cried, all of them, so thankful to be *saved*. And they made it through the last mile, sunburned but committed to devoting themselves to only higher pursuits—no more pretend fart sounds during *satsang*, no more mouthing *d'oh* instead of *om*, no more resenting all the time they spent reflecting on their higher selves and then half-heartedly pushing these selves to detach. "And one whole day of silence," Krish suggested. It was what the adults did to acknowledge their gratitude.

None of them except Arjun made it even the full day. And then he went two, then three, then four days. On the fifth day, Simrin was terrified that he would stay forever silent. She went to Jyoti and demanded someone make him speak, but Jyoti laughed and said this was his journey, so Simrin found him herself and pinched him hard on the inside of his arm. He didn't yelp, but his eyes shot daggers at her. And then he said, calmly and coolly, "Was that necessary?" And she broke down and cried, so glad the divine hadn't made him mute.

"I have the pictures," she says now. It is a stupid thing to say, but so is the silence, and really, what else do they have to talk about right now?

"When this is over, you and Quinn will have to come back," he says.

This takes her by surprise, and she realizes that she has wrapped this encounter up neatly in her head without realizing it. She will leave, and he will disappear again. Or she will leave and intentionally never come back. She moves away from things, a linear progression that hasn't, up until now, been altered. But that isn't exactly true; she went back to Ananda once. Quinn had just turned one, and for some reason, it seemed momentous enough to mark with a tidying of her past. But the return wasn't momentous. Yes, her mother was there. She fawned over Quinn and introduced her to everyone at Ananda as if she had something to do with Quinn's creation, but then she was gone again, needing to get the tomatoes in the ground and aghast at the suggestion that she could skip her meditation even for one day. So Simrin had wandered around Ananda, noticing how everything seemed smaller and everyone older. It was more like an amusement park ride through her childhood—lots to gawk at, everything going by so quickly—than a mending of old wounds. She knew enough to understand that anyone left would never see the wounding, and anyone gone was, well, gone.

Except Arjun. He isn't gone now. But he will be soon, she thinks, and the realization is enough to spark the first flickers of panic. She feels her heart speed up, a sheen of sweat surface.

"Mama, River made me a card!" Quinn says. She holds out a piece of paper with markered rainbows and flowers.

"Cool," Simrin says.

"She said my voice is rainbowed, so she drew a rainbow. Her voice is pink-and-yellow lines. And Darcy's is just kind of whitish. But Ash and Jessie's are nothing." She gestures to the other girls. Juniper is sitting on the porch, watching.

Juniper's voice is a shimmery blue, Simrin thinks, like a mermaid's tail.

"And Juniper's is also nothing," Quinn says.

"Really?" Simrin says. She doesn't mean to say it out loud, but she is genuinely surprised. Hasn't Quinn already told her it is blue? Colors are the way they are, and they do not change. "I thought," she begins, but then she stops. She knows who this girl looks like. There is this show Quinn likes to watch, some late-'80s sensation Simrin missed out on altogether. That girl is shimmery blue. That girl is a mermaid tail. That girl looks intensely like Juniper.

"Do you want to take Quinn to the art room?" Arjun says. "She can draw your voices."

"Okay!" River says.

The little girls run off, but Juniper stays, and Simrin can't help but stare. They look so much alike, don't they? She wants to google that girl, but she doesn't know her name. Simrin's knowledge of pop culture before the 2000s is basically nonexistent, and Tom, who was an adult by then, is the only boyfriend who never teased her about it.

"We can go to the office," Arjun says. "Look at the pictures there."

"I want to see," Juniper says.

It is the hair. And the eyes. Not like Arjun's at all.

Arjun runs his hands through his hair. "Junie, I'll show them to you when we're all done. This is the boring stuff."

"I want to see." She can hear the whine in her voice, but there is something else behind it, something forceful.

"See what?" Bethany comes out, and Simrin feels her body stiffen. She met Bethany briefly yesterday, and then she disappeared. Simrin found it odd, and at the same time, she was grateful. Children she could imagine, but the idea of Arjun with a wife makes her chest harden. She expects that Bethany feels the same, and Simrin wonders if she knows the full story of their past.

"See what?" Bethany says again.

"Simrin's brought the pictures," Arjun says.

"Let's take a look," Bethany says.

Simrin looks from Juniper to Bethany and sees them mirrored in each other's features.

Juniper stands. "Come on."

Bethany stares at Arjun, but he looks past her. There is silence, and Simrin understands that something else is being communicated, and both the communication and the tenor of whatever message is being sent make her uneasy. She watches Arjun. She has always been so good at reading him. One look at his face and she knew exactly what he was feeling. But now, he seems inscrutable, the seams where she used to scramble in stitched tight.

"Okay," he finally says. "Let's do this."

BETHANY

She watches Juniper from inside the common room, has been watching her all morning in fact, watching because she didn't watch her yesterday. And she should have. What the hell was she thinking, letting all of them, but particularly Juniper, out of her sight with this photographer around. Yesterday, it had felt reasonable. There was something deeply uncomfortable about knowing all of Meadowlark was watching her watch Aaron and Simrin. But more than that, she wanted no opportunity to police them. Aaron promised no pictures of the kids, and despite the fissure between them, Aaron never broke a promise. She knew that and wanted him to know it too. So Bethany hid out in the loft, trying to convince herself that staying out of the way was a way of healing the rift between her and Aaron.

I will trust you with this, she was saying. But it is a tenuous trust. Years ago it was easy to convince herself that unrelated acts altered outcomes, but her mother's strain of magical thinking has eroded over the years. Her mother was the supreme believer in "do this, and this will happen." When they discontinued the exact hair dye they used on Bethany, her mother trekked all over Los Angeles, bullying hairdressers into selling her the last bottles of color lest their empire be lost to a slight ashiness. She used the same pen for every contract, wore the same oxidized metal charm bracelet for every table read, made Bethany say the same "Good morning, chief!" to every set's director before speaking to anyone else.

Now it is harder to believe in causation rather than correlation, but she is desperate to be done with this disconnect, so she lay in the loft, windows open, listening to the familiar sounds of Meadowlark—laughing, crying, screeching—and let the time pass. Finally, she heard River and Darcy shouting goodbyes and looked out. From one window she could see the group of them making their way to the gates, River cartwheeling over herself to get there first. She watched Simrin and Quinn leave, then watched Aaron struggle with the gate and the new tin sheeting. She watched until the girls ran off somewhere and Aaron took Blaze into Bodhi two floors below her.

Then she walked to the other window. She saw the huge swath of yard, dusty and empty. Then Juniper. Standing all alone. It was more than Juniper's isolation that made Bethany feel like she had been sucker punched. It was watching her alone at Meadowlark. She gritted her teeth and tried to will away her own discomfort.

If nothing else, she hopes her children will never feel the burden of their mother's emotions. But it is so hard to keep the boundaries rigid, particularly when Aaron has erected his own impervious borders. She doesn't know if it's the fact that Juniper is her firstborn that makes Bethany's heart wring itself out particularly for Juniper, or the fact that they are so much alike. Of course they look similar, but it is more than that. Bethany can see her own hypervigilance in so much of how Juniper approaches the world, the same cost-benefit analysis of nearly every situation. So much of what Bethany has always assumed is nurture—she is surprised to find—is nature.

As a child, Bethany was the ultimate observer forced center stage, but at Meadowlark, Juniper is free to be a bystander for as long as she needs. Bethany assumed this autonomy would breed confidence and sense of self, and it isn't that Juniper isn't confident—it's just that lurking below is always that concentrated scrutiny. Bethany imagines it is exhausting. It was exhausting for her, is still exhausting despite the fact that Aaron and Meadowlark have eroded some of the layers of disconnect. Still, that fiery swallowing of experiences, that knowledge that the world will always meet your needs that is there in Aaron and River, will always be absent in Bethany. And it looks like absent in Juniper. That certainty is pure Aaron. And pure River. River, who shouts, "Hello, world!" every morning when she steps out of the house. River who articulates exactly what she is feeling like some kind of seven-year-old psychoanalyst. River who has never approached anything cautiously or without utter confidence that it will be "Amazing!" Bethany doesn't know about Blaze. Even though they created Meadowlark as an ungendered space, Blaze seems so dramatically different from both her girls, so eager to throw himself into a pile of dirt and turn all toys into vehicles. But what this means for his future self she doesn't know. He still seems such a baby, and she isn't eager to wish this away. In fact, it worries her more than she allows herself to admit. They built Meadowlark for the children, but what happens when the children aren't children anymore? She and Aaron discussed having one last baby up until a month ago, but now even if everything settles down, this seems unlikely. The stability of what they have built now feels threatened. And it makes her not only scared for her children but for herself.

Watching Juniper by herself in the middle of the yard yesterday did nothing to alleviate this. So she hurried down to see her. But when she came into the side yard, Juniper was gone. Bethany wasn't able to find her until dinner, and then when asked, Juniper said she had been with Sammi. Which wasn't true. Bethany knew because she herself had been with Sammi, helped her make bracelets out of embroidery floss rather than do what she wanted to do—press Aaron about the photographs. It was alarming because Juniper never lies. In that way, she is like her father. Bethany tried to reason that eleven-year-olds lie. It is a healthy developmental milestone that marks independence and a need for separation, but there has been too much separation lately. And now, she doesn't want Juniper out of her sight, no matter what child psychology she spouts at herself.

She looks out the window and watches the little girls run off, hears the murmurs of conversation and then Juniper's whine. She can't make out the words, but there is something unfamiliar in the tenor, something that makes her get quickly to her feet and hurry outside.

"I want to see," Juniper whines.

"See what?" Bethany says.

"Simrin's brought the pictures," Aaron says.

Bethany can feel the tired antagonism, a tightness in his voice. "Even now?" she wants to ask. If the story he wants to tell is one of loving-kindness, he better make his way back from anger pretty quickly. Her patience with his processing is beginning to wear thin, and she can feel her own anger building. But it is easy to attach herself to anger. The truth is much more layered. Anger, yes, but just as clearly detachment, that familiar feeling of being unmoored, alone and far, far away from anything to hold.

"Let's take a look," Bethany says.

Juniper stands. "Come on," she says.

Aaron stays still. Bethany tries to meet his eyes, but he is looking out and over the landscape, increasing the immense distance between them. It's always fine, she tells herself. It's always just fine. She tries focusing on Juniper, watches her watch her father, until he finally speaks.

"Okay," he says. "Let's do this."

Aaron leads the way, and Bethany lets Simrin and Juniper follow him before moving. It feels safer at the back, Juniper sandwiched between, but safe from what? The pictures are nothing but insurance, in case this brouhaha escalates. Brouhaha. That's what Aaron called it, and she rolled her eyes. She supposed *hullabaloo* would make it seem even more unsubstantial, but *brouhaha* is pretty close. In the chain of events, she feels they are a few steps closer to mayhem than brouhaha. Still, everything has been peaceful for several days. Simrin walked in this morning, and last night, Malik and Dan just walked out, bought groceries, then walked back in. Nevertheless, she still feels her heart echoing loudly around her body, and she places one hand on her chest and presses. It is how she calms the children when they are distressed. "You know," she tells them, "when you breathe deeply, you activate the parasympathetic nervous system, particularly the vagus nerve, which reverses the stress response in your body and slows down your heart rate." Aaron loves that she is teaching them how to use their bodies as tools for comfort, but Bethany knows it is just the big words, just the authority with which they are conveyed that is calming. Someone who loves you knows more than you do, she is saying, and that person has it all under control.

It's always fine, she tells herself. It's always just fine.

They walk down the long hallway, up the back stairs, and toward the office. It is a small room used mostly for paying bills and playing grown-up computer games, but it has three huge monitors and no outside light.

"Thank God for the monitors," Simrin says. "I've been working with my tiny laptop screen, so the postproduction may not be perfect, but I think they're okay." She pulls a flash drive off her key chain. "Which computer?"

"Here," Aaron says. He takes the drive, and for a moment, Bethany wonders if he will just pocket it. It's a silly thought, but there is something unsettling about this moment. Bethany imagines it is the strangeness of the four of them together. She can feel the tether between Simrin and Aaron, and then Juniper and Aaron, but she feels unfastened, and she grips the back of one of the two chairs.

Aaron sits down and plugs the drive in. There are only two seats, and Simrin takes the other. Juniper is bouncing on her toes, leaning on both chairs and making them swivel, and Bethany puts a hand on her shoulder. Juniper shrugs her off, and Bethany feels the sting of the rejection harder than she should.

"I want to see my pictures," Juniper says.

Bethany hears the words, hears her say *my pictures*, but it isn't until she sees the change in Aaron's body, sees his hand clench the mouse, that she actually understands what *my* means, what *pictures* means.

"You let her take their pictures?" she says to him.

"Beth," he says. He swivels his chair to face her, and for the first time in days, he looks her in the eyes.

"You promised," she stumbles. "You said." She can't get a meaningful sentence out, and he must sense this because he interrupts her, grabs her hands. The sweat blossoms under her armpits, dampens her palms. She tries to pull away, but he holds her firmly.

"I know this is hard," he says, "but we need to tell our story, and our children are part of that story." He makes it sound like a condolence, but she can feel something behind it, something even worse coming to get her. He tilts his head, and he looks as charming as he did the day she awkwardly asked him for coffee.

"And we need the publicity; we need to reveal who their mother is," he says.

She feels her body go heavy, her head light.

"What are you talking about?" Juniper says.

There are spots in her eyes, spots on the ground.

"Wait," Simrin says.

Bethany tries to pull away, but he is holding her there. She is caught like a fish, and all she can see are the headlines: "Cassie Campbell Found Living on Commune!" "Cassie Campbell Discovered with Her Own Little Angels!"

Her breathing is speeding up, trying to outrun her, and she's caught between impulses—to grab Juniper and run, to fall to the floor and beg, to yank the flash drive from the computer and stomp it. Too many choices and her body a useless husk.

"No," is all she can say.

"We need the world's attention," he says. "This is how we get it." His eyes are shining. He is on fire with the prospect of her exposure.

"No," she says again, but all he does is tilt his head, squeeze her hands, and smile like she is some obedient child.

"It'll all be fine," he says.

And then, like a punctuation mark, his phone rings. He hurries to answer it, and with the release of her hands, Bethany feels the shock inside her churn and turn to fury. This betrayal, the sacrifice of her children, her entire world offered up on a website.

"How could you?" she says, and it is such a predictable line that she is almost embarrassed, but he hasn't even heard her. He shoves his phone in his pocket and stands.

"Stay here," he says.

"Wait," Simrin says, but he is gone.

JUNIPER

The grown-ups are taking forever to get to the pictures, arranging themselves and talking about computers. She wants to tell them to hurry up, that she needs to see herself.

Yesterday, she'd been so excited about the possibility of her photos being seen by people she didn't know, but now she feels a thread of uneasiness pulling inside her. What if she looks stupid? What if she looks like a little kid? And then, why are these pictures making everyone so nervous? Particularly her mother. She can feel the anxiety coming off her like static. It's making Juniper nervous, too, which her mother notices because she puts her hand on Juniper's shoulder, and the touch feels like a shock. They are a wire sending current back and forth, and Juniper wants it cut.

"I want to see my pictures," she says because maybe, if they show them already, everyone will just settle down. But that's not what happens. What happens is that the room becomes electric. Her mother's hand seems clamped to the chair.

And then her father is talking. And Simrin is interrupting. And Juniper doesn't know what's going on until her mother turns to him and says, "You promised."

And then Juniper understands. That's why her father closed the bedroom door. That's why her mother was missing. Her mother didn't know Simrin would take pictures of them. But why would her mother care? Suddenly she is furious with her mother. Why did she disappear like that? Why did she not know? You were not vigilant, she wants to yell at her. It's your fault. But then her father is saying something about who her mother really is, and Juniper cannot get them to slow down and tell her what he is talking about. She tries to make them, but then her father's phone rings, and then he is gone, leaving the room spiky and jagged. Juniper cannot see emotions, but she feels this, and it makes her want to run.

Her mother is pushing her hands through her hair, pulling at the roots. "You cannot post those pictures," she says.

"What did Daddy mean?" Juniper asks. But her mother isn't paying any attention to her. She is gripping Simrin's hand now, repeating herself over and over, and Simrin is doing the same, saying, "Why can't I post them? Why? Why?" again and again. They don't even remember she is there.

"Why did he say that about you?" Juniper demands.

"You can't let him post those," her mother says. "Do you understand? Do you understand?" She is repeating herself again, and the more times she repeats herself, the higher her voice gets, the shakier it gets. Juniper has never seen her mother like this, and she doesn't want to see her like this, but she wants to know what her father meant. What could her mother possibly have to reveal? She tries again, but no one is paying any attention to her. It is as if an alarm has been set off, and no can hear her over the noise of their own panic.

Her father seems the only one left who is not panicked. The only one who knows what's going on. Yes, he lied to her mother, but he has never lied to her. It is a pledge he makes each of his children on their birthday: "I promise you love, truth, and freedom." He makes them wait to blow out their candles until he has held their faces in his hands, looked into their eyes, and sworn this oath. Juniper always pretends to be annoyed, but it is really her favorite part of the celebration, all that affection wrapped up in solemn ritual.

She knows her father will tell her the truth, and he will be calm and in control when he does it.

She is only a few feet from the door, and it is simple to take a long, easy stride and then disappear around the corner. And then Juniper is running, hard and fast. She hears her mother call after her, but it is a flat, faint "Juniper." She knows she won't follow her, and if she does, she can't possibly catch her.

Juniper takes the stairs quickly, feeling the blood pulsing through her limbs, and flies into the common room, where there are a bunch of oblivious people doing oblivious things. She pauses at the bottom of the stairs, not sure where to go next. Jennifer is sitting on the floor with Justice and Blaze, and she looks up.

"Where you going so fast?" she says and smiles up at her.

"Where's my dad?" she says.

"He went out the front."

Jennifer is still talking, but Juniper couldn't care less about being kind and respecting all people right now, so she runs out the door, off the porch, into the middle of the yard. And then she stops.

In front of her, she sees Gavin and David at the gate. She scans the yard for her father and finds him. He is fiddling with something on the side of Rudraksh and then lifts open a hatch she has never seen before. He is pulling things out, doing something with his shirt. He doesn't see her, and Juniper feels stuck, debating with herself about what she should do. She doesn't know why, but this moment feels dangerous. It's not just what he might say to her about her mother but what he might say about all of this. And then he turns around.

At first he doesn't see her. He strides quickly toward the gate, but a few steps before he reaches it, he spots her. He stops, and when he does, Gavin also turns, then David. Gavin points angrily at her and then at the house, and then David joins him, but her father takes a moment and looks at her. And although it can't be more than two seconds, it feels much longer. It feels like there is an invisible current that runs from her father's hard stare into her chest. It hits her solid in the sternum until she *can* feel what he is thinking, not in her brain but in her chest, and it is something strong and certain. She doesn't know if she wants to take a step back or forward, and in that moment, he motions for her to come to him, and that something strong and certain pushes her forward.

She runs, her heart beating her hard from the inside, and when she reaches him, he pulls her close. She can smell the stink of his under-arms, rotten and reassuring at the same time. He hugs her tightly and murmurs something into her hair that she cannot hear, but she nods anyway. They have somehow moved beyond anything spoken in that room. And the thought of there being something bigger than a secret her mother carries is frightening. Still, there is a joy in feeling the risk, knowing it's real but also scary.

And then he is pushing her, gently, toward the gate. Gavin says something, and David agrees, but she is not paying attention to the words because her father is positioning her directly behind the entrance.

"Unlock it," her father says.

Gavin mumbles something back but does as her father says, and soon there is a gap in the gate the size of a small person, a person like her.

Outside there are a bunch of people, a bunch of police. They are the same ones she watched yesterday, but now they look like giants. Her heart is pounding and her ears are buzzing and her knees feel rubbery, but her mouth is a hard, tight line. There are three policemen and one policewoman standing directly in front of her, but a whole giant's length away. From the inside she feels her father's hand on her back.

"Junie," her father says, "just repeat what I say." He rubs her back in soft, even circles, keeping his body behind the shield of the gate. "We have done nothing wrong."

"We have done nothing wrong," she says.

"Louder," her father whispers.

She tries again, forcing her voice to imagine her throat a megaphone.

"We have broken no laws," her father says.

She repeats.

"All we ask is that you leave us in peace," he says. She says it, and then there is a creepy silence, so many people staring intently at her, frozen. Gavin and David move to shut the gate, but the short policeman speaks.

"We have a search warrant," he says. "We have a legal right to enter the premises."

Juniper knows he is not talking to her but to her father.

Her father repeats, "We have done nothing wrong. We have broken no laws. All we ask is that you leave us in peace."

Juniper tries again, but this time, the short policeman interrupts her. "Open the gates. We have a search warrant." He is not even looking at her, is just staring right over her head.

"Try again," her father says. "We have done nothing wrong . . ."

Juniper tries, but the short one shakes his head, mutters under his breath, and it makes her angry.

"Listen!" she yells. She watches a small wave of movement in the people behind.

This time it's the tall policeman who speaks. "Honey," he says. "Let us talk to your daddy," and it is the way he says it, as if she is five and not eleven and an actual human being.

"This is all just a grown-up misunderstanding," he says. And the rage she feels is magnified by the fact that she knows *this* is not a misunderstanding. She feels her anger spin out from the place her father has stung her, up from her sternum and into her mouth.

"Fuck you," she yells. She has never said these words aloud, and they make her feel big and powerful. Her father believes she can do this, and so she can. Behind her, David says, "Fuck yeah." There is movement in front of her, and her father pushes up behind her and rests his elbow heavily on her shoulder. She cannot see him, but she knows something big is happening from the movement in the crowd, and very quickly the tall policeman yells, "Hold your fire, hold your fire!"

Juniper looks up and sees her father is holding a gun. She has never seen a gun up close in her whole entire life, only knows what one looks like from a kids' encyclopedia they have. It is smaller than she thought it would be, but the strangeness of it in his hand makes it look big and clumsy, like he could drop it at any moment. She tenses, and he grips her other shoulder with his free hand.

"Now listen here," her father says. His voice is different. Mean. She doesn't think she has ever heard him like this, and she feels him grow a hundred inches behind her.

"This is our property. These are our children. They are well cared for, well loved, and we will not let them be taken into your world of limitations and restrictions."

"No one's trying to take your children, Aaron." This is the tall policeman, but now his voice is softer and slower, put on the way Juniper puts on when she wants some of River's ice cream.

"We both know that's not true, so cut your bullshit," her father says. "You can either get the hell out of here. Or you can risk hurting a bunch of innocent kids."

And now Juniper is scared. A big part of her wants to run back to the safety of Bodhi, but her father grips her tightly with one hand, and with the other he does something to make the gun click.

"We have thirty-one children in here, thirty-one children who are not leaving our sides." He pauses and snakes his forearm on top of Juniper's chest. "I think you understand what I'm saying. So get the hell off our property." He takes a step back, pulling Juniper with him. David and Gavin slam the gate closed, and as soon as they do, Juniper starts to cry. She lets out a single sob, and her father clamps his hand over her mouth.

"You can't do that now, Junie," her father says. "You've got to be strong."

This has never happened before. Never. They are taught to feel their feelings, feel them in their bodies, their minds, their art, their movement. And this makes Juniper cry more.

"I'll take her back," he says. He hands David the gun, and it is then that Juniper notices the gun Gavin is holding and the other gun strapped to David's back—a long, pointy thing. She is struggling to keep the sobs in, but the guns and her father's hand are making them come out. He picks her up and pulls her to him like he did when she was a little girl pretending to be asleep.

"I know it's scary," he says. "I know. I know." He is running now, trying to run, but Juniper has grown tall this summer, and he has to pause halfway and put her down.

"I need you to do something, Junie," he says.

She is still crying, but there is something underneath her fear. Something that bubbles closer to the surface when her father looks at her now. She cannot see music or taste words or call the oncoming, but she can do this. She can do not-a-brouhaha. She takes a deep breath and straightens her spine like she has been taught, like her vertebrae are reaching for the sand and the sun, making space in her body for whatever's already there.

"Tell everyone to get inside Bodhi and stay put," her father says. "Make sure everybody knows."

She wipes her eyes, nods, and is quickly off and running, first to Cedar's porch, where Candice is standing. "My dad said to get everyone in Bodhi and stay there."

"I'll go round up the houses," Candice says.

"No," Juniper says. "He told me to do it." She thinks Candice will push back, but she doesn't. She just grits her teeth and lets her have her way, as if this is just another part of being a Lark. And Juniper doesn't question. She runs. First to Tule, then to Willow, then to Hawthorne, and finally to Bodhi, where Rowan and Rory have pressed their faces against the front window. There are a few people behind them, but

Juniper doesn't stop to notice who and instead runs to the front door. Dan swings it open as soon as she reaches for the doorknob.

"My dad says to stay in Bodhi," she says to him.

"Damn," he says. "The police are at the front gate?"

"Yes."

Blaze is behind Dan, and he reaches his arms out to her. Juniper picks him up and holds him tightly to her like her father just held her. And she feels strong.

"We have to all stay here," she says.

"Where's your father?" Mary asks.

Juniper turns around, searches for him out the open door, but can see only David and Gavin facing the gate, what she now knows are guns at their sides.

"We have to go inside," she says.

More people are coming up the porch, holding babies and little kids who are whining and dragging their feet. They are never told they have to do anything, and here they are being forced into Bodhi. She gives Blaze to Jennifer and lets the people stream by her.

"Get inside," she says. She is surprised by her own ability to take charge. No discomfort or awkwardness. And then there's something else. A slight pleasure fizzing up inside her.

Everyone is here, or at least it looks that way. The community room is full of crying little kids and adults trying to soothe them. A bunch of the bigger kids are crowded at the front windows. She sees Ash and Jessie and remembers that they went to the art room with River and Quinn, who are not here. Her mother and Simrin are also missing, but she knows where they are. They are technically in the house, and Juniper doesn't want to go anywhere near the panic of that room, does not want to hear anything more about those pictures or what they have to say about her father, who is still the only person who seems to be in control of himself and isn't ignoring her.

She makes her way through the living room to the kids at the window and looks out. Her father is still missing, but she can see David, and if she squints, the long pointy gun across his back, something else in his hand, probably her father's gun. She's glad the others can't see the guns because she knows that every single person would freak out.

"Where's River and Quinn?" she says to Ash.

Ash shrugs.

"Weren't you with them in the art room? Did they come out with you?"

"I went to the bathroom. Then Mama got me."

"Ugh," she says. She had one job, and she's already messed it up. She knows she has to go get them before her father comes in and finds out she couldn't do this one easy thing.

The art room is under Cedar, a basement converted into a massive messy space for kids to do whatever they want with paint and glue and glitter. It's probably faster to go out through the front door, but she's worried her father will come in while she's going out and find out she forgot her sister, so she runs down the hall, past the TV room, past the bathroom, and out through the laundry room.

Outside the laundry room there is a pile of old buckets, and some kid has taken a bunch of clothespins and wire and made what looks like a person hanging from the clothesline. It's wearing an old torn baby onesie. She would have thought it was kind of cool a week ago, but today it looks freaky. Everything is looking freaky, and she starts to get scared, but this is not the time to want to go back to being oblivious. "Fuck," she says aloud. It's only the second time she's ever said it, and it feels good to say. She thinks maybe it holds some power. And she wonders if this is what her father is talking about when he asks what a word tastes like. Maybe she just *feels* the words, words like *oblivious, secret, fuck*. Maybe. But no. She doesn't know. And she can't just stand here wondering, so she picks up a bucket and throws it at the clothespin baby. It swings on the clothesline but doesn't fall, which makes it look even freakier, so she says it again, "Fuck," then takes a deep breath and runs to the edge of Bodhi.

She peeks out, looking for her father again, but the whole front of Meadowlark is empty now except for David pacing in front of the gate. It's never been this empty before. And quiet. Sort of. She can hear the static of the police scanner, but that's it. She rounds the corner and is about to go left toward Cedar when she notices the people on Bodhi's porch. It's Dan and Candice and Mary and Gavin, all clustered together.

"We're fucked," Gavin says, loudly, and then the others are shushing him. Juniper wants to hear what else they're saying. She's committed to this cause now, and if there is info to be had, she wants to have it, no matter how scary it is. She'll leave River and Quinn in the art room for two more minutes. Two minutes won't matter.

She crouches down and watches Candice run her hands through her hair, then say something, but Juniper can hear only a low garble of words. There are a bunch of shrubs that bump up against the porch. They're actually juniper bushes, which, depending on the day, make her feel either special (no one else has their own bush, except Sage, but they weren't planted for him) or embarrassed. Today she just feels lucky they're here. They've grown almost as big as she is, and she can creep down and shimmy under them and get close to the group on the porch. Part of her wonders why she's even hiding. Larks can do pretty much whatever they want to do unless it involves severe physical or emotional danger. But something is changing, and she just knows that they will stop talking the minute she walks over.

She lies down and tries to get her body as low and far away from the scratchy juniper branches as she can. A juniper is a stupid plant to be named after. It's pokey, and you can't even eat the berries (or you can, but they're disgusting). But they can grow anywhere; they're strong and resilient, "Which is what we wanted you to be," her father says; "And you are!" her mother always adds. She does feel strong. And probably resilient. She thinks this will be a good test of her strength and resilience.

She is almost flush with the porch, hidden from sight. It's not hiding, she tells herself; it's secreting. From where she settles, she can see legs and feet, and she can hear some of what they're saying, which basically consists of people wondering what is going to happen. Gavin keeps saying, "We're fucked," and Mary keeps saying, "Do we have to comply with groundless accusations?" And then there is another pair of legs, and Juniper knows immediately they are her father's. Everyone quiets and immediately turns to him, and Juniper feels something like a smile swell through her body.

"Okay, listen," her father says. "Right now, we have no reason to believe they're not going to leave."

"They're not gonna just *leave*," Gavin says.

"We don't know that." This is a woman's voice, but Juniper can't tell if it's Candice or Mary.

"They're fucking cops. Cops don't just leave." This is Gavin again. He is shifting from foot to foot.

"Calm the fuck down, Gavin," Dan says.

"Calm down?" Gavin says. "Have you not heard of Waco?"

"Gavin." This is her father again. She is sure he's putting both his hands on Gavin's shoulders. "That's exactly why they're going to leave. They don't want Waco."

"Christ," Gavin says. She can see his feet crossing the length of the porch, then returning, then crossing again.

"We just need to wait them out," her father says.

"Or let them in," Mary says.

Someone scoffs. Then there is silence. Finally, her father speaks. And again, it is the voice she's never heard before today, the one he used with the police. "You can get your kids and go, Mary," he says. "No one's stopping you from leaving."

Without the safety of his body behind hers, this voice scares Juniper. Her father does not talk this way. He has never raised his voice. Ever. The grown-ups at Meadowlark are not supposed to yell or scold, but of course it happens. Marsha will screech out the window that the baby is trying to sleep, or Kenny will complain that they've ruined the strawberry patch *again*, and don't they have eyes to see where their feet are going? Even her mother occasionally falls into the "toxicity of shame." "You're old enough to know better," her mother will say, and someone, usually her father, will steer her mother back with a "toxic waste alert!" It's not okay to hit people with your hands *or* your words. And that's why this voice, her *father's* voice speaking to someone *at Meadowlark*, feels like a hard fall from the trampoline. But worse. Because no one is reminding him that "Shame breeds fear; love breeds growth." No one is acknowledging that he has just done something very, very wrong.

And then Dana comes out. Juniper can tell because of the bare feet and chipped blue nail polish.

"Oh God," Dana says. "This is all my fault."

"Of course it's not." This is Mary, but Juniper can't help but think that Dana is right. If she hadn't gotten in the fight with Kevin, none of this would have happened.

"Let's go inside," her father says, and his voice is back, her father again. "I'll let everyone know what's going on."

The group shuffles in, and now Juniper is torn about what to do. She needs to get River and Quinn, but she really needs to hear what her father is going to say. She puts her cheek on the warm dirt and tries to make a decision. With the heat and the smell of juniper all around her, she feels like she could just close her eyes and take a nap. But this would be actually choosing to be oblivious, to fall asleep when there is so much needing to be aware of. If she sneaks in behind everyone, she can listen and then sneak back out again to get the little girls.

She shimmies out of the juniper and pulls herself up onto the porch. There are a lot of people in the doorway, and she has to push through. She wants to hang out on the edge of the crowd, but more people push through the door, and she ends up on the bottom corner of the stairs, a bunch of grown-ups in the way of her and the front door. They meet often in this room, but now it feels like the population of Meadowlark has doubled. Juniper usually slinks behind something during community meetings, braiding the fraying edges of a chair or using the back of a couch as resistance for her backbends, not really paying attention, but now she feels like she has too much attention, and she puts her hand on her heart to try to hold it quiet.

She leans against the banister and looks around for David or Gavin. David must still be out front, but now she sees Gavin. He is standing with his back to the front door, arms crossed. Juniper has never particularly liked Gavin. People are always giving him "toxic waste alerts," and he is always grumpy with the kids if they're not asleep by nine, but more than that, she's not sure *he* sleeps. Every time Juniper gets up in the night to pee, she can see Gavin outside, walking the yard and smoking cigarettes. She has only ever told Sammi this. "Maybe he's a vampire," Sammi said, which is dumb because he is awake during the day too. And there are no such things as vampires.

Her father is now in the middle of the room, and people are shushing each other. "I have some information," her father says. He sounds weird, not that same angry voice as before but still somehow different.

"Yes, the police are at the gate," he says. People start to ask questions and talk to themselves, and he shushes them.

"Please don't worry," he says. He is saying something about the power of community and the strength of children. He doesn't say anything about the search warrant or the guns. But at least he is calm. At least he is in control.

"What did the police say?" someone asks. It is Malik, his arms wrapped tightly around Aria from behind.

"They don't want anyone hurt," her father says. People are restless, and there are a number of little kids still crying.

"Did they say that?" Dana asks.

"Everyone wants to settle this as quickly as possible," her father says.

"Do they have a search warrant?" Star asks.

There is a pause, long enough that Juniper, who has been scanning the room to see if her mother or Simrin has arrived, is surprised and looks back at her father.

"No," he says. "No search warrant."

Juniper can hear Star start to reply, but she feels the blood rush to her feet, a dizzy upside-down feeling that makes her lean hard against the banister to keep from slipping away. She looks up, and Gavin is staring at her. She looks quickly at the floor and doesn't move. Maybe she imagined the search warrant. Maybe she didn't hear the police say they had one, or maybe her father thought they said something else. There is no evidence. Except Gavin's hard stare. She can feel it like molten lava, slowly lurching toward her. She is afraid. The thought makes her eyes fill with tears. She doesn't want to blink, or she knows they will run down her cheeks, and then what? Then Gavin will know she is scared, scared of what is happening all around them, but even more so, scared of him. She realizes she's never been scared of one of her grown-ups, and now, now she is terrified. And this thought is even worse, worse because it reminds her of why she's scared. Because of her father. Because of the lie. Her father values truth above all else. Her father is the one who is always talking about the thousands of tiny threads between them and how when you lie, you cut them all. And now he has taken very sharp scissors and snipped straight through everything that connects him to Meadowlark, everything that connects him to her. She feels it like a slice through the chest. The lie. And the truth. That there is something really very wrong here. That there is something dangerous outside. And in.

And so she runs—down the hall, through the laundry room, and out of the door to Hawthorne's roof, where she can secret herself away.

SIMRIN

Simrin tries to locate herself. She is in this weird computer room. Bethany has disappeared to her bedroom. Quinn is in the art room. And Arjun is God knows where doing God knows what.

Clearly Arjun has changed. Or hasn't changed. She doesn't know, but she does know she needs to get out of here quickly, and then she will have a whole ten-hour drive to contemplate these questions. Whatever magnetic pull he still has on her, whatever understanding she was trying to glean by coming here, whatever secrets there are to unsecret have to be left unknown. Legally, she can't post the photos without explicit consent, and she doesn't have that. In fact, what she has is explicit refusal. Bethany is not only refusing but frantically refusing, adamant that no pictures of her children be posted and adamant that she specifically told Arjun not to take the children's pictures.

"There are things I can't talk about," Bethany said. "Things that have nothing to do with Aaron."

Simrin tried to push her for more information, but Bethany refused to say more, her frenzy rising with each question Simrin asked.

"Please," Bethany begged and grabbed Simrin's hands. "Help us leave. Take us with you."

Simrin felt herself recoil at Bethany's unconcealed desperation, so raw and ugly. She has seen this kind of panic before, has felt it in herself at fifteen, the terror and the urgency, the animallike scrabble to escape. There is something more than simple betrayal here, something more insidious. "Okay," Simrin said. She will meet Bethany and the children at Rudraksh in fifteen minutes, then drop them in Reno or wherever else they want to go that is on the way back to sanity. Christ. *This* is a betrayal. Arjun has created what they spent their childhoods longing for, and here she is helping disappear it. But Simrin sure as hell doesn't need more devastation on her conscience. Meadowlark is nothing like Ananda, but Simrin can recognize Bethany's panic like it is her own. The irony is that Jaishri never panicked, not even the night they escaped. She was scared, yes, but all it took was Arjun's arms around her small shoulders for her to calm and then follow. And Arjun, Arjun wasn't even scared. At the time it seemed noble and inspiring, a boy with the confidence to lead them anywhere, but now Simrin cringes at his bravado and stupidity, his desire to be the hero, no matter the cost. Just like his fucking namesake, the archer whose pride was his greatest failing. And it is happening again. Bethany can see it. "This isn't *our* story," Bethany said to Simrin after Arjun left that claustrophobic room; "this is *his* story."

And that word, *story*, kicked at something inside Simrin. Simrin tells stories—directs viewers, pairs images. It is something that sometimes pricks at her conscience. Choose this image but not this one. Crop this but not this. Manipulate pictures to form a narrative. Her narrative. Her story. But not hers. Because she doesn't place herself at the center, not in her work and certainly not when others' lives are at stake. It is one thing for a boy to cheat and manipulate his way into staying the golden child. It is another to keep the camera trained on your grown-up self, no matter the cost. Now they are the adults and responsible for these little people. These little people who aren't chips to rake into a growing win. You don't get to decide someone else's story, but that's what he is trying to do. And what the hell is she doing? Her heart squeezes. Taking pictures to help a man who betrayed her, while the cops wait outside the gates and her daughter draws random kids' voices. What is this if not deciding Quinn's story?

Her heart quickens. She doesn't know where the art room is. The second floor seems unnervingly empty. No one to ask for help. But it's okay, she tells herself. She will find Quinn on her own. She will go down the stairs, go outside. It won't take her more than ten minutes, five if she asks someone. But who? She wonders who else is complicit in Bethany's betrayal.

She tries to remember the positioning of the houses. The girls ran away from the house she is in now to get to the art room, toward Rudraksh. She winces. Even the name in her head makes her squirm. She grabs her camera bag and winds her way past bedroom after bedroom. Either this will all magically resolve and they can meet again and she will tell him about Jaishri. Or it won't. The cops will escalate. Meadowlark will resist. The standoff will end in some cataclysm of media good fortune. It would be nice to leave him with what happened to Jaishri, one lasting wound, but Simrin is more concerned with the possibility of imminent disaster—when will it begin? Tonight? In two hours? Now? She feels the predictable clench in her stomach, then the inevitable pounding of her heart, the same old panic beginning to swell. *Cakravat parivartante duḥkhāni ca sukhāni ca*, she tries: pain, then pleasure; pleasure, then pain. When she was little, she imagined an old-fashioned wagon wheel spinning around in the sky, half the spokes shooting knives, the other half candy hearts. Pain, then pleasure. Pleasure, then pain.

She walks down the hallway toward the stairs and hears the noise before she reaches the landing, a growing murmur of worried people, and then, as she turns the corner, Arjun's clear, solid voice.

"Let's all just hold tight," he is saying.

She stands on the landing, trying to go unnoticed. There are a lot of people here, way more than before, and she wonders if everyone at Meadowlark is now in this room. There are women swaying with crying babies and lots of little kids pulling on their parents. She searches the room for Quinn, and when she can't find her, she feels a moment of relief—the noise and the density of people would overwhelm Quinn—and then fear.

"It's all going to be just fine," Arjun says.

Simrin feels the lie plunge through her like a lead sinker. Everything is very definitely not fine. There are too many nervous people packed in one room, but Arjun is not one of them.

"We all need to remember what Meadowlark stands for," Arjun says. "Why we're here." He is standing in the center of the room, the crowd circling him like he's some goddamn guru. "Why are we here?" he asks. He puts his hands out in front of him, inviting answers.

"To raise children who know their truth," someone says.

"Children who aren't influenced by the world's bullshit," someone else adds.

Simrin can sense the undercurrent of anger in the room. It's building, and it makes her uneasy.

"Yes," he says and pauses. "But don't forget the bigger reason. These children are Larks." There are yeses from the crowd. "They will shape the world," he continues. "And we need to guard them for it."

He is luminous, hair like a halo around his head, eyes shining, light seeming to literally emanate from his body. "Who will protect them if not us?" he says.

There are murmurs.

"No one," he says. He looks down at the ground, shakes his head as if he is contemplating the answer, then looks up slowly. "Do we want our children to live their truth?" He waits for the affirmations, then asks again, but this time louder. "Do we want our children to live their truth?" The crowd is louder now too. There are yeses and hell yeses. He waits a moment, holding out for complete silence, then finally speaks. "Then now is the time for us to live ours."

There are shouts and cheers from the audience. He is dazzling them, and he is radiant, awash in his people's adulation. Simrin feels her stomach drop. He is everything they as children were warned against, the prophetic guru in love with his own power. How did they get here? Him commanding focus, her complicit in his demands. And what if she refuses? She feels the knives of the wagon wheel spinning increasingly closer.

She tries easing herself down the stairs. She takes a step, then another. She tries to remember which building the girls ran toward, but she was so eager to show Arjun the photos. She didn't even bother to see where her daughter went. What kind of mother leaves her daughter alone with people like these? What kind of mother takes her daughter into a secluded compound? She feels the panic rise higher, and she tries to focus on the path to the front door. Down the stairs, slight turn right, then four steps ahead. She will go out the front door and turn left. And then? Someone calm and kind will be there to direct her, or she will run frantically around yelling Quinn's name.

She makes it down, then weaves her way around a group of adults, her camera bag knocking into people's backs. There is a man with his back to the door, and she tries to avoid eye contact as she reaches around him for the doorknob.

"Excuse me," she says, but he doesn't move, his body solid against the closed door.

"Please," she says.

He doesn't move, and then she feels a hand on her arm. She turns, and it is Arjun.

"Come with me," he says.

"I have to go."

"This way." He pulls at her, and she tries to tug her arm away, but he holds tight, and she feels the threat through his fingertips, real and terrifying.

"I need Quinn." She hears the crack in her voice, the announce-ment of her weakness, and then her knees begin to buckle. He grasps her under her arms, and she falls into him, her head resting against the familiar plane of his chest. But now he doesn't tug her to him, doesn't gather her into the space of his body. Instead, he pulls her to stand, then whispers something to the man in front of the door.

"Let's go upstairs," Arjun says and walks her down the hall.

He steers her past the TV room and up a rear stairway. They pass bedrooms and bathrooms, and Simrin can feel her body grow heavy, like she is underwater, and her head go fuzzy, like it is full of dryer lint. She tries to convince herself that her body has it wrong. He just wants the photographs. There is no threat here. He is just Arjun. But her body seems to be separating itself farther and farther from her head, and she realizes the immense difference between emotional and physical danger.

They stop when they reach the computer room they were in before. He leads her in, and she notices now that it is barely even a room, more like a closet—long and thin with double doors—overpacked with computers. More like a control room than anything else. The thought is actually calming. People in control rooms are in control. She is going into the control room. And isn't she the one who is actually in con-trol? She has the pictures, the passwords to her blog and social media accounts, everything he needs to tell what he thinks is his story.

"Get me Quinn," she says.

He turns, shuts the double doors, and looks at her. He is silent, but she holds his stare.

"Get me Quinn," she says again.

"I need you to post the photos. Now." He is calm and direct. "And then you can get Quinn."

"I need my daughter."

"First the pictures."

"No."

"Just put the pictures on the blog," he spits.

She can see the flash of anger, a split second, but enough to feel the rage simmering underneath, a white-hot fury that is boiling closer to the surface. And now it isn't a boy who is directing it at her. It is a man.

She won't post the pictures of his kids, she tells herself. She'll post the others, get Quinn, help Bethany, and then get them all out. She takes the flash drive out of her pocket, inserts it into the port, and navigates to her site. She logs in, opens a new post, and begins to drag and drop.

"Wait," he says. "I want to see them."

She hesitates.

"I'll do it," he says and reaches for the mouse.

"No," she says. She doesn't want him anywhere near her site. It is hers. And even though she feels bullied and manipulated, the pictures are hers too. They are fine work, and she won't let him have even the small pleasure of clicking "post."

She navigates back to the flash drive, opens the folder she created for him, and then clicks on each image, giving him a few seconds to see each picture full screen. They show normal, happy kids doing normal, happy things. A boy in shorts and rain boots working on a block tower. A girl with face paint doing a backbend. They are beautiful on this giant screen, the children dazzling in their unblemished perfection. And she can't help but see her own artistry, her skill for him to admire. She steals glances at him, but his face is vacant, and she tries to focus on the work. She is surprised that she didn't choose any of Blaze or River but also relieved. Still, there is the last shot in the series, the stunning picture of Juniper. But before it appears, she quickly clicks over to her site.

"Wait," he says. "There was one more."

"That one isn't for the blog."

"I want to see it."

"I can't—"

"Show me," he interrupts.

She hesitates. Bethany has explained nothing, only insisted that Simrin not post her children online and not let Arjun say anything about them. "Especially Juniper," she kept saying, and Simrin understood that there was something more going on than that instinctive desire to protect your child. She recognized it in Bethany, like she recognized it in herself, Bethany's fear of being seen as obvious as Simrin's fear of not being seen, both passed down onto their children like an unwanted inheritance.

"Show me," Arjun says, and there it is again, the flicker of unconcealed rage.

Her fingers hover over the mouse. She takes a breath and navigates back to the folder and clicks, and there is Juniper. Those giant blue eyes even more brilliant on a large screen, her hair a tumble of gold. She feels Arjun's body tighten beside her.

"Transfer them all to the computer, then upload," he says.

"I can't," she stumbles. "I can't upload the one of Juniper."

"Of course you can," he says.

"It's illegal. I need consent."

He laughs, a hollow forced sound, and then he is silent. He looks at her, and she forces herself not to look down.

"Remember," he says, "why we ran."

"That's not . . ."

"Why did we run?" He grasps her hands, and she feels that contradictory desire to meld and sever. All it takes is his hands on hers, his tug on the frayed rope of their youth. She is disgusted with herself, how easily he can still sway her.

"Why?" he says. And in that moment, she doesn't know why. Why had they run? Because Ananda was a horrible place for a child, a place where adults forced dogma and conditions on children, a place where everyone was supposed to have a voice and a child had none, a place that pushed them to detach from themselves before they had even discovered who they were? But that wasn't the reason then. The reason then was that they were terrified of being sent off to India, of being separated, disconnected from the only warmth they had ever swum in and out of. Arjun, Simrin, Jaishri. The three of them a sanctuary together.

"Because they wanted to separate us," she says.

"Yes." His eyes light up like flames, and she has to look away. "That's what they want to do to my family," he says.

She hears his words, the way he takes what she has said and manipulates it to fit his needs, and she feels her anger whistle through her. "That's what you did to us," she says.

He winces. He obviously wasn't prepared for this, had thought that after yesterday, when she had let it go, he was forgiven. He grits his teeth and squeezes her hands, tight and uncomfortable, and she feels her panic rise. But then, just as quickly, he looks down, knits his eyebrows, tilts his chin, and looks up at her. And it all seems so contrived, so manufactured—put out stimulus A to elicit response B—that she feels sickened.

"*We* were your family," she says. "You separated us."

"No." He shakes his head.

"Yes."

He is trying to maintain a look of great benevolence and compassion, but Simrin can see the strain, the lines at the corners of his eyes growing deeper, the white hairs at his temples highlighting the sweat on his forehead. The boy she so revered just as human as the old men they hated.

"You abandoned us," she says.

"You had your father," he says, "and Jaishri wanted to go back."

"You could have made her stay."

"She needed to go back."

"She worshiped you," she says. "She would have done anything you told her to."

"She did," he snaps.

And then there is silence. It takes Simrin a moment for the words to make sense, but then they do, and it feels like the air has been violently sucked from her. "You sent her back?" she asks.

"You think she would have done it on her own?"

She opens her mouth, tries to speak, but there is nothing.

"She threw up in the bathroom when we sent her to the lobby to ask for more towels," he says. "She peed her pants trying to cross the street by herself! You think she could have survived outside Ananda?"

"She had us!"

"I couldn't help her."

"You could have tried."

"I did."

"And when it didn't work after two weeks, you just gave up?"

"Yes," he says.

It is not what she was expecting, this shameless admission, and his disinterest in even pretending the admission pains him enrages her. She can feel the many years of anger roil through her, the sediment of loss and anguish and, yes, guilt dredge up from every crevice. "She killed herself," she spits. "She went back and hung herself from a beam in Rudraksh."

He pulls his hands away, and there is nothing manufactured about the motion.

"No."

"Yes," she says, remembering the phone call. Six months later, settled at her father's and finally able to call and hope they would let her talk to Jaishri, Simrin had been transferred from Ruta to Lakshman and finally to Jyoti, who told her, clicked her tongue and said, "Oh, honey, you didn't know?"

Jaishri left no note, said nothing to anyone, just slipped out one night and hung herself with the dirty bedsheets from her laundry duty. "She's released," Jyoti said on the phone. "*Mrityorma amnitam gamaya,*" she said. "*Om Shanti, Shanti, Shanti, Om.*" The words made Simrin's stomach seize, and she retched, nothing coming up, over her father's kitchen floor. Now, those same words reverberate in Simrin's head: "*Om Shanti, Shanti, Shanti, Om.*" Peace. Peace. Peace. But this, this is the opposite of peace. This is pain, and she refuses to spin the wheel.

"You sent her back, and she killed herself."

He is shaking his head no.

"She worshiped you," she says. "*I* worshiped you. And you betrayed us because you couldn't 'handle' us." And when she says it, she can see that this has struck him far deeper than anything she has said before, and she refuses to let up. "You think you're something special. The hero, the great protector. But you're not. You betrayed us, you betrayed your wife, and now you're betraying your own children."

"Put the fucking pictures up." He strikes, grips her wrist and yanks, and she cries out. And then her tears come quickly, spilling over her cheeks and down her chin, and he holds her tight, but she can hear the tremor when he speaks.

"Please," he says. "Please don't make me hurt you."

But he already has. Her wrist is throbbing. Still, it is only an irritation, nothing compared to the fracture inside her, the slicing of all the ties between them.

It is her left wrist, and so with the right, she takes the mouse and does as he says, transferring, then uploading, even the last one, Bethany's child for all the world to see.

"And one more thing," he says. "You need to upload something else."

"What?"

"Something I wrote."

She doesn't care anymore. At one time she thought she would have fought anyone who tried to sabotage her work, but now, all she wants is Quinn. All she wants is the two of them together and gone. He directs her to a folder, then a document, then a file titled, simply, "Meadowlark." She copies and pastes and tries to let the words blur into a fuzzy shadow. She doesn't want to know what he's written, how he plans to devastate Bethany, what his absurd reasoning is for bringing down this chaos onto all of them.

"Post it," he says. "Social media too." And she does, and the pages refresh, loading slowly like presents leisurely unwrapping for him. He stares at the screen, and she watches his eyes flick across the text, each sentence giving him back some of the strength she has drained. She looks down at her lap. Her wrist is starting to swell where his hand has been, and she stares at the thick red marks circling her arm like a cuff.

"I want my daughter," she says.

She refuses to look at him, but she can feel his eyes on her. He waits a moment, then pulls his phone from his pocket. She can hear the phone ring, then connect.

"Bring Quinn to the front gate in ten minutes," he says.

BETHANY

She knows she needs clothes and the kids' birth certificates, but what else? Her mind is racing, and she is afraid she is forgetting something important, but what is more important than just getting the four of them out?

She looks out the window. The yard is empty, except David, pacing at the front gate. She is supposed to meet Simrin at Rudraksh, the only point at Meadowlark where it is possible to see everything—the gate, the houses, the yard. From there they can leave together. If she isn't there yet, she will be. Bethany is sure of it, but perhaps this is more magical thinking—binding herself to a woman she doesn't know simply because Simrin, too, is a mother; simply because Simrin, too, was betrayed; simply because Simrin, too, once lost everything. Bethany has been given no reason to trust this woman, this "sister" who was bent and shaped as Aaron was. Or rather, Arjun. That was his name, and when he first told her, it seemed so exotic, the way the softness of the *r* bled into the severity of the *j*, that she rolled it around her mouth like a candy, tasting the possibility of his childhood. She said it—"Arjun, Arjun"—until he scowled and said, "That name is cursed." And then she felt horrible, understood the pain of a name given in a life you hated. But later, when she actually read the *Mahabharata*, struggled through it just to know him better, and then read the *Vayu Purana*, where Arjun also appears, she understood that he truly meant it. In the *Vayu Purana*, Apava the sage curses Arjun, saying whoever holds his name will never be king and always the servant of others. It was such a tiny part of the vast collection of literature about her Arjun's namesake that she laughed, then thought it endearing that of all the great mythological things Arjun had done, this tiny curse was the one Aaron held on to. But thinking about it now, it seems far more insidious.

She tugs a flat sheet from the tangle of bedcovers, spreads it on the floor, and throws clothes into the center. Everything is always a mess at Meadowlark, but now it seems even more so, and after trying to find three pants, three shirts, and three sets of underwear for each of them, she gives up and just throws things onto the sheet. Clothes, plus Blaze's dolls and multiple lovies, River's stuffed animals and rock collection, and what of Juniper's? Juniper seems to have outgrown herself overnight, and Bethany isn't even sure what she prizes anymore. She grabs Juniper's penny collection and her journals. Is that enough? She looks at the almost-empty cubbies and feels the sharp tug in her chest, a building pain for her uncertain girl. Or for herself? Jesus. She is starting to unravel, mixing herself in with Juniper like some kind of optical illusion—from this angle she's a crone! From this, a young girl! She shakes her head again, then grabs the dictionary in Juniper's cubby and throws it on the pile.

There is a box in the closet, a plastic storage thing where she has carefully packed each of her babies' tiny hats, their first drawings, a baby curl, a lost tooth. It is too big to carry, but there is something at the bottom she needs. She has hidden it here because she knows how unsentimental Aaron is. "Why do I need souvenirs?" he says. "I have the real things right here." He has this idea that the infant stays in the person, as does the baby, the toddler, the child—a Russian nesting doll of a person. "We all have access to these parts," he says, "but the world forces us to forget." But Larks! Larks can be taught to keep these selves near the surface, access them when needed. He often asks the girls to tell him about their births, as if they can do more than just mimic the details they have been told. Bethany finds it charming, how love drunk he can get as they "remember" their newborn selves. But this, too, is intentional delusion, not his but hers. To see the charm but not the danger. To think that his form of magical thinking is any less poisonous than her mother's. And what kind of fairy-tale cognitive dissonance did she have to indulge in to ignore the other "less conventional" theories?

"Less conventional," that's what she's told herself, what she explained when Star confided that there were ideas being explored that concerned her. Healing through thought? Just a "less conventional" way to say they were teaching the children to think positively. Calling on the oncoming? Another "less conventional" way to say they were helping the children be mindful of their intuition. But the truth is she has kneaded these theories like dough, plaited them into neat little braids rather than see how they were expanding, dangerously, around her. And why? Because she loves Aaron. Because she loves Meadowlark. Because where else could she go that didn't involve any risk of discovery. Jesus. It is nauseating to think about, but she won't ignore the truth just because it incriminates her. She is terrified of being discovered first; she is terrified of her children being discovered second. There it is. And what if he's right? That she is selfishly putting herself before the children? Then he'll have to be right. She can't allow herself to be found, and she can't allow him to decide this.

No. No more relying on Aaron's assurances or taking faith in his supposed devotion to her as evidence that everything will turn out peachy keen. If the best predictor of the future is the past, then Bethany has been an idiot to imagine her future had the potential to be some idyllic wonderland.

She pulls the box from the back of the closet, carefully digs her hands to the bottom, and finds Juniper's receiving blanket, the one that wraps and conceals the passbook. Banks rarely use these anymore, and the teller laughed when she was there last, telling her he'd only ever seen one of these and that one belonged to his grandmother. But Bethany wants nothing online. No email accounts, no photo storing, no social media, and no online banking. She unwraps the book and tucks it in the front of her jeans. If she has to, she can leave with nothing but the children, her ID, and the $234,876.34 the passbook proves is hers. $234,876.34 collected over nine years, each year feeling like a criminal, constructing some lie about silent meditation in the desert and instead going first to a post office box in Layton for the residual checks and then to the bank in Clearfield.

She finds the manila envelope with all their important papers on a shelf in the closet. She pulls out the homeschooling paperwork, their "marriage certificate." It isn't legal. She wanted nothing official, but as a joke, Aaron hacked into the county clerk's office and downloaded the template, filled in their names, and added Juniper, whom Bethany was pregnant with, as a witness. Juniper had kicked when he showed Bethany, and they had both seen it as some auspicious sign that even the baby knew they should be forever together. Now, she feels a wave of disgust at her own willful ignorance. She thinks about ripping up the certificate, then decides she won't give him a keepsake of her anger and drops it to the ground. She pulls out the birth certificates, the baby footprints, the deed to Meadowlark. It carries only Aaron's signature, for obvious reasons, but now all his decisions seem suspect.

She throws the birth certificates into the center of the pile, ties the corners of the sheet together, and wrenches it tightly so the bundle is manageable. It is heavy, but after it is hoisted over one shoulder, she can hold the ends with one arm and leave the other to carry Blaze. He is with Jennifer, and River is in the art room. They will be easy to find, but Juniper could be any number of places. Juniper runs, just like her mother, and the thought makes her heart clench. She wishes they had told the kids they had to stay inside until all this was over, but Candice thought that was putting the cart before the horse, and Dan argued they were ceding control to the state if they stopped living their lives exactly as they had before the cops came.

She would rather take the rear stairs, avoid the questions and subsequent shock, but usually Jennifer sets the babies up in the community room, so she makes her way to the front stairs and sees the crowd. Something is going on. She takes the stairs quickly and scans the room for Jennifer. Everyone seems to be here. The room is dense with people, and she wants to stop and ask someone what is happening, but she knows if she does, it will be harder to start again. Her heart is beating hard, and she tries to think about the parasympathetic nervous system and stay moving. She scans the room for Jennifer, but Dana stops her.

"It's all my fault," Dana says. "I'm trying not to say it in front of Marley, but I just keep thinking if it hadn't been for me, the cops wouldn't have come, and then we wouldn't be here."

"They're trying to get in?" Bethany asks.

"Yes. Aaron says they'll leave, but what if they don't? What if they come in?" And then Candice is there.

"What's that?" Candice points at the sheet.

"Where's Jennifer?" Bethany asks.

"She took the babies into the hall," Dana says.

"I need to go." Something has definitely happened since she has been upstairs. She needs Blaze. Then River. Then Juniper. It is like picking up pennies from the bottom of the pool—dive and grab. She repeats their names in her head—Blaze, River, Juniper—and swims.

JUNIPER

She runs hard to Hawthorne. She swipes the key and unlocks the door, but before she tucks herself behind the rain barrels to not just secret herself but hide, she takes a quick look behind her. She scans the yard to make sure no one has seen her, and then she sees Rudraksh. She has seen it every day, many times a day, since it was completed when she was six, but now she really sees it, not just the shady overhang where they sleep sometimes in the summer or the expanse of concrete floor they draw chalk pictures on. She sees what she only sort of saw before—the hiding spots, an entire crawl space of secret storage. This is where her father got the gun, where the other guns were probably hidden. Who knows how long they've been hidden, lying and waiting, neither here nor there, invisible, while Meadowlark swirled up around them? And who knew they were there? Obviously her father. Definitely Gavin. Probably David. Her mother? Maybe. But probably not. She didn't even know about the photographs of her own daughter. She can feel the burn in her chest, the embarrassment of her mother's not knowing. And then her own embarrassment for not knowing. About many things. But right now about Rudraksh. How could she have missed such an important hiding spot? How could she have been oblivious to what lay directly under her feet as she ran around playing super tag and making up dumb dances? It is too painful to stand. She needs to see what she's missed, own that information for herself.

The only person outside, besides her, is David. And his gun. He's still pacing at the front gate. Back and forth, back and forth. But he's looking down at his feet, watching the dusty path he's worn into the dirt. If she sneaks to the bottom of the stairs, then runs when he pivots away from her, she can make it to Rudraksh without him seeing her. She waits, balancing on the balls of her feet like a cat, the sting of her ignorance making her brave.

And then she sprints—eight, ten, twelve strides—and then she is there, crouching next to Rudraksh, running her hands along the exterior lower wall, feeling for an opening. And then she finds it, a panel that is set into the wood. She pushes the sides, the bottom, and finally the top. She presses hard, and the bottom of the panel comes up, but she isn't tall enough to open it all the way, isn't strong enough to get enough leverage, and she needs to shove her foot between the ground and the edge of the panel to keep it from closing. She is barefoot, and it is heavier than she thought. It digs into her foot, and she knows it will leave a bruise, but she manages to get her fingernails, then fingertips underneath and lift it enough so that she can crawl in. The panel bangs her calves, hard, on the way down, and she wants to cry out, but she grits her teeth and tries to be thankful the door didn't slam behind her.

She sits up and looks around. It is incredibly hot down here and surprisingly dark, and she has to blink a bunch of times and wait and wait until her eyes adjust. But slowly, she can see. It's a pretty big space, and she thinks it must span the whole length and width of Rudraksh. She stands up and reaches up, but there's still a good foot of headspace between her fingertips and what she assumes is Rudraksh's floor. All those nights spent asleep on top of a whole secret room she didn't even know was there. She kicks her foot into the dirt floor and searches for what else has been hidden from her—a few tall bookcases at one end, a heap of cardboard boxes at another, and then two tall metal cabinets, part closet, part safe.

She walks to the closest one. It's closed, so she tests the handle, but it doesn't turn. There is a keypad, and she presses random numbers. Each glows with her touch, but the handle stays stuck, so she tries the second cabinet. This one has double doors, and one of the doors looks open. She creeps closer and pulls at the door. It is heavy, like steel heavy, but it opens, and now she is standing right in front of a gun rack—two long guns and two short guns staring back at her. She can't believe that there are at least seven guns at Meadowlark, and she never even knew. For someone who prides herself on collecting information, this is a really depressing realization. A whole secret room and seven guns that she was completely oblivious to. It is humiliating. More humiliating than when her father finds a quiet space under the old sycamore tree and asks her to sense the cards he holds up to her forehead. "Eight?" she guesses. "Three? A king?" And then when he decides he will make it simpler, ask just the color, she tries, "Red? Black? Red?" Once she didn't guess even a single one right, and her father accused her of intentionally guessing wrong. "It's statistically almost impossible to get fifty-two out of fifty-two wrong," he said. She had felt the shame blossom in her chest and flower up into her throat until, despite telling herself she would not cry, her chin had shaken and the tears had fallen, and her father had pulled her into him and rocked her side to side, telling her it was fine, she had other talents, she would find her magic. But she had felt the stiffness in his arms, the too-high pitch of his voice, and she had known that she was pathetic. But now, the memory of his lie burns in her head, his denial of the search warrant scorching her as savagely as if he used a hot iron, and the pain of it turns her shame to anger. If he can lie so easily about the police, who have guns and are going to come inside their home, then what else has he lied about? She can feel the anger blossom through her, her skin vibrating with fury.

"Fuck," she says. But it doesn't work.

So she takes a gun. She chooses one of the small ones and pulls it from the rack, and when she does, she feels the weight of what she is doing alongside the weight of the gun. There is danger everywhere, and everything is a lie.

And then she is moving again, holding the gun in one hand, using the other to push the panel up an inch and wait for David to pivot away from her, and then she shimmies, then sprints, eight, ten, twelve strides back to Hawthorne, where she climbs the stairs, shuts the door behind her, and sinks down behind a rain barrel.

She's breathing hard, sweat dripping from her face, and she wipes the back of her arm across her forehead and then sucks on the skin. She examines the gun carefully. She knows guns are dangerous, so she keeps her finger off what she's pretty sure is the trigger, keeps her distance from where she assumes the bullet comes out. If it even has a bullet. She knows guns have to be loaded, and she has no idea if this one is. She turns it in her hands, braves a look into the cylinder, where the bullet comes out, and then she feels the fear rising.

A bullet could shoot straight out of this space and straight into her head, and then she would be dead. She knows dead—obviously—has found dead birds on the perimeter of Meadowlark, saw Marsha's bloody dead newt baby, but for the first time the idea that you could exist one moment and then not exist the next floods her. The truth of this surprises her, but what surprises her more is that it makes her more angry than scared. People out there want to shoot her and her family. They want to make River and Blaze dead; they want to kill her mother. Thinking of her mother dead is excruciating, like her heart is opening up and turning inside out, a pair of bloody socks, and she has to push the fist that's not holding the gun into her chest, think about the whatever-it's-called nervous system, but it's hard when it is not her mother saying it, when it's not her mother doing the pressing.

She tries to think less about the dead people and more about the people who want them dead. This is what strong and resilient people do, she tells herself. And what else do they do? Assess potential hazards and secure protections. This is from Crow Seekers. The crows scan for danger, and the Rolen protect the tribe. Sammi is always wanting to pretend she's a crow and Juniper a Rolen, but Juniper is the one who is good at watching for danger. It is Juniper who knew this was not a brouhaha long before anyone else did. Everyone except her mother.

The thought of her mother makes her chest tight. She loves her mother, loves her so viscerally she can barely feel what it means to love her unless she thinks about not loving her, and yet she recognizes that this is not completely true, that there is something stiff knit into the weave of her love. It is tight and hard to stretch, and she wonders if it has to do with what her father said about who her mother is. What if her mother isn't really her mother? But no. That's impossible. Everyone says they look exactly alike, and she knows about genetics, knows that wouldn't be possible if her mother wasn't actually her mother. If this were a normal day, she would be back there pestering her parents about what her father meant. "We don't hide things at Meadowlark!" she'd announce. But today isn't a normal day, and instead, she's sitting here, holding a gun, and trying to figure out when that pokey feeling with her mother first started. It might have been when she saw Marsha's newt baby. Or it might have been when her father started TMF. She was maybe eight. It's hard to remember exactly, but she does remember it was winter. There were a bunch of them in the Bodhi common room—Sammi, and Devon and Micah, and River, and probably some other kids—trying to fill a pillowcase with cut-up pieces of white paper. It was her father and Kara, and maybe Mary? They had taught them a game—Touch-Mirror-Feel they called it then, and now, just TMF. "Turn around," her father had said, "and tell me which part of my body I'm touching."

"Hand! Head! Butt!" they had shouted, but Kara had sat them all down, had them breathe and breathe and breathe, and then her father had told them to imagine his body was their body.

"Feel where I'm touching you," he said.

And Juniper had tried. She closed her eyes and imagined her father's huge arms outlined over her arms, his head a halo over hers, and she had felt it! He was touching his chin; *her* chin! She could feel the warmth of his palm cradling her face, and she had shouted it out, amazed at herself, then turned around to see him with his hand on his knee.

"Try again, Junie," he said. "You just need to settle yourself. You just need to practice."

So she had tried. Elbow. Nose. Ear. She had felt each one, and she had been wrong each time. More wrong than Devon, or Sammi, or even River, not because she had guessed less right but because Meadowlark had been built for her and she was failing it. The failure had sunk deep in her stomach, but along with it, the twitch of doubt. How could she feel someone else's body when even the grown-ups couldn't do it, and hadn't they been practicing their whole lives? And it was at that moment that she had looked up and seen her mother on the stairs, her mother's hand gripping the railing, her face a confusing mix of something. She knows it's impossible, Juniper had thought; she'll come down and tell them to stop being ridiculous. But the moment her mother had seen Juniper watching, she had turned and gone back upstairs as quietly as she had begun to come down. And Juniper had felt the hard poke of something stiff work through her.

But there have been other times. She remembers now, a wash of moments coming back to her: her mother suddenly absent whenever her father leads them in exercises to call on the oncoming; the pinched look she gets when Candice encourages the kids to play with all dimensions of their feelings. Every time her mother leaves, a tiny splinter forms between them. Every time her mother grimaces, one more slivered thread. If lying cuts the strands that join them, what stiffens them? Lying but not lying? Seeing but not seeing? Is this what her mother has done? It is a horrible thought, to think of how much time Juniper has spent trying to figure out if what people *say* is real is real, or if there's actually a *real* real, or if one makes the other, when her mother has known what is real all along but just not said. But this is impossible. Her mother built Meadowlark right alongside her father to grow "children who know their truth." This is what is posted near the front door of every house, written in her mother's own writing! "Listen to your head," her mother tells her; "listen to your heart." But her head and her heart just chatter; they bounce truth around like a Super Ball, a blur of red neither can catch. Her father lied about the search warrant. He lied about the pictures. Therefore, he is a liar. Her mother may have lied to her about who she is, and she may have known her father is a liar. Therefore, is she a liar? But her father lied to her mother too. But she is a grown-up! If a grown-up can't even know the truth, how the *fuck* is she supposed to? And this is what tips her from the murk of scared-angry-confused to outrage.

She wants away from all these grown-ups. She needs to assess potential hazards and secure protections. She crawls across Hawthorne's roof, scraping her bare knees, and hides behind the third rain barrel, right next to the drain that is missing a pipe. If she lies down flat on the roof and puts her eye to the hole, she can scan all of Meadowlark and beyond. The gun is awkward to crawl with, but it's doable, and when she gets there, she realizes the hole is bigger than she remembered. She can actually see out of it with both her eyes. The front yard is still quiet, still only David, but now he is standing motionless, his back against the gate, pointy gun hidden behind his body. But she can also see over the gate. There are still police, but the people without uniforms are gone, and the ones in uniform have all moved back. Before, they were so close she could see the dust on the policewoman's shoes, but now they're almost at the driveway, and there are more of them. And there are also more vehicles, four jeep-looking things and a small truck. She's too far away to see what anyone is doing, but for sure no one is walking up to the gate. David could stop his pacing already.

She lies there for a few minutes, watching, but nothing changes, so she creeps along the wall, examining all the other drains. Each one has a firmly attached drainpipe except the far right one on the back wall. That one is loose, and she wiggles it slightly, then wipes her hands on her shorts, and is about to wiggle it again when it falls. It bangs against the building, and she freezes. But everyone is in Bodhi. The yard is still empty except for David and his gun. She doesn't move, tries to quiet her breathing just in case, waits for one alligator, two alligator, ten alligators, and is about to exhale a big sigh when Gavin is there. It's as if he has read her mind and beamed himself here, he's appeared so instantly below her.

He looks at the drain, and she can see him in telescopic detail—the rip in the left front brim of his baseball cap, the thick black hairs on the back of his neck, the gun—the same as hers—snug in his hand. He kicks at the drain and then looks up. He is staring directly at her, the place where the drain was, and she can feel his eyes like icy claws. They dig into her until her brain feels like it is racing and jumping inside the cold, dead thing of her body. She thinks he will take the stairs, find the door unlocked, and then stand above her frozen body and shoot her. But he just fiddles with his baseball cap. He looks down at the drain again. Then he looks up. He scans the whole of the building. And then he leaves.

She can't hear where he has gone, and she wants to crawl to the other open drain, but she's not sure she could even get her hands and feet to work, and she's terrified he will hear her scrabbling across the roof like a giant rat. Or a mouse. That's what she feels like, a tiny squishable mouse. Once they found a mouse in a cereal box. River slammed a plate down on the bowl it had landed in, and Juniper piled books on top. They ran to get their mother, but when they came back, it was gone, escaped out of the quarter-inch space between plate and bowl. Squishable, yes, but maybe that is okay. A mouse can squish through a hole, squish through a gate.

Hawthorne is the house closest to the back fence. She scans it, looking for holes or maybe secret panels like the one in Rudraksh, but she sees nothing, just long stretches of dirty wood covered in chalk drawings and mud and fairy staircases. Maybe she could climb the fence, but no, it's too tall. She'd need a ladder, which she could get from the shed if no one was watching, but Gavin is there, and David, and there will probably be others soon. And then, as if it's one of those crazy optical illusions in that *National Geographic* book they have, she sees the men. They're invisible, and then they are there. One, two, three, four, five, six, seven, eight, nine—lying on the ground and spread evenly beyond their fence. They are all in black with round black helmets and big black sunglasses, and they have giant black guns. And she is the only fucking one who knows. Her heart speeds up. It is pounding in her chest and her throat and her head.

She wishes River were with her. She is only seven, but at the moment, everyone older than seven, including Juniper herself, seems to be losing their minds. It's not that River would know what to do, but she would do something, not just watch her breath come faster and faster until her heart explodes before anyone has a chance to shoot her. But still, that something would probably be standing up and shouting at the men, asking them what they are doing and if they are hot and why they don't just go back into the shade if they're just lying around waiting. And then she would show them her Purple Land necklace.

Obviously, it's not going to help to imagine what River would do, but it's calming to realize she knows her sister so well, unlike her father or her mother or any of the other grown-ups. Maybe her father is right, and the kids are the ones with all the power. Or should be. But then, River's idea of power would be claiming she needs to consult with the people of Purple Land, who live on the other side of the fence in Mr. Turner's yard.

If she squints, Juniper can see that section of the fence. It looks fastened now, but she's pretty sure the plastic is just set against the hole. Beyond there, she can see over the fence into Mr. Turner's yard. There's the chicken coop, and some abandoned vegetable beds, a couple lawn mowers and lots of wood, and a bunch of really tall trees that make a sort of zigzag pattern at the back of the property. She's pretty sure there are no men with guns back there. She makes her eyes watch each tree for a count of ten, scanning for black helmets, and then she does it once more, just in case, but the yard is empty. Even the chickens are hiding in the coop. But there's no way to get down to the hatch anyway. She'd break her legs if she jumped over the side, and there's no way she's going down those stairs with Gavin nearby.

So she waits, brings the gun up close to her chin, watches the men with the big black sunglasses, thinks about River, and listens for what's going to happen next.

SIMRIN

They take the front stairs this time, descending into the room full of people and chatter. She knows she will never be back here, and she looks hard at everything, trying to absorb it so she can make some kind of sense of this place later. There are mothers and fathers and kids, families that would fit in seamlessly at Quinn's preschool. She thought Star was funny and smart, someone she could easily be friends with, and Star gave her tips on good kids to take pictures of (the adorable boy with the missing front teeth, the one girl who could do a handstand) and steered her away from certain adults (that man who blocked her at the front door, some woman named Candice). Simrin didn't ask why, but now she wishes she had. She wants the full picture, wants to understand where Arjun stands in the frame. Now it is too late, and Simrin will have to piece together the story to tell herself. And it won't be accurate. That is what happens when someone gives you only what they want to.

She follows a length behind Arjun, her left wrist pulsing, a reminder of what he can do if he wants. All the frames of their childhood are methodically splicing together so what she sees now are not the individual snapshots—the troll doll he stole as a birthday gift for Jaishri, the white of his skull after he shaved his head in protest against their high school dress code, his two-day fast when the children were required to do only one day. No, not the snapshots but the film of their youth, a narrative of a boy desperate for everyone to make him special.

Simrin watches as Arjun calmly assures people, squeezing hands and telling everyone just to hold tight. There are a number of people who rush to talk to him, and it is easy to put herself back in time—Simrin trailing behind the golden boy. They move slowly toward the front door.

The man who stopped her before is gone now, and Arjun gives final assurances that everything is going to be just fine and just to stay put while he checks on a few things outside. She follows him out, suddenly uncomfortable alone with him again, and focuses on her feet, the layer of silt covering her sandals. It is eerily quiet, and she realizes that the sounds of the police scanners are gone. Have they really left? That's impossible. She read the comments this morning, saw the media presence rising. She wonders if the blog has been noticed yet. It doesn't take more than fifteen minutes for something to go viral. All Arjun cannot have in real life is possible on the World Wide Web, at least until the next viral sensation. Poor Arjun, only days away from being upstaged by a skateboarding cat. Or, if she is honest, upstaged by her. Whatever he has written, whatever manifesto he has made her post, will have to be dealt with. She will have to write some explanation, which she never does, preferring the ambiguity of photographs. You can frame and direct all you want, but what is finally left is the viewers and their own filters of meaning. Words are so much more directed, managing the reader like some kind of baby nurse. But she will have to explain this time—the hijacking of the blog, what it was like inside the compound. Every minute she is inside, his story grows. Every minute she is out, it shifts to her. And probably to Quinn, the real innocent.

Simrin has no idea what is happening beyond the compound, but if the story is growing like she thinks it will, Quinn will be part of it, forever caught in the narrative of those crazies at Meadowlark. And the ironic part is that Quinn *is* their Lark. Simrin doubts any of these kids are synesthetes, never mind the more-impossible talents Arjun seems to be convinced are hidden within these children. Simrin wouldn't wish those "gifts" on any of these kids. She already carries the ache of the snags that lie ahead of her exceptional kid. In ten minutes they will be out. In eleven hours they will be home. In seven days Quinn will walk into a world where she is the weird one.

They stand for a minute on the porch, and she can see the compound spread out before them. That horrible Rudraksh at the center, now surely as sickening a reminder for him as it is for her. How did Jaishri climb those giant supports?

Once, Simrin had hauled the camera up there, but she was too scared to use both hands to take the pictures, so Arjun had climbed after her and wrapped his legs around the beam, shot the landscape beyond Ananda. The next day he paid the extra money for one-hour developing and stood there until the Fotomat girl handed him the envelope. He refused to let Simrin look at the pictures, but she read the disappointment on his face before he ripped them to pieces. Jaishri had tried to save the scraps, later taped them together and tried to convince him they were wonderful, but Simrin secretly gloated—the perfect boy couldn't do everything perfectly. But now she sees his tantrum for what it was, the budding rage when the facts betrayed his vision of himself. But also, another uncomfortable truth: how hard Jaishri worked to keep him on his pedestal. Was that what Simrin did? Probably. Still, there was something untethered about Jaishri. Ananda worked them hard, forcing detachment from the self like daily medicine, but Simrin somehow always held tight. Once, a journalist asked her what drew her to photography. "It's proof," she said. "That what you're shooting really happened?" the journalist asked. "No," she said, "that I was there."

She spent her life proving this, working to be seen. But Jaishri. Jaishri was always in danger of disappearing, a tiny wisp of a girl. And Arjun offered proof that she existed, his reflection a cloak of visibility. Without it, she was invisible. Or at least felt invisible. Why else would she have picked Rudraksh? There were a million places with less possibility of failure. Why not Ambar? Or the stairwell in Vaayu, or even one of the bathrooms with their industrial showers? Rudraksh was an intentional choice. Only an invisible girl would climb up there by herself with a sheet and probably a ladder. Except Jaishri had it wrong. No one saw her, not because she was invisible. No one saw her because no one was looking. Tiny, cautious little Jaishri, their sheltered little sister. How horrible to go back to a place where no one noticed you gone. How horrible to feel that was the only place you belonged.

Now, they stop at the bottom of the house steps, and Arjun looks around the yard. There is a man at the front, his back to the gate. The rest of the landscape is empty.

"Wait," Arjun says. He listens for a moment, then unpockets his phone, swipes, and puts the phone to his ear. He holds it there, then palms it again, swipes. Holds it, palms, swipes.

"Shit," he says.

"What?"

He says nothing. He looks to the left, sees nothing, and then whistles—strong and loud—to the man at the gate. The man stands up straight, and Arjun holds his phone above his head and shakes it. Simrin can't see clearly, but the man seems to reach for something in his pocket, and Arjun stares at his phone. Nothing. He waits, and when nothing happens, he swears again.

"What?" she says again.

"They turned off the phones."

"Who?"

"The cops."

"What?" She has been at other standoffs—two, actually. One when the cops surrounded a man who was waving a machete, keeping his family hostage inside his apartment. The man was high, and it took the police two hours to talk him out. They didn't cut the phone lines then, used cell service to make sure the little girls were okay, to assure him they wouldn't shoot. The fact that she had been there at all was a total accident. The man lived on their street, and Quinn was with Tom.

Simrin had stood across the street and tried to shoot with a telephoto through his window. The other time was a bank robbery. She never would have been allowed anywhere near that one, but a friend of a friend had a police-issued press pass and brought her with him. She knew he only wanted to date her, but the opportunity was too good to pass up, and so she left Quinn with a neighbor and went. And got great shots. That time SWAT was called in. They droned in a phone and communicated that way. Maybe that is what is happening now. She looks around for a drone, for any sign of police presence. Jesus. If that is happening, things have intensified quickly.

How many minutes have gone by since Arjun called for Quinn? How many minutes does she have before SWAT establishes a line of control and that line becomes impenetrable?

"Where is Quinn?" she says, but he isn't listening. Instead he is looking around the yard for someone or something. He hadn't expected this, and Simrin feels a wave of nausea, the realization that not only has she completely ceded control but that she has no idea to whom.

He runs his hands through his hair, scans the yard again. And then he freezes. And Simrin turns. And she sees what he sees. Bethany is heading out a side door, walking quickly past the house next door and toward Rudraksh, their baby on one shoulder, a tied-up bedsheet on the other.

Oh God, she thinks, and when she realizes she has said it out loud, she turns quickly away from him, tries to bolt out of reach, but in one quick movement, he grabs her arm.

"Quinn!" she screams.

"Don't."

"Quinn," she yells again. He pulls her close to him, and she can see it all come together for him—Bethany and the children gone, Simrin stealing everything he has. And then she hears the horrible expulsion of breath, his raw grunt of rage, and sees his face in hers ready to spit or strike.

"Quinn," she tries again, but now it seems a plea, just something to speak between them. He says nothing, but she can see the rage mutate when she speaks Quinn's name, the reflection of her own fear and desperation hovering on his face.

"Let us go," she says, and how can the irony not stab at him? Her abandoning him, him clutching at her. "Please," she says. "Let us go."

"You're trying to steal my children, Sim."

She shakes her head. "No."

"I'm not gonna give you yours." The words are unbearable, but his face softens, as if this is a kindness. "Quinn's perfectly safe where she is," he says.

"No."

"And I need to make sure my children are safe."

"Please," she begs.

"I need to make sure all the children are safe."

"Quinn!" she screams. He grabs her by both arms, and for a moment, she thinks he will shake her like a doll, but instead, he brings her in close enough that she can smell his breath, the stale coffee and simmering rage.

"She's safe," he says. "But she doesn't have to be."

She stiffens under his hands, and he turns her toward the gate. "That's David. He has two guns." He turns her around. "And under that house is the art room. Quinn is there. So is River. And so is Gavin. Gavin also has a gun. Do you understand what I'm trying to say?" He readjusts the grip on her arms, and she feels all strength drain from her body.

"Do you?" he says.

She closes her eyes and nods. He takes a slow breath, and she feels his hands soften on her arms and then his fingers gently holding her face. She opens her eyes and grits her teeth to keep from crying.

"I created a place where children are extraordinarily powerful, and I need to keep it safe. I need to keep them safe. Do you understand?" His eyes are huge, a giant green swamp of delusion. She makes her head nod, and he pulls her to him. "Simrin," he says. She feels his arms around her, and with her name, she sees those damn copper streamers. "Just wait."

BETHANY

She finds Blaze asleep on Jennifer's lap in the quiet of the hall and manages to get him settled on her free shoulder without waking him. He is her only deep sleeper, and she knows as long as there are no loud noises, he will stay asleep despite the jostling and shifting.

"What are you doing?" Jennifer asks.

Bethany doesn't want to answer, but here she is with a sheet full of stuff and desperately in need of help. "I have to go," she says.

"Where?"

"Do you know where the girls are?"

"No, but what's going on?"

River is probably still in the art room. If she goes through the laundry room and out the side door, she can go past Hawthorne to Cedar, get River from the art room, and then find Juniper. *If* Bethany can find her. She wasn't able to yesterday, and the guilt of having let her disappear again today makes her jaw clench.

"I have to go," she says.

The sheet is heavy, but Blaze is heavier, and she has to constantly adjust the two of them to keep moving. There are a few people in the hallway, but she focuses on the laundry room ahead of her and walks through them. This will be the last time she walks down this hall, the last time she navigates around some child's cardboard box invention, the last time she looks away from the sharp wall corner River cut her forehead open on. She walks through the laundry room and out the side door and past the clothesline and stops in front of Hawthorne. Her arms are trembling from the weight of Blaze and the sheet, and she realizes she won't be able to find the girls without putting one, or both, of them down. She squints and tries to see if Simrin is waiting for her at Rudraksh. If so, she can hand Blaze over to her and go find the girls, but she doesn't see her, which doesn't mean she's not there. Simrin could easily be standing right around the curve. Bethany will have to circle the building and, if Simrin isn't there, wait for her to come before she goes looking for River and Juniper.

With the yard so empty, Rudraksh seems forever away, but she knows it is only two hundred feet, exactly the same distance between every house's front door. They built it symmetrical, a perfect semicircle of houses, a smile, a sun. She feels a lump rise in her throat, the desire to cry and the well-trained absence of tears. "You only cry on camera," her mother would say. "*That* kid has something to cry about." And she is right. Even this isn't worth crying over—the loss of the elaborate and hard-earned fiction of her life. This is what happens when you are made visible. This is what happens when you think you can disappear.

She is wearing her flip-flops, and she stops to kick a stone out from between her toes, and then she sees David. He is at the front gate, watching her, and she pauses and looks at him. She wants to put her finger to her mouth, to beg him not to say anything, but her arms are full, and all she can do is plead with her eyes. "Please," she mouths, but he isn't looking at her. Instead, he is looking over her shoulder, his eyes intently focusing, his mouth open, and then closed, and then open again, and then she hears Simrin scream.

She turns back to Bodhi and sees them, hears the next scream, but then Blaze lets out a cry, and Bethany turns her back, drops the sheet, and wraps her other arm around Blaze. She tries to soothe him. "Shh shh shh," she says, rocking, rocking back and forth. Please don't wake up, she begs. Please. And he doesn't. He quiets, still asleep, his baby mouth sucking at nothing. She tries to pick the sheet up again, but Blaze is awkward on her shoulder, and she thinks she might drop him if she bends down, and besides, where can she go with only one child? How will she get there with no one to help her? So she turns and stands, like a woman tied to the train tracks, no Technicolor angel coming to rescue her, and watches Aaron and Simrin walk toward her.

They walk slowly, and she watches him take in the sheet filled with his children's things, his son on her shoulder. It is obvious she is leaving, and his hold on Simrin means he understands who they are leaving with. She has never seen him lay his hands on anyone, but here he is gripping Simrin. It makes Bethany's breath quicken, and again she doubts her own judgment. But that isn't exactly true. Her judgments have been right, just inconvenient. Once, when River was only a few months old, she thought about leaving. It was silly, a postpartum hormonal breakdown over toothpaste. She didn't want Juniper using a fluoride toothpaste; he did. But she worked herself up until she could visualize the long list of things he was doing to harm their children. If she didn't leave now, she told herself, they would be irrevocably damaged. So she sat him down and told him she was leaving, and in typical Aaron fashion, he pulled her to him and told her they would use whatever toothpaste she wanted. But he also said something else, held her tightly and said, "I'd never let you leave me." It was sweet, just like the mama bunny says to the baby bunny in the book, but she had the same visceral association she had to those long-ago furious words: "You threaten my authority, I threaten your life." And now, here she is threatening Aaron's authority, just like in that movie. That woman didn't listen to her intuition, and that woman got burned. But if Bethany's intuition told her anything, it was to stay, to love this man, to give him everything. And yet not everything. She can feel the passbook in the waist of her jeans, sticky and tight against her belly. She planned for this—bathed babies and built compost bins and hashed out community philosophies—all the while, year after year, socking away money. Now she just needs to let the calm take over.

It is painful to watch them approach and just as painful when he stands in front of her, saying nothing. She knows the silence is intentional, this game of his, so she waits, clenching her jaw to keep from saying anything, focusing on detailing his reactions to crush her own fear: two blinks, one lip twitch. She always breaks their silences first, but what does she have to say to him now? Yes, we're leaving. No, there's no discussion. She tries not to see his grip on Simrin, how intentionally he is keeping her here, but Simrin's fear radiates from her, such a contrast to Aaron, how calm he looks, how confident in the face of their world falling apart. And finally, he speaks.

"Let's all go back inside," he says, and Bethany feels his words like a win.

"We're leaving," she says. She sees Simrin cringe, then sees the tears begin to pool in her eyes. Don't cry, she wants to say. This is not worth crying about.

"No one's leaving," Aaron says.

"Yes, we are," Bethany says.

"Beth."

"We're leaving." She modulates her voice, enunciates, calls on everything that was once so innate. "Simrin and I are going to get the children, and then we're leaving."

"If you need to go, go. But the children are staying." He knows this will anger her, the idea that she would ever abandon her children, and she snaps.

"I'm taking them, and we're going." She is louder than she means to be, and Blaze stirs.

"You will not steal my children," he says. He reaches for Blaze, and she takes a step back.

"Don't touch him," she spits.

He stands for a moment, taken aback. She has never spoken to him this way, the words infused with so much venom she can taste it pooling in her mouth.

"Do you have any idea what would happen if you posted . . . ," she says. She stumbles for the words. My identity? Our children's identity? Which is it, or does it even matter? He has already betrayed them, destroyed their world. What does it matter who would have been hurt worst by posting? She waits, can feel the power that comes with restraint, and then something thick and nauseating descends. She glances at Simrin, but she is staring at the ground, her shoulders heaving with each breath.

And then Aaron speaks. "Oh, Beth," he says. "I posted everything." He says it with such kindness, as if it is an act of mercy, that it takes her a moment to reconcile the words with his tone, but when she does, she feels them like a punch. Still, she already feels so beaten; what difference does one more punch make? She looks at Simrin. "You promised," she says, and it is such a stupid thing to say, as if this woman owes her anything.

Simrin shakes her head. "It's not like that," she says. The tears are falling now, and Bethany wants to shake her. You do not get to cry when you're an accomplice to someone else's unsecreting. You do not get to cry if it isn't your show.

She feels her body go heavy, her head light, feels the ringing in her ears. She takes a step back, stumbles, and Aaron is there to catch Blaze. There are spots in her eyes, spots on the ground. She puts her hands on her knees, lets her head hang, and sees the lens of the microscope descend on their lives, tightening, tightening, tightening until they are smashed between glass plates, forever specimens. And her children's childhood sold for advertising space.

She stares at Simrin's sandals, the sun glinting off the buckles, and hears Blaze cry.

"Mama," he cries. "Mamamamama." It is what he always says when he first wakes up, a repetition of *Ma*s strung together until the sleep has fully lifted, but now she hears it like a roar. She takes another step back, and then Aaron is beside her, his arm reaching around her back. She straightens, wanting to jerk away, but she feels unsteady on her feet.

"It doesn't have to be like this," he says. "Think about what you're doing. Remember what *we're* doing. This world that we created is worth fighting for. Our children are special, Beth. And we're helping them stay that way."

They are familiar words, the same ones he uses whenever she doubts their great experiment, but now she hears the *I* beneath the *we*.

"We created them," he says. "And we need to protect them." He turns her to face him, and Blaze reaches for her, but her arms still feel weightless.

"Think about Juniper," he says. "Remember how *she* ran out of preschool, how *she* told us how to parent her. Remember how *she* saw my voice, how *she* told us it looked like copper streamers."

And she does. At least the preschool part. Juniper first told Aaron about the streamers, how warm they felt, how bright they glinted. "Tell Mama," Aaron said. "Tell her about how you see my voice." And she had. "Like stretchy pennies," Juniper said.

"We created this place for them," Aaron says. "And now we need to fight for them."

I am fighting for them, she wants to say, but what does it matter? He doesn't care if she is fighting for them, as long as she doesn't put up resistance to his fight. This is not about you, she imagines him saying, and then she realizes this is what he has actually been saying. "This is not about you," he said the few times she expressed concern over what they were teaching the kids. "This is not about you," when she wanted to open the gates for the police. "This is not about you," he will say, when what he really means is, "This is about me." The pictures, her exposure, the confrontation, Meadowlark itself, all in service of her husband. The smoky lens she sees him through has been slowly clearing, but now it seems to disappear entirely, leaving her with the irrefutable truth that she has traded one huckster for another.

"Let's all go back inside," Aaron says.

She can feel the rage begin to bubble, the heat of it expanding her resolve. "No," she says. And then she screams it. "No." Every speck of strength she can cobble together pushing out that one tiny resistance. She screams it again. "No." And this time she can hear her echo, loud and clear from above, Juniper on the stairs shouting, "Stop," her baby, her daughter, her lark.

JUNIPER

Everything is still and quiet. The sun is superhot and beating down hard on her bare arms and legs because there is nothing to shade her on this roof. She is thinking about the men with the guns and wondering how they can stand wearing those long black sleeves and long black pants when she hears Simrin scream. Then there is silence. Then "Quinn!" It is a scared scream, a terrified scream, and Juniper scrabbles to the other side of the roof and finds the empty drain hole.

It takes her a minute to orient herself, to find Simrin, because she is right below her, standing with her mother and father. Her mother is holding Blaze, and she looks to see if her father still has the gun, but it's not there, and she feels a bolt of pleasure at the realization that she has something he doesn't. Then she remembers that her father gave his gun to David when he carried her halfway to Bodhi, and the pleasure sizzles away. That feels like years ago—when he carried her, when she felt that invisible current binding them together. Now even the memory of it makes her shrink in on herself. He was lying to her then, and she didn't even know it. How stupid of her. They've been taught never to call anyone stupid, particularly themselves, but now this seems just something else to doubt. She does feel stupid. And embarrassed. Because she didn't even know, because she is oblivious.

They are arguing below, but it's hard to hear what they're saying until her mother raises her voice. "Do you have any idea what would happen if you posted . . . ," she says, and then Juniper understands that at least some of this is about the pictures.

"Oh, Beth," her father says. "They're already posted."

Her mother's body shifts: the realization that she has been betrayed. Juniper knows it is horrible, but she can't help the small grin that escapes. Here is unmistakable evidence that her mother knows her father is a liar. And what about the other stuff, Juniper wants to say. Did he lie about everything? Find out, she wants to shout. But things are shifting so quickly beneath her. She sees her mother crumble. She sees her father catch her brother. She hears Blaze's familiar *Mamamama*, and then she hears her name.

"Think about Juniper," her father says. And then, "Remember how she ran out of preschool, how she told us how to parent her." Juniper has heard this story lots and lots of times. Daisy Preschool, running to Wren's house, et cetera, et cetera, et cetera. Everyone at Meadowlark knows this story along with the one about the copper streamers, which is, as expected, what he says next: "Remember how she saw my voice, how she told us it looked like copper streamers." Juniper hates this story, has hated it since before she can remember. She hates the way it makes her stomach bob, hates what always comes next—the reminder that Meadowlark was built for her, because of her. And she's sick of all the other reminders—the rust-colored swirls in the mouths of those dumb larks on the Meadowlark mission statement, the shiny pennies they all give her to remind her she is loved, and all that stupid "gentle encouragement" to just be Juniper, to not be frightened of her birth power, to get back to her infant self.

It reminds her of that last Crow Seekers book, how the Rolen boy loses his power and stops being able to see what his crow sees. He spends the whole book devastated. Until the end when he finds the broken digascope embedded in his dead crow's brow. "You deluded me!" he screams at the tribe elder. She was fascinated with the idea that you could put a belief in someone's head like you could a digascope, and they would never know you did it. They would never remember.

And then, it's as if all the questions and uncertainties and doubts that have always swum around inside her settle like a dirty sludge, and she can finally see out. The reason she can't remember those copper streamers is because they never happened. They are just a made-up story, just another lie. And if the copper streamers are a lie, then Larks are a lie, and if Larks are a lie, then she, herself, is a lie, and if she is a lie, then who is she? It is the worst thought she's ever had, worse than the thought that she could be alive one minute and dead the next. But behind this horrible, terrible thought is the glimmer of another thought.

She knew.

Not completely, not perfectly, but a little. Those questions, and uncertainties, and doubts are proof that she is not oblivious, that she could sense herself beneath this other made-up self. And if she could sense herself then, she can more than sense herself now. She is strong and resilient but also smart and the complete and total opposite of oblivious. And angry. Angry at her mother for the hard slivers between them, angry at her sister for pretending she was special, angry at the Meadowlark grown-ups for being so stupid, angry at Simrin for coming here in the first place, but mostly, angry at her father. All those games, and lessons, and walks and talks, each one another delusion pounded into her forehead. She can feel the anger blistering within her. It grows. It takes up every inch of her insides until it strains her skin, and then she hears her mother scream.

"No," her mother screams. "No. No."

And then Juniper is on her feet, the gun warm and solid in her hands. She shoves the door to the roof open, stands at the top of the stairs, and points the gun at all three of the grown-ups.

"Stop," she shouts.

And they turn. "Oh my God," someone says. "Junie," someone says. She can't tell who is saying what, but her mother looks white, and Simrin takes a step back. "Where did she get a gun?" someone says; "Where did she get a gun!"

Her father is still holding Blaze, but he puts his free hand out in front of him like he is about to ask for a hug. He takes a step toward her, and she shouts again.

"Stop!" she says, and he does. She can feel the strength this gun gives her, the power to impose herself on all of them.

"Junie," her father says. "That gun is really dangerous." He is being very careful with his voice, trying to sound casual but serious. "Put it gently down on the steps."

"No," she says. She doesn't know what she wants to do, but she knows what she doesn't want to do.

They all stand frozen, and she realizes they are waiting for her to say something, to do something, but she doesn't know what to say or what to do. She knows only that she feels herself in this moment and won't give that away.

"That gun can kill people." Her father tries again. "Just put it down."

I know that, she wants to say, but she doesn't say it. He has taught her that there is power in silence, but she knows there is even more power in standing silently, wielding a gun from above. She doesn't move, but she can feel her arms begin to shake. Her shoulders are tired from holding the gun up and still, so she keeps her forearms out but tucks her elbows to her body, and her mother jerks. It is a small movement, but Juniper can feel it. Her mother is scared.

"Juniper," her father says. It sounds like a warning, and it is clearly meant to be because he tries another step toward her, and this makes her angry. He has spent her whole life not listening to her. And now he's not even paying attention to how terrified her mother is or how he's putting Blaze in the way of a gun. He takes another step forward.

"Stop it!" she screams. She screams it as loud as she can. And he does. He stops. And she can see a tiny bit of his fear now; his face has gone flat. He slides Blaze to the ground, and her mother slowly puts her arms out. Blaze is still whimpering, thrashing his head back and forth like he does when he's tired, but he throws himself at their mother, and she pulls him back onto her shoulder and closes her eyes for a moment, rests her forehead on his baby head, and for the first time, Juniper realizes she has a gun pointed at her mother, a gun pointed at her baby brother. Blaze is not afraid, but Juniper knows he should be. If he were older, he would be, and this makes her heart catch. He can't see the danger, doesn't even know it's there. But she knows. She also knows it's not the danger of the gun that's really making her heart hurt for him. It's the danger that every day he is being deluded, that every day he is being inched a little closer to thinking he is someone else. Just like her, just like River.

She wants River here, wants to scream her name and have them all together in one place. And then what? Then she will get them out of here—use the gun to get them and her mother through the broken back fence, through Mr. Turner's yard, and away. They will leave and never see their father or this place again. It hurts so much to think this, and she can feel the fear creeping inside her and starting to swallow her strength, swallow her resistance. She knows she needs to do something, so she points the gun directly at her father, imagines it a digascope that will force him into truth.

"You're a liar," she says to her father. She thinks this will make him angry, but he unstiffens. He takes a breath and almost smiles.

"Junie," he says. And then he makes his face serious. "I would never lie to you."

"You said there wasn't a search warrant."

"I didn't say that to *you*." And the way he says it, the emphasis on *you*, she can feel the tingle of that current between them.

"You lied about the pictures."

"Not to you," he says.

The tingle grows, and she wants to shake her head, scratch it out of her body. "You said I was special."

"You are special."

"You said I could see things." He cannot deny this. She knows more fully than she's ever known anything that she can't and never could. If he lies about this, she has complete and total proof that he is a liar and that Meadowlark is a lie and that everything she's ever known has been created just to delude her.

"You can," he says.

"I can't."

"You can."

"I can't!"

"Of course you can."

And then, because there is nothing more she can do to force it out of him, she pulls the trigger.

SIMRIN

It is instinctive, the slowing of her breath, the way she stabilizes her arms against her body to steady the camera, the continuous and indiscriminate shots. She clicks a hundred clicks, two hundred—the fierce recoil of the gun, how it punches Juniper in the stomach and slams her against the stairway wall; the moment of stillness before the commotion, Juniper motionless, gun dripping from her hands. The shutter barely has time to close before it has to open again, and Simrin gathers it all, safe behind the lens, barely visible but buzzing in the moment. This is the shot, she thinks; No, this one, this one, this one. It is only when she hears Arjun groan that she is jerked back to her presence in the landscape. He is on the ground, gripping his leg, groaning, and they all watch, Bethany, Juniper, and Simrin, each of them one millisecond away from a changed narrative.

And then there is chaos.

There is screaming, and people, and then Simrin is scanning the compound for Quinn. There are people pouring out of the main house, huddling together and spreading out, none of them noticing her, none of them seeing Arjun down on the ground. Quinn would be coming from behind her, so she turns, looks, looks, but there is no one. There is no one at the gate now either. She turns back around, scans the main house and the yard again, and then looks to the staircase. Juniper is gone. And so are Bethany and the baby. Vanished.

Now it is only Simrin and Arjun, tucked into the shadow of Hawthorne. And then she sees the gun. Juniper has dropped it at the foot of the stairs, ten feet from where Arjun lies. She takes a step toward the house, edges toward the stairs, where she can see him better and where she is closer to the gun. His eyes are closed, and he is holding his thigh, rocking back and forth and gripping the wound, blood slowly seeping from his closed fists. Juniper has shot him, yes, but the blood is coming sluggishly. He'll live, she thinks, and she is both relieved and angry. All the trauma he has caused, all the lives he carelessly forged and abandoned, all in exchange for a small, neat scar. She takes a step closer to him, then another, until she is standing almost on top of the gun. She wants it close, beneath her, where he cannot get it, but she doesn't have to touch it. If she picks it up, she is afraid she will shoot him, not dead, but maybe give him a matching scar, her mark forever on his body.

"Simrin," he says, and as always, the russet shimmer appears. His eyes are open, and the green seems more vibrant than before, blazing like he has manufactured an illusion. He is pale, but his hair fans out like an angel's, and she hates herself for recognizing how beautiful he is. She badly wants to lift the camera, but she knows this is madness. She does not need to keep this moment. She does not want her own souvenir. And she doesn't need to unsecret his secrets. They're all laid out before the both of them.

"Simrin," he says again. There are streamers, and they linger longer than usual. She can hear the commotion behind her, feel the tug of Quinn somewhere close by, but her body feels stuck in this moment, the two of them alone in their insulated glass bubble.

"Give me the gun," he says.

She opens her mouth, but she can't speak. He is crazy to think she would hand him a gun after all this.

"Please," he says.

And then there is an ear-piercing siren. She flinches, instinctively covers her ears, tries to locate where the sound is coming from, and sees the police funneling through the now-open gate. There are dozens of them, all in black, protective shields covering their bodies. Quinn, she thinks. Just her name. It ricochets around her skull; it pounds with her heartbeat. She needs her. Still, she is surprisingly calm, as if she is still watching this all through her viewfinder.

She looks back to Arjun. He has managed to heft himself to a half crawl, and she takes a step backward, shuffling the gun with her.

"Don't," she says.

He looks up at her. "I'm done," he says. "Just help me be done," and then she understands. He wants the gun for himself. He wants to put an end to his story if someone else is going to tell it. The realization should make her furious. Why should he get to choose when to stop this fucking wheel? But it actually strikes her as profoundly sad. After fighting so hard to catch hold of themselves, here he is, begging her to help him let go, get off the ride, detach completely.

"Please," he begs. "Please."

She watches him, the twitch of his eye, the tremor of his lip. He is scared. And it seems so obvious now. No matter how much bravado he is able to cloak himself in, underneath is the same fear that rises, so obviously, in Simrin. It is just shoved down, buried beneath the swagger and need for devotion. The night they ran, yes, there was anger—the destruction of the information center, his spit on the ground just after they crossed the property line—but there had also been fear. Deep fear of what would happen to them, to him. And maybe something else? An understanding that he wasn't who they all believed him to be—Ananda's golden child with the extraordinary talents, Jaishri and Simrin's savior. What kind of terror rose up when you realized you weren't who they thought you were? What kind of panic when you were convinced you needed to be?

She is straddling the gun; one small kick is all it would take. A gift. A cruelty. His hair hangs in his face; the sun beats on his bare neck. It is so easy to still see the boy.

There is an image Simrin comes back to, again and again, whenever she's thought of him these last twenty years. They had climbed to the beams of Rudraksh—Arjun, Simrin, Jaishri, Gautam, Priya, and Krish. It had been hot, over a hundred degrees, and the boys had taken their shirts off and launched them like parachutes. Jaishri had squealed and closed her eyes, not wanting to be reminded of the drop, but Simrin had watched, thrilled with the terror. "That could be you," Gautam had teased and pretended to shove Arjun. "Except I wouldn't fall," Arjun had said. They had rolled their eyes, and Priya had thrown her headband at him. "Maybe I can fly," Arjun had said, and he had said it so seriously and with such complete assurance that Simrin had, for more than a moment, thought maybe he could. This is the image she's seen when she's thought of him—chest broad, eyes wide, the sheen of confidence covering him like sweat. Now, she sees it like a glossy in front of her, colors saturated, pure beauty and bravado, a diptych that clings to the broken man in front of her. And then she hears Quinn.

"Mama!" Quinn screams.

And Simrin kicks the gun.

Now is a mess of flip-book images. Simrin feels stuck in staccato motion, tripping over herself to get to Quinn, who is running toward her but also toward Arjun and the gun, toward the police in black. Quinn has lost her shoes, has a streak of blue paint across one cheek, a fistful of papers in her hand. Her eyes are wild and terrified. And then Quinn's small body slams into Simrin's, and Simrin picks her up, almost loses the camera dangling from her shoulder, and then bangs them both against the house and into the hollow of the entryway, where it is safe. She holds Quinn tight against her, muffles her sobs into her chest and rocks her like she is still a baby, still her little newborn mouse. And she watches.

The police have come closer, but they are careful. They move slowly and in formation, like birds. Someone is yelling into a bullhorn, "Don't move. Keep your hands up." And Arjun has closed in on himself, his back to the police, cradling the gun like a wound. She watches him, tears coming, knowing this image will now be the one forever rendered when she thinks of him. She waits for the moment, but it doesn't come. He doesn't turn the gun on himself. Instead, he twists, slowly, as if he is matching his movements to an imagined movie score. He stretches his arms out in front of him, extending the gun toward the police like a lens, and the weight of what he means to do crashes down on her. He will not shoot. And he doesn't. Instead, he waits. It is only a millisecond, but it is enough time for Simrin to remember.

She sees it before her, that defining, long-away image again. The lot of them, up on the beams, Arjun shining like a golden idol. He throws his chest out and lets his torso, legs, arms jet behind him. He flies off the beams, suspended in the air, and Simrin is both terrified and rapt. He is a god, capable of all things. And then he falls, somehow tumbling down so that he lands on his feet, letting out a sickening yelp from the ankle that turns under him. They scramble down. Someone runs for the grown-ups. Simrin rushes to him, wanting to claw her fingers down his back. "Why would you do that?" she screams. "You could have died!" His face is a grimace of pain, his ankle already swollen twice its original size, but he manages to grin up at her. "The boy who died flying," he says. "You'd never forget."

Now he stretches, the gun an extension of his body. He leans. He flies. And then he is vaulted back, his body contorting with each of the four bullets, and Simrin raises her camera. And shoots.

QUINN

Quinn gets the plates down, fills the water glasses. Her mother's bringing Chinese, but she'll also want salad. She always does. There's a bag of lettuce in the refrigerator, and she pulls it out and empties it into a bowl.

They've been doing these Tuesday-night dinners for years now, but tonight her mother is coming to her, and it feels momentous. She's an adult! With her own apartment! No roommates and an actual couch! But it's not just that. It's also that tonight Quinn carries something she hasn't before. And she's not sure what she wants to do with this new information.

It is, of course, about Meadowlark. For the most part, Quinn has learned to leave it alone, to not pester her mother for details. Her mother will reluctantly talk about Meadowlark in interviews, but how can she not? Those photographs are her most recognized work, the ones that won her a *National Geographic* Photo of the Year award. And earned her twenty million followers. And changed their lives pretty significantly. But when Quinn asks, her mother goes silent.

And Quinn does understand her reluctance to talk. It's not like her mother doesn't have her critics, the supposedly unbiased interviewers who ask whether she thought twice about bringing a five-year-old into a standoff and how she could have risked her daughter's life just for some pictures. What kind of mother would do that?

The badass kind, Quinn wants to answer.

No. Quinn's questions are much more boring: "Did I go to the art room on the first or second day? Did River lend me those socks, or was it Juniper? What was the baby brother's name?"

But the answer is always the same. "Why would I want to rehash two terrible days?" her mother says. "It was a tiny part of my life."

But it isn't tiny, at least not to Quinn. It is, in fact, a daily portion, inked on her inner wrist.

The tattoo is a small line drawing of a lark. And yes, she knows that after everything that happened, it seems kind of creepy. Her mother was aghast. "Why would you want that on you? And forever!" But her mother is not in Quinn's head. She's not in Quinn's body. Her mother can't hear the words Quinn hears when she traces the lark. Her mother can't feel the warm swell that comes next.

"You're special," the voice says in her head. "You're special."

She has never told anyone about this. The voice—and this is where she pauses because admitting it, even if just in her head, is humiliating— the voice belongs to her mother's "brother," a man she can't remember except through the photographs, the crazy cult leader the world knows. "You're special," the voice says. "You're special." Touch the lark, hear the words, get the fix. It comes like liquid heat, her own unique drug concocted just for her, a little bit of synesthetic heroin.

But it hasn't always been the tattoo that prompted all this.

When she was little, she would make her mother read *The Lion, the Witch, and the Wardrobe* to her, over and over, but it was really only the part where the children are told about the great lion Aslan that she wanted to hear. Aslan's name is so intoxicating, so heady and true and overwhelmingly lovely, that although the children didn't know why, they wanted to hear it again and again.

"Yes!" Quinn said the first time her mother read it, but when her mother questioned her on why this part was so riveting, Quinn didn't know what to say. It wasn't Aslan's name that she wanted over and over; it was Arjun's voice. And then how to explain this? *I hear something* too lovely for words? I feel something too true to explain? It was much too embarrassing to say out loud. And too baffling.

At first the words in Arjun's voice seemed to come randomly. "You're special," when she traced the letters in her phonics book. "You're special," when someone clapped a hand over her eyes and everything went black. But eventually she figured out the triggers—a particular thickness of line, a certain shade of black—that generated the words that produced the feeling. So she started drawing, filled sketchbooks with shapes, and then animals, and then shape animals, trying to find the right black, trying to arc the line correctly, until she finally did it— drew a single-line lark that conjured the voice. She was ten then, many years away from a tattoo, so she kept the drawing under her bed, traced the lines before she went to sleep. "You're special. You're special. You're special," playing like a mantra and spreading something too lovely to put into words right through her.

It is her secret, her lovely, uncomfortable companion, the reason for all her questions and why she requested the files.

Two months ago, the Meadowlark records were finally unsealed. It has been twenty years, and all the babies are grown up now, ready to deal with the producers and directors that are sure to be clamoring for interviews and sound bites. She knows because there is already a producer who's been emailing her, asking if she'll talk to them about what she remembers. But she barely remembers anything. And what she does remember has little to do with the chaos—peeling bark off twigs for fairy shoes, drawing with Smell-o markers, stroking the ponytail holder tangled in the mess of River's hair. And his voice.

It has taken two months, but yesterday, the whole thousand-page document appeared in her inbox, a mess of interview transcriptions and badly taken pictures and police reports and evidence sheets. And then the children's records with meticulous notes on the developmental achievements of all thirty-one Meadowlark children, all written in Arjun's tiny scrawl.

Plus one more.

There, nestled at the end, is a log devoted to Quinn followed by pages and pages of childhood history: medical records and court filings, child-support documents and school forms.

At first she didn't understand. How did he get all this? And why? But then she read his handwritten log, each entry a date with milestones: "8/4/16—reports being able to see and taste words (like S); 11/4/17—neuropsych finds mild developmental delays, possible dyspraxia, dyslexia, and sensory integration disorder (inherited from S?); 8/5/18—contact established!!!" And it was the exclamation points that shook her, his excitement at the possibility of contact. He wanted her for Meadowlark. He wanted them.

The doorbell rings, and she almost drops the salad bowl.

"It's me," her mother calls.

Quinn opens the door, and her mother is standing there, dwarfed by too-big overalls.

"You're too old to wear those," Quinn says.

"Which is exactly why I'm wearing them," her mother says. She hands Quinn the bag of takeout and pulls something from another bag.

"I got you a plant," she says.

It is a lucky bamboo.

"You need some greenery," she says and puts it in the window.

"And luck?"

"God, no."

Quinn puts the takeout on the table.

"You're the luckiest person I know," her mother says. She hugs Quinn from behind, and Quinn feels suddenly small and shaky. It is what happens when she is overwhelmed by too many erratic colors and flavors and sounds, but there is none of this now, just her body stiffening in her mother's hug, and her mother must feel it because she asks what's wrong.

"Nothing," Quinn says. "I just have a headache."

Her mother places her head on Quinn's shoulder. "Want me to rub it?"

Usually Quinn would come back with a funny quip and then let her, but she doesn't have the energy.

"Sure," she says.

Her mother sits on one end of the couch, and Quinn sits on the floor, lays the back of her head in her mother's palms.

"I did this all the time when you were little," her mother says and pushes her thumbs into Quinn's temples. "It helped calm you."

"Did you do it at Meadowlark?"

Quinn says it before she can even decide to say it, the contradiction of wanting to be simultaneously seen and hidden too much to hold.

Her mother pauses. "Quinn. Please." There is a catch in her voice. Usually there is annoyance, even exasperation, but tonight she just sounds tired. "Okay," her mother finally says. "Ask what you want to ask."

Quinn feels the quiet, sees it like a fog, a dense gray cloud around them.

"I . . . ," she starts. But the questions seem to have evaporated. What does it matter if River was taller or shorter than her, if Arjun gave her chocolate chip or peanut butter cookies?

"Why did we go there?" she says. She has never thought to ask it before, has always thought she knew the answer. Because her mother is a rock star who didn't let her kid get in the way of her career or her career in the way of her kid, but now it seems the only question to ask.

"Because," her mother says, "because he needed me." And then there is her mother's sharp inhale, her breathy exhale, the soft hiccupy echo of pain and guilt laid bare, and Quinn knows. Arjun's exhaustive log may come out at some point, the twist in some director's docuseries, but she won't be the one to tell her mother.

◆ ◆ ◆

After dinner, they watch a movie, and then it is late.

"I'm so tired," her mother says.

"Just sleep here," Quinn says.

"I should go," she says but lies down on the couch.

"Poor Mama," Quinn teases. "Should I rub your elderly head?"

Her mother bats her away, but Quinn scoots onto the couch so her mother's head rests on her lap. She presses her thumbs into her temples.

"Relaaaax," Quinn chants.

Her mother smiles and closes her eyes. "My mother used to rub my head like this."

"Really?" Quinn asks. She rarely hears about her grandmother, a woman she met only twice, and what she does hear is usually followed by a sigh and a "I suppose she tried her best."

"Mm-hmm," her mother says.

Quinn runs her fingertips across her mother's forehead, smoothing the wrinkles that are normally covered by her bangs.

It is quiet, but now it is colorless, just the dark and a streetlamp shining a pool of light on the living room floor. She presses her mother's temples, smooths her forehead. She presses and smooths, presses and smooths until she hears her mother's rhythmic breathing and feels her head like a warm stone in her lap. She pauses and waits for her mother to move, and when she doesn't, Quinn touches the birthmark on her mother's lip, the age spots that dot her cheeks.

Once, when Quinn was fifteen and in full teen rebellion, she had stood in the kitchen and yelled at her mother: "You don't listen to me. You don't even see me!" Normally, her mother was a beacon of calm. "I will talk to you when you stop screaming," she would say, but this time, she seemed to fracture. She pushed Quinn against the refrigerator, held her shoulders in her hands, her anger and grief gusting puffs of yellow behind her. "I see you, Quinn," she cried. "I do nothing but see you."

Now, Quinn looks at her mother, tries to lock focus and see the whole. It is hard. To see the love and the hurt in a single frame, but when she does, the space between them seems to expand and contract, and Quinn can see it, a rosy gold between them. She reaches for her wrist, traces the lark, and warms.

ACKNOWLEDGMENTS

Thank you for help with research to David Sullivan, Rachel Neumann, Graham Norton, Aria Simpson, George Fong, Natalie Arnold, Michelle Legro, Sheriff Ben Troter, Jim Simpson, Mikal Condon, Nancy Barillaro, Cory Jackson, and Marvi Lacar.

Thank you to Maria Hummel and Caroline Rhame for reading drafts and giving invaluable feedback; to Janet Miller for spending inordinate amounts of time talking about characters as if they actually existed; to Sloane Tanen, Jennie Durant, Melissa Hillier, Samantha Moss, and Amy Ahlers for support and fortitude; and to Laurette Schiff Gennis, who taught me to stay curious.

Thank you to my agents—Christy Fletcher and Sarah Fuentes. Christy for always being a champion of my work and Sarah for her thoughtful insights and spot-on guidance.

Thank you to my editor, Vivian Lee, for loving this baby as much as I do, and to Laura Van der Veer and Emma Reh for stepping in and seeing it across the finish line so wonderfully. Thanks to Stephanie Chou, Kimberly Glyder, Merideth Mulroney, Kristin Lunghamer, Laura Costantino, and Adria Martin for all your wise oversight and help turning a mere manuscript into a beautiful book.

I'm not sure what this book would be, but it would not be this book without the editorial prowess of Laura Mazer, who loved it and me from the very beginning. Enormous thanks.

And thank you to Vikram, whose steadfast belief in me as a writer and insistence that the writing (almost always) come first buoyed me through writing a novel while raising small children. And to those not-so-small children, Leela and Darshana, who taught me what it means to see and be seen and about the fierce and luminous power of love.

ABOUT THE AUTHOR

Photo © 2019 Niki Stefanelli

Melanie Abrams is the author of the novels *Playing* and *Meadowlark*. She is an editor and photographer and currently teaches writing at the University of California, Berkeley. She lives in Oakland, California, with her husband, writer Vikram Chandra, and their daughters.